BERWYN

By David Mansfield

'Berwyn': First Published 2023

Berwyn *is dedicated to the loving memory of my mother and father. Their love for this wonderful part of North Wales was passed on to me and provided the inspiration for this book.*

CHAPTER 1

The blast boomed down the tunnel, belching black dirt and dust into the darkness deep under the hillside. Three minutes earlier, John Roberts had lit the fuse. Then he had waited, slowly counting to fifty, but nothing had happened. He cursed and walked back along the tunnel. The rock face exploded before he reached it. Rock fragments ripped into his body, and he was hurled backwards through the air. The gaffer, Ben Hopkins, and another man carried him into the daylight. Their sweaty faces and arms, black from the muck and dust, were now also covered with John's blood.

'Misfire,' Ben Hopkins shouted to the navvies waiting at the tunnel entrance. 'But he's alive. We've got to get him to the doctor.'

***

It was the last Sunday in May 1864, and Dr Richard Lloyd had been to church with his fiancée, Sara. He had heard the blast as he left the churchyard but had thought little of it. The railway tunnel at Berwyn had been under construction for several months and the explosions had become commonplace. Richard and Sara strolled alongside the river, followed by his brother Evan and Elizabeth who were to marry later that year. As they paused at the Horseshoe Falls to look at the water cascading over the low weir, Elizabeth's father, Sir Clayton Davenport, caught up with them.

'It's a fine day for a walk, especially after an hour sitting on those church pews. How are you both?' he asked Richard and Sara. 'Have you set a date for your wedding yet?'

'Not yet. I need to build up my practice before we can afford to settle down,' said Richard.

'The day will come, and it will be all the sweeter for your patience. But don't be too cautious and wait too long. Sometimes you need to follow your feelings and take the risk,' said Sir Clayton.

'There would be no risk if Richard returned to surgery in London rather than scrape a living here,' said Sara with obvious annoyance.

'Sir Clayton doesn't want to hear about all that,' said Richard.

Evan tried to make light of the awkward moment. 'Our wedding will be quite enough excitement for Berwyn this year. We don't want to be beaten to the altar by my younger brother, do we, Elizabeth?' Elizabeth smiled back at Evan, but Sara looked on, stony-faced.

They heard a girl's voice calling for Richard. Sian, the young housekeeper from Ty Celyn, the Lloyds' family home, was running down the field towards them with one of the navvies.

'There's been an accident in the tunnel. Someone has been badly hurt,' said Sian. 'He's at Ty Celyn.'

Richard was tall, fit and in his mid-twenties, and he ran up the steep hill to his home and surgery.

The navvies had carried John Roberts almost a mile from the tunnel to Ty Celyn, and Sian had shown them to a back room that Richard used as an office and surgery. John was laid on the bed, and Richard carefully removed his bloodstained shirt and trousers and inspected the wounds. John was in and out of consciousness, but

Richard reassured him as best he could. Sian brought in jugs of hot water and cloths that had been boiled.

'Thank you, but I'll need more cloths. All these cuts need cleaning. Some sharp bits of rock have also gone deep under his skin.'

About an hour later, there was urgent knocking on the front door. Sian went to see who was there. A young woman with a flushed complexion and a worried look spoke quickly.

'I understand that John Roberts is here. He's had an accident on the railway.'

'Yes, he is with Dr Lloyd now,' said Sian. 'Who are you?'

'Elin Roberts is my name. Can I see John? How is he?'

Sian asked Elin to wait in the hall and said she would inform the doctor.

Richard came out of the surgery, wiping his hands. 'I can't stay long to talk now. He's badly injured, but I'll do all that I can for him.'

'Might he die? What's happened to him?' asked Elin.

'The blast has shot several pieces of rock into his body. Fortunately, it seems that they have missed his heart and lungs. He has several cuts, resulting in blood loss, and is very weak. His wounds need cleaning and the pieces of stone removed.'

'I can help clean him. Is he through here?' Elin pushed past Richard into the back room.

'You can help, but you must first wash your hands and arms. There is hot water in the jug by the washstand. I'll then show you what to do.'

Richard bathed one of the wounds and exposed the shard of rock in John's arm. Elin joined him at the bedside.

'I can take over now.' Her attitude was neither rude nor arrogant, just matter-of-fact and businesslike.

Richard looked at her. 'Have you been a nurse? You seem very confident.'

'No, but I have looked after my family when they were sick, back at home.' Elin blushed and avoided his gaze. 'I am sorry if I have been rude, but I want to do all I can for John. I want to help you.'

'Your help will be welcome. Now go to the other side of the bed and start cleaning the wounds on his leg. I am going to release this stone and then stitch and bandage the wound.'

Richard lifted John's head slightly and made him take sips of morphine solution. He took his surgeon's knife and deftly started to remove the rock. Richard and Elin worked together quietly, the silence interrupted only by John's cries of pain.

From time to time, Richard looked at his new assistant to see how she was getting on. He became aware of how beautiful she was, with her jet-black hair and dark brown eyes that showed such love and concern for the patient. Inevitably, their eyes met, and she smiled back at him. Richard complimented her work.

Almost two hours later, Richard told Elin that they had done as much as they could and that they should now let John sleep.

'Can I stay with John tonight?' asked Elin. 'If he wakes in the night, he might want a drink or be confused about what's happened. I'll be no trouble, and I can rest in the chair by the bed.'

'Yes, of course, and you can have supper with us, too. You must be hungry after all the nursing you've done.'

***

Elin sat down with Richard, Evan and their father, Edward, for supper. Edward, a widower, was in his fifties, still with a good head of hair but now very grey. An illness a few years earlier had resulted in him handing over the running of Ty Celyn farm to his eldest son, Evan. The old stone, whitewashed farmhouse stood high above the Horseshoe Falls with views over the Dee Valley to the hills and forests beyond. The farm had been passed down through the Lloyd family over many generations. Similarly, Welsh remained the language of the home.

Edward asked where she and John were living.

'We're in lodgings in Llangollen, near the bridge. We've been there since John got the job with the railway. But we're from Rhuddlan. Mam and Dad and my two sisters still live there.'

Elin was interested in Richard's work and asked him why he had become a doctor.

'Since I was a boy, I wanted to be a doctor. I trained at the London Hospital and became a surgeon, but my dream was always to return home to Berwyn and be a physician in this valley.'

'So you've achieved your dream. People can spend their entire lives seeking what they want.'

'Well, I'm working hard to build up the practice in order to make a decent living.'

'You'll succeed. I know you will. You're a wonderful doctor – you've saved John's life.'

'The early signs are promising, but he still has a fight on his hands.'

'I know, but without you, I would have lost him today.'

'Don't go flattering him,' said Evan. 'It's my hard work managing the farm that puts the food on the table. If we relied on Richard's income, we'd be on bread and water.'

Evan looked at Richard and broke into a broad smile. Richard laughed and admitted that for now anyway, his brother was right.

Evan's looks were similar to his younger brother: tall with dark brown hair, but he was broader in build. He was good-looking, but not quite as handsome as Richard. Richard had always been the more serious brother, and Evan the light-hearted one.

'And what is your dream, Elin?' asked Edward.

'Right now, I would thank God to return John to us healthy and strong again. I don't think much beyond each week, or even each day, really. If we can send some money home to Mam and Dad, pay our rent and eat, then that's all I expect.'

Elin went on to explain that she worked at The Hand Inn, a coaching inn at Llangollen. She cleaned rooms, served at tables and did other similar duties.

Elin stifled a yawn and rubbed her eyes.

'Are you alright?' asked Edward.

'Just a bit tired – I think I'll go and see John. Thank you for being so kind.'

'I'll come with you and check him,' said Richard.

A few minutes later Richard rejoined Evan and his father in the parlour.

'Elin's a lovely young woman and very devoted to John,' said Edward.

'She's very determined. She worked so hard this afternoon and didn't stop until the job was done,' said Richard. 'She's intriguing.'

'Very beautiful too,' said Evan. 'But remember that you are engaged to be married. Don't forget Sara.' He grinned at his brother.

'Of course not,' said Richard. 'And anyway, Elin is obviously in love with John.'

'How are things between Sara and you? Things seemed a bit tense after church when we met Sir Clayton.'

'What happened?' asked Edward.

'Clayton asked if we had set a date for our wedding yet. I explained the situation, but Sara got cross about the practice again. It was a bit embarrassing.'

'You need to sort things out with her,' said Edward.

'I've tried. Sara is determined that our future lies in London. She wants to be married to a hospital surgeon and enjoy London society, or so she thinks. I'm not leaving Berwyn. I valued my time in London, but I'm not going back.'

'But you still love Sara, don't you?'

'I have always loved her. I would marry her tomorrow if she would have me as I am. But she does not want to stay here, and I can't consider a future without Berwyn and my practice.'

Evan looked at his brother. 'It seems to me that you have two loves, Sara and Berwyn, and the question is, which love is the greater?'

'I cannot choose between them,' said Richard. 'I have to persuade Sara to stay here.'

CHAPTER 2

Before breakfast, Richard went to the surgery. Elin was sitting at John's bedside, and Richard asked him how he was feeling.

'Like I've been blown down a tunnel backwards. But thank you, doctor, Elin has told me everything you've done.'

'Elin played her part as well. You'll be with us here for a few more days. You mustn't be moved until those wounds start to heal.'

John was going to live, and with relief in her heart, Elin left the two men at Ty Celyn and walked the two miles or so into Llangollen to get ready for work. She followed the canal towpath into town, passing the noise and bustle of the slate works at Pentrefelin and the navvies working on the new railway line alongside the canal.

Richard attended to John's wounds and was relieved to see that most were clean and there had been only minor bleeding overnight. In the kitchen, he asked Sian to arrange some breakfast for John.

There was a heavy knocking on the back door. Richard opened it to see an unshaven, thickset man, probably in his early thirties, standing there. He wore a long black coat that had seen better days.

'I need the doctor,' he said.

'I am Dr Lloyd. What can I do for you?'

'You must come with me now.'

'I have a sick man in the house and visits to make,' said Richard.

'They'll have to wait. My mother has fallen and cut her leg badly. She's passed out. You must do as I say and come right now.' He stepped forward and stared Richard in the eyes.

'There is no need to threaten me. If it's an emergency, then I shall come immediately. Where is she?'

'At our farm about two miles up the Glyn Ceiriog road.'

'I'll go and get my bag. You wait here.' Richard closed the door and beckoned Sian. She followed him out of the kitchen.

'That man wants me to attend to his mother. I think he's one of the James brothers. I want you to tell Evan that if I'm not back by midday then he must get help and come and find me. I shall leave my horse tied up somewhere visible near the farmhouse. I'm sure I'll be fine.' Richard wrote down the location of the farmhouse.

'I'll tell Evan as soon as he comes in. Takc care now.'

Richard was right; it was Jed James that led the way up the rough road. Jed and his brother Will had a reputation for hard drinking and even harder fighting. Some people believed that the brothers were responsible for the robberies from carters heading north to buy coal. There was no proof that it was the James boys, but many said that the thieves had fled into the forest above Berwyn, after the attacks.

Jed and Richard rode their horses as quickly as was possible on the steep lane. Richard realised that he may be heading into an outlaw's den, but his growing concern was partly offset by the note he had left for Evan. They rode mainly in silence, although Richard did ask about his mother's injury.

'She fell in the yard on some old metal,' Jed told him.

'How long ago was this?'

'It's about an hour since I found her. I tied a piece of cloth around her leg to try to stop the bleeding.'

The isolated farmhouse came into view. At first it looked run down and empty. The smoke from the chimney was the only indication of habitation.

Richard quickly dismounted and tied his horse to a post in the yard where Evan would be able to see it from the track. He grabbed his bag and followed Jed inside. Will was standing next to his mother, who lay on an old couch near the hearth. The room was sparse but warm and tidy.

'Mam seems the same,' Jed said to his brother.

'She hasn't woken up.'

Richard examined the leg injury. He took her pulse and temperature. He didn't like the look of the patient. She had been unconscious for some time and the cut on the leg was deep and long. Despite Jed's attempts, she had lost a lot of blood.

He applied a fresh tourniquet and temporary bandage, but the look of the wound worried him. While Will set about getting hot water and a clean sheet, Richard asked Jed to show him where his mother had fallen. In the yard, he saw the bloodied ironwork, and his concerns grew when he saw the dirt and rust on the jagged metal.

'I shall do my best to save her leg, but it may be a choice between her life or her leg.'

'Mam will have no life if she cannot walk,' said Jed. His tone of voice had become one of despondency, losing the aggression he'd shown at Ty Celyn.

Richard told them to clear the long trestle table and to lift their mother carefully onto it. Then he went to work. There was a need for absolute concentration with no room for any thought of failure. Richard cleaned the wound and stitched the nine-inch gash on Mrs James' leg.

As Richard bandaged her leg, Jed asked about his mother's chance of recovery.

'I've done what I can,' said Richard. 'Time will tell whether it's worked. Your mother is still with us, and there is hope.'

The door opened quickly. A pale-faced Evan stood in the doorway with Will behind him, holding a shotgun.

'I found him in the yard,' said Will. 'He says that he's your brother.'

'He is my brother,' said Richard.

Jed told Will to lower the shotgun. Will put the gun down, and the colour slowly returned to Evan's face.

'So we just wait now?' asked Jed.

'We wait and we pray,' said Richard. He was pleased to see Evan but knew that he had now put his brother at risk as well.

Richard's eyes did not leave Mrs James. Jed sat in a chair next to his mother, and Evan stood by the window looking out at the yard. A large tomcat carried a dead rat out of a half-derelict barn. Will came back in to see if there had been any change. Jed shook his head.

An hour later, Mrs James regained consciousness and her sons laid her back on the couch to rest. The tension of the past hours, and the relief that their mother was still alive, proved emotional for these hard men. Will tried to hide his tears.

Richard provided medicine and gave instructions as to what they should do for her. He said that he would be back in the morning, then he and Evan rode homewards.

'Thanks for coming to my rescue,' said Richard. 'Although I was never really in any danger. They needed me to help their mother.'

Evan raised his eyebrows. 'Will's shotgun in my back felt quite dangerous. I hate to think what might have happened if she had died.'

'Jed James knew that I had done all that I could to save her.'

'You see the best in everyone. I'm not so sure about those two. What if she dies tonight? Are you really going back tomorrow?'

'Of course I am. I have made a promise to see her, and I'll need to examine the wound and change her dressings.'

'I'll come with you,' said Evan, 'and I'll bring my shotgun.'

'There's no need, and I'll be fine. Keep your gun for the pheasants.'

***

As he arrived back at Ty Celyn, Sian told Richard that Elin had come to visit John. She also gave him a letter that had been delivered earlier in the afternoon. It was an invitation to dine with Sara and her family tomorrow. He grimaced at the thought of an evening with her cousin William. He could only hope that the weather would be good so that Sara and he could escape outside for a walk.

Richard went to the surgery, where Elin was sitting at John's bedside. He lay motionless with his eyes closed. As he heard Richard's voice, he tried to sit up but immediately fell back with a groan.

'I'm well enough to leave soon. I'd go now, but Elin says that I'm too weak,' said John.

'You're making progress, but Elin is right. We'll review things daily, but I think that you should stay here for at least two more days. Those wounds are deep, and I want to see some healing before we talk about you leaving.'

'I'll stay one more night, but that's all. I know you mean well, but I need to be back at work.'

'We'll talk further tomorrow,' said Richard.

Richard offered to take Elin back to her lodgings. They rode back together in the gig.

'Why is John so determined to leave? He could easily set back any progress that he has made.'

'He needs to get back to work. My wages don't cover the rent, and he's also worried about your bill, if he stays too long.'

'The charge will be the same whether he stays for two days or two weeks, and I shall not require payment until he's back at work.'

'Are you sure? That would be a huge weight off our minds.'

'I'm sure.' Richard smiled at Elin. 'All that matters now is to get John well again.'

As Richard brought the gig to a halt, she took his hands and squeezed them in hers and kissed him gently on the cheek.

'*Diolch yn fawr*, thank you so much,' she said.

As Richard drove the gig back to Berwyn, he could still feel the slight touch of Elin's lips on his face. The warm, pleasant sensation stayed with him until he reached Ty Celyn.

This is nonsense, he told himself. *She is a married woman and her husband is my patient. It's nonsense brought about by a hard day.*

***

Richard was awake early. Perhaps it was the thought of revisiting Jed and Will James. At breakfast, Evan repeated his offer of accompanying his brother, but Richard was insistent that he would go alone.

As he arrived at the James' farm, Jed was in the yard.

'How's your mother?' asked Richard.

'Bad headache and a pain in the leg, but she seems alright.'

He was pleased to see her sat up on the couch, holding a cup to her mouth. She was talking and looked quite bright, despite her ordeal.

'Your mam is a fighter,' Richard told Jed. 'She's made of tough stuff.'

'I've had to be tough,' she remarked. 'I've brought these two up on my own since my husband died over twenty years ago. I've had to be mother, father and farmer too. To be fair, they've helped on the farm since they were little boys.'

Richard told Mrs James that she must rest for a few days and not climb any stairs until she felt steady on her feet. He wished her a quick recovery and went outside with Jed. Will came out from a building in the yard and walked over to them.

Jed reached inside his pocket and took out some banknotes. 'You saved our mother's life. We can never repay you for what you have done, but this is for you.'

Richard looked at the money. He couldn't tell the exact amount in Jed's hand, but it was several pounds.

'My full fee for two visits is fifteen shillings. I cannot take any more than that. I wouldn't charge Sir Clayton Davenport at Berwyn Hall a penny more either,' said Richard. 'I thank you for your offer and don't want to offend you, but fifteen shillings is all that I shall accept.'

'Very well, but if you ever need our help, you only have to ask,' said Jed.

Richard thanked them and rode down into Llangollen to visit another patient. He smiled to himself when he remembered Evan's concern that he might get shot by Jed. Instead, he had received the most generous offer of payment made by any of his patients.

***

At Ty Celyn, John Roberts received a visitor: his gaffer, Ben Hopkins, who had helped him out of the tunnel after the accident.

'How are you?' asked Ben. 'You look a lot better than when I saw you last. We wondered whether you would see another day.'

'The doctor wants me to stay a few more days, but I'll be back at work soon.'

'That's good news. Listen, I don't like to ask, but you couldn't lend me some money, could you? I only need a few shillings.'

'You're joking, aren't you? I can't help this week. No work, no wages, and Elin must find the rent for the lodgings. Have you got a card game?'

'No,' Ben lied, 'but I've got a man pressing for a debt to be repaid. I thought you might be able to help. Not being a drinking or gambling man yourself, you usually have some money to spare.'

'Not this week.'

John knew that Ben wanted the money for gambling. It wasn't the first time that he had bothered him for a loan. Ben often used his position as the gaffer to bully the navvies into lending him money. John had always resisted and quietly disliked the man for abusing his status.

Ben Hopkins looked disappointed. He'd have to find his stake for the card game elsewhere. After a quick look around the room, Ben headed back to the railway.

***

Later that afternoon at Ty Celyn, while changing John's bandages, Richard asked him about the dangers of working on the railway.

'As a miner, the most dangerous is the misfire, and that's what happened to me on Sunday. You set the blasting powder and then light the fuse. If nothing happens, then you've to go back and check it. Usually, the fuse has gone out, but sometimes it can relight due to a sudden draught of air. Damp fuses are a real problem. Mining is always risky. You also have the chance of a roof fall with supports giving way.'

'Is this railway any more dangerous than others that you've worked on?' Richard asked.

'No, I've had worse conditions on other lines. In my time, there's been only one death here, when a navvy was trapped under a falling wagon.'

'I remember. Dr Bevan attended as I was in Corwen.'

'There's pressure on everyone to get things done quickly, and that can lead to shortcuts or rushing the job. That's when the accidents happen. Company profits, not workers' lives, are what interest the bosses.'

'Does drunkenness cause accidents?'

'Many do drink hard, I suppose. The navvies are a tough bunch, but they take pride in their work, mostly. They work hard and they play hard. I don't live in the trackside shanties, so I don't have to put up with the poor conditions. But if I didn't have our lodgings and Elin for company, I'd no doubt drink myself to sleep as well.'

Richard thought about what John had told him. Perhaps he had something to talk to William about this evening, after all.

CHAPTER 3

William Griffiths-Ellis lived just outside Llangollen at Plas Gwyn, one of the finest mansions in the Dee Valley. He had inherited the large estate, with its white country house, after his father's death some five years earlier. William's father had been a self-made businessman, and he had instilled in his son the same driven need for success and power that had motivated his own life. William's mother had died when he was very young.

Soon after William's tenth birthday, his cousin Sara came to live at Plas Gwyn after she had lost her parents. Sara was two years younger than William, but the cousins became good friends. They played together during the holidays when he returned home from boarding school. In later years, William remained protective of his cousin, who continued to live at Plas Gwyn with their Aunt Grace. Over the years, Grace had become more of a mother than an aunt to Sara.

William had invited to dinner a business colleague, Samuel Vaughan. William had several business interests, including a major shareholding in the new railway, and Mr Vaughan was also considering investing in the venture. William and Vaughan entered the dining room while continuing their conversation about the line. The other diners, Sara, Richard and Aunt Grace, were already seated at the table.

'May I introduce Mr Samuel Vaughan,' said William. 'Samuel is planning to buy into the next phase of the railway; the extension from Corwen to Bala.'

'I already know Dr Lloyd through our work at the Corwen Union,' said Mr Vaughan. 'As Chairman of the Union, I appointed him as our medical officer. How are things at the workhouse infirmary?'

'As well as can be expected given the age and frailty of many of the inmates,' replied Richard. 'Poverty and homelessness have taken their toll on their health. The infirmary is always busy.'

'Well at least they have a roof over their heads and food to eat,' said Mr Vaughan. 'I am surprised that you've stayed at the infirmary given the low pay. I'm sure you could earn far more at a proper hospital.'

Sara whispered 'exactly' to Richard.

Tucking into the main course, Samuel Vaughan asked Richard for his opinion on the railway.

'I believe that it will be really good for the valley. We've seen the benefits since Llangollen Station opened, and the same will no doubt happen for Corwen and the places in between, like Berwyn. If the line is extended to Bala and eventually to the coast, then travel across Wales will be greatly improved. But we mustn't forget that it's had serious downsides too. Some people in Llangollen have lost their homes and their access to water from the river, due to the construction of the railway.'

William frowned at Richard's negative comments.

'There is always a price to pay for progress,' he said, 'but there are huge advantages for the majority. The railway provides great opportunities for our businesses to expand and prosper through improved access to markets. We can transport coal, livestock and materials to our factories and markets quicker and cheaper than ever before. The railways have already revolutionised the transport of people and goods for the cities, and now it is our turn in the smaller towns and countryside.'

'You make a good argument,' said Samuel Vaughan. 'You also provide an excellent dinner.'

'Well perhaps, but I don't accept that people should suffer as a consequence,' said Richard. There were polite smiles around the table, and a pointed look from Sara, but Richard kept his attention on William. 'If the company needed those houses because they were in the path of the railway line, then new homes should have been provided for those who were evicted. The company promised new houses, but broken promises don't deliver homes. As usual, it is the poorest who suffer most. But I do agree with Mr Vaughan that the dinner is very good.'

Everyone laughed, except William, who was getting increasingly irritated. 'Those houses will be replaced, and we have not broken our promises.'

When annoyed, William would repeatedly take off his spectacles and then put them back on again. Being slightly overweight, he also went red in the face.

Richard decided to bring up John Roberts' accident.

'I have a favour to ask of you, William. I am very concerned about a patient of mine who was badly injured from an explosion in the Berwyn tunnel. He has told me of the dangers of working on the railway, and the many risks of injury, that are made worse by the time pressures placed on the workers. I want to raise these issues with the company board at its next meeting.'

'No, that will not happen. I am not wasting board members' time with such matters. Of course, there are pressures to get the work done quickly. The railway has tough targets to meet. If the Berwyn tunnel is delayed, then we risk missing our opening date.'

Richard pressed his point further. 'Of course, I accept that the railway is a business. But the safety of its workers is a business issue, as well as one of welfare. John Roberts' injury stopped work on the tunnel for several hours. Accidents cause delays as well as injuries. I disagree with you that your board members won't be interested in what I have to say.'

William's annoyance with Richard was obvious. As his neck turned almost as red as his wine, he downed his drink and summoned the servant to refresh his glass.

'You may disagree, but I refuse your request to attend the meeting, and that is the end of the matter.'

'Come now, William,' said Samuel. 'The doctor has a professional duty to raise these issues with the board, and he makes a good point about the cost of delays.'

'Thank you, Mr Vaughan,' said Richard. 'My request is not unreasonable, but I can see that I'll get nowhere with it tonight. My neighbour, Sir Clayton Davenport, is a reasonable man and a vice chairman of the railway company. I shall ask Sir Clayton for permission to attend the meeting.'

The dining room fell quiet. William was livid but said nothing. He emptied another glass of wine, glowered at Richard and stood up.

'I ask that you excuse me for a few minutes.'

'Request granted,' said Richard with a smile.

'Oh, Richard, don't antagonise him,' said Sara after William had left the room.

'I'm sorry, but if he had agreed to my request, then I would not have to go over his head. Anyway, let's change the subject. I apologise for causing any indigestion. This lovely meal should have more appetising conversation to accompany it.'

Aunt Grace laughed. 'You are quite right about the indigestion. It looks as if poor William has already succumbed.'

The meal passed without any further awkwardness. Afterwards, William and Samuel withdrew for further business discussions, while Richard and Sara went into the garden for some fresh air. It was a lovely evening and the low sun enhanced Sara's attractive blonde hair and very light complexion. She took Richard's arm.

'Have you given any more thought as to our future?' she asked. 'On Sunday, it was embarrassing not to be able to give Sir Clayton a proper answer to his question about our wedding. Evan and Elizabeth have been engaged less than half the time that we have, and their wedding is planned for October.'

'Evan is older than I am, and their future is more certain. He has Ty Celyn to manage, and Sir Clayton is giving them a house on his estate.'

'I love you, Richard, but I am not happy with the way things are. When we got engaged, I thought that you would stay at the hospital in London and we would be married and buy a house. And then you bought your practice here. You have not been fair to me.'

Richard took Sara's hand as they walked on slowly towards the fountain. 'I'm sorry, but you knew my plans from the beginning. You knew that I wanted to return to Berwyn. We could be married now if you would be willing to accept a simple life while I build up the practice. We could live at Berllan. It's small, but dry and comfortable.'

'I will not live in that little hovel in the hills.'

'It's a lovely cottage and only a mile or so out of Llangollen. It would be a good home until we could afford something bigger. My grandparents lived there most of their lives and brought up my mother and her two sisters.'

'It has only got two bedrooms and is very basic. The practice is so poor that we'd never be able to afford anything better. Face reality – we'd be stuck there forever.'

'I'm a good doctor, and I will grow the practice. Already I have twelve more patients than two years ago, and I've acquired the work at the Corwen Union.'

'But they don't pay, do they? The workhouse salary is nothing. You need to get a decent practice, and you need money for that. You don't have it and I can't see how you'll get it.'

'Thanks for the vote of confidence.'

'But I do have confidence in you.' Sara's voice softened from her previously critical tone. She knew that Richard would get defensive and stubborn if she kept up her attack. She smiled at him and held his hand. 'I know that you will make a fine surgeon and have a great career if we go to London. I want this for you as well as me. You are wasting your talent staying here. What a life we could have. We have nothing here.'

'I have *everything* here. I love Berwyn and the Dee Valley. It is where I was born and where I want our children to belong, with their family around them. I want them to know their land, their heritage and their language. That is more important to me than being some fancy surgeon and living in a big London house. I am not wasting my time here. My patients have the best treatment, and many would have died if it had not been for me. These are my people, and I am proud to care for them even though many are poor and cannot pay much for their treatment. Don't they deserve help too?'

'Of course they do, but it doesn't have to be you, does it? Dr Bevan in Llangollen can help them, or a doctor in Corwen. Why you, when you have talents that those doctors could only dream of?'

'Those doctors will not treat them if they cannot pay. Why can't you understand that this is about doing what is right for me and what I believe in?' Richard had lost his usual calmness; he frowned in frustration and held his head in his hands.

Sara was similarly exasperated. She snapped back at her fiancé. 'Right for you – what about what is right for me? Doesn't that count for anything? I have waited two years for you to realise that there is a better way, and I am not wasting another year. Please come to your senses before it's too late.'

This was not the first time that Richard and Sara had argued over their future, but past discussions usually ended on a happier note with one of them believing that the other's viewpoint was softening. Tonight was different. They kissed goodnight but not as passionately as usual.

***

On his way home, Richard stopped at The Chain Bridge Inn at Berwyn. He wanted to reflect on the events of the evening over a brandy. The riverside inn took its name from the old chain bridge that crossed the river at this point.

Ben Hopkins, having managed to borrow some money, was having a drink with a fellow navvy. Jed James and Dan Williams, a local carter, also sat at the table. Richard remembered Hopkins as the man who had helped John Roberts, and raised his glass in acknowledgement.

Jed came over to Richard and asked the landlord for another brandy for the doctor. Richard thanked him.

'That's from Mam,' said Jed.

'How is she today?'

'She seems to be doing well.'

'Good. I'll check how the wound is healing in a couple of days. Thanks again for the brandy.'

Dan Williams lived alone in a house with a large yard from where he ran his haulage business. It was at Dan's place that the card games took place, after the gamblers had assembled at The Chain Bridge Inn. That evening, the four men made their way there across the bridge.

After playing several hands, Ben Hopkins had met with some success and trebled the small amount of money he had brought with him. The other players, keen to win back their losses, had no intentions of quitting and another round was dealt. Ben looked at his cards – another good hand. He raised the stakes and looked at the other men.

Jed grinned back at him. 'Now we're getting somewhere. I'll raise it too.'

Ben looked again at his hand. Surely Jed James couldn't beat it.

Dan was the next to fold.

'Right. Let's see what you've got,' said Ben.

Jed laid his cards on the table. Ben watched each card as Jed turned them over. His heart sank as the last card was revealed.

'That beats mine,' he conceded. 'And I'm out for the night too.'

'I'll give you a chance to win some of it back, if you want to carry on,' offered Jed. 'You can borrow another five shillings if you want to keep playing.'

'I owe you enough already.'

'All the more reason to play on.'

Ben was tempted. He also owed money to two other men, including Dan, and they were pressing him for repayment.

'Alright, I'm back in.'

Jed James dealt the cards. Ben's hand was good. Everyone laid bets to stay in the game. Jed eyed each player in turn, watching for signs of confidence or bluff. It was his turn to play.

'I'm out. One of you must have a better hand than mine,' he said, putting his cards on the table.

Only Ben and Dan were still playing. Ben confidently raised the stakes and was swiftly matched by Dan.

'Four queens,' Ben announced, and laid the cards on the table.

'It's a good hand,' said Dan, 'but not quite good enough against my four kings.' He collected his winnings. 'I'll get us all a drink; some of you look as if you need one. I take it that we're finished playing cards this evening.'

Ben wanted to appear calm in defeat but his stomach reflected his true feelings. The final pot was a big one, and a win would have helped his problems. Instead, he now owed Jed a sizeable sum as well.

He left Dan's house a worried man.

CHAPTER 4

Sian put the note on the hall table so that Richard would see it when he returned home from Plas Gwyn. The man who had delivered the note appeared anxious and had insisted that the doctor should see it urgently.

The worried man was Merryman Christmas. His family meant everything to him and his wife, Mary. Despite their low income, he would not hesitate to ask the doctor to visit if the children showed any sign of illness. So, when Dafydd developed a high temperature, his father decided to walk the two miles to Berwyn to ask Richard to call.

Despite his visit to The Chain Bridge Inn, Richard arrived home still in a despondent mood. He felt Sara slipping away from him unless he gave in to her demands.

He saw Sian's note on the hall table, and as he read it, his own problems were forgotten, for the time being. The first visit tomorrow would be to the Christmas family.

Merryman Christmas lived in the middle of a row of small, run-down houses with two rooms downstairs and two bedrooms in the loft. The approach to the houses was down a lane of even poorer homes. Richard tried to avoid the thick dirt on the road. It was as much animal waste as it was mud. He despaired over this breeding ground for disease and human misery that the poor had to endure and most of the rich cared little about.

Merryman let Richard in. Everything was clean and homely. Merryman was almost forty but looked a few years older, partly due to his short and stout figure.

His fullness of face and beard normally lent him a jovial appearance but not on this day.

'Thank you for coming so early, doctor.'

'You are first on my list. How is your boy today?'

'Dafydd has had a fever since yesterday. He seems to be no better.'

They went upstairs to where Mary waited at Dafydd's bedside. She was wiping her son's hot face. Richard placed his hand on the boy's forehead. He checked his heart and breathing, and then his body for any swelling or signs of a rash.

'Apart from a high temperature, Dafydd is alright.' Richard smiled at the boy. 'I'm afraid you'll be back in school in a couple of days. There are quite a few children affected by a nasty cold at the moment. Keep him warm in bed, give him plenty to drink and tell me if there is no improvement.'

'Thank you, doctor,' said Merryman. '*Duw*, that is a weight off my mind. Dafydd's fever took me back all those years to what happened with our first two children. We get so worried when any of them are ill.'

Mary was clearly upset. 'They were so very, very young when the fever took them, you see. I often wonder what they would be doing now if they had lived. They would be fifteen and seventeen years old. It's been eleven years, but the pain of losing them is still bad.'

Richard put his arm around Mary's shoulder to console her.

'I am so sorry,' said Richard quietly. 'However, I can reassure you that there is no smallpox or scarlet fever in the town at the present time.'

Richard's thoughts were with Mary and the other parents who had lost so many children in the 1853 epidemic. In the small town of Llangollen, over one hundred and fifty died that year. Two thirds were young children.

'Myfanwy was spared, thank God,' said Mary. 'It was a miracle really, as she was younger than her two brothers. She's thirteen now and in her last year at school.'

'How are things at work?' asked Richard.

Merryman was foreman porter at the Old Vicarage terminus and had been one of the station's first employees when the railway had arrived in Llangollen from Ruabon two years earlier.

'I can't complain, really. It's the best job that I've ever had, and I've had a few over the years, you know. It's regular work and pay, and what more can you ask for? I don't suppose I'll ever be prime minister, but it's honest work, and you meet some interesting people.' He stroked his beard and chuckled.

Richard smiled at the thought of Merryman as prime minister, and wished the family well.

***

Richard rode the few miles to Corwen to visit the workhouse infirmary. He had been appointed as the medical officer for the Corwen Poor Law Union eighteen months ago. The workhouse was a bleak building that reflected the lives of its inmates. It was the last resort for the poor and frail of the local area. It had a small infirmary that Richard visited at least twice a week and for which he received a small salary.

Richard met the workhouse master, Enoch Evans, and asked him whether any new cases had been admitted to the infirmary. Evans, in late middle age, had metal spectacles with small round lenses that perched near the end of his nose. He looked over them at Richard.

'One of our old inmates, David Lewis, was given a bed yesterday,' said Evans. 'He was evicted from his farm last year, and with no money or relatives, he lived rough for several months until the winter took its toll. He hasn't been well since but has got worse in the last few days.'

'I'll take a look at him,' said Richard. 'Is there anyone else?'

'One of the boys, Bob Morgan, had a bad fall in the yard and cut his leg. Ann Jones dealt with it, but she wasn't happy with the wound. We'll get him out of the schoolroom when you want to see him.'

Ann Jones was one of the infirmary nurses. She was also a workhouse inmate. The workhouse infirmary did not have properly trained or paid nurses. The master, or his wife, selected the nurses, and they learned their duties from others or through common sense. Richard always provided guidance during his visits.

Richard went up to the infirmary where there were two rooms, one for the men and one for the women patients. Ann Jones took him over to David Lewis, whose breathing was laboured and interrupted by severe coughing. Richard examined the old man.

'Your chest is very congested. I'll give you some medicine.' He paused and looked down at the old man, lying weak in the bed. He sat down beside him. 'Mr Evans tells me that you used to farm.'

'Yes, in the hills above Cynwyd.' He spoke slowly, so he could catch his breath and avoid coughing.

'Don't speak too much now. I shall see you again in three or four days and you can tell me all about it when your chest is a bit better.'

Richard checked the other patients with Ann Jones. He had got to know Ann quite well and he regarded her as one of the better nurses. She had been in the workhouse for two years since her husband died in a quarry accident. Forced to leave the quarry cottage, she ended up homeless and penniless. She was put to work in the kitchens when she first entered the workhouse, but the master's wife thought she would be better suited in the infirmary.

Ann mentioned that a young, single girl had been admitted to the workhouse yesterday. She was nine months pregnant, homeless and had nowhere else to go.

'She told me that she'll give away the child as soon as it's born,' said Ann, 'but wanted to make sure that it was safely delivered.'

'I know you'll look after her, but if there are any complications then send for me. It must be a worrying time for the poor girl.'

'Thank you, doctor. Yet another poor soul disowned by her family.'

Finally, Richard attended to poor little Bob Morgan's knee. For being a brave boy, he gave the six-year-old a sweet. Bob's eyes lit up, and he asked if his brother could have a sweet, too. Richard laughed and gave him another sweet out of his pocket. As Bob was not yet seven years old, he stayed with his mother in the women's dormitory, but his older brother was in the boys' wing and his sister in the girls' section of the workhouse. Their mother did not see her older children, and she would have been separated from her husband, too, if he had still been alive. He had died five years earlier. The segregation of family members was just one of the harsh realities of workhouse life. Secretly, Bob managed to give the sweet to his brother in the schoolroom.

It was lunchtime when Richard left the infirmary and felt the sunshine on his face. It was a pleasant change after the confined greyness of the workhouse. The severe austerity and hopelessness of the institution was a different world from the bustle of life in Corwen square. Market day in the town meant that the inns and taverns were busy. Richard entered the Owain Glyndwr Hotel and ordered some food. He noticed Mr and Mrs Edwards and their son and daughter, Llewelyn and Angharad, at a table at the back of the room. The Edwards family were Richard's patients, and Mrs Edwards had recently recovered from illness. He went over to their table and asked after her health. Mr Edwards, a farmer, was in town for the market and farm business.

'Llewelyn and I are meeting the land agent in ten minutes, so you can have this table,' said Mr Edwards. 'Llewelyn wants to take over the farm and we are hoping that he can get the tenancy. He has lived and worked on the farm all his life, and there will be no one better to follow me when I'm too old to carry on.'

'I'm getting married to Mary next month,' said Llewelyn, 'and the tenancy will give us security for the future.'

Richard wished them good luck with the land agent. Angharad looked at her parents as if she had a big favour to ask.

'Please can I stay and talk to Dr Lloyd about my plans to become a nurse? It will be so useful to have his advice about what I should do.'

'I am sure that the doctor wishes to have his lunch in peace,' said Mr Edwards.

'I'll be pleased to discuss Angharad's plans,' said Richard.

'Let her stay,' said her mother.

As Mr and Mrs Edwards and Llewelyn were leaving, William's business colleague, Samuel Vaughan, entered the hotel. He joined a couple of acquaintances at a table quite near where Richard and Angharad were sitting. Richard had his back to Mr Vaughan and didn't see him. He was only interested in Angharad's ideas to train as a nurse.

'I really admire Florence Nightingale, and I am going to see if I can have a place at St Thomas' Hospital. She has a training school for nurses there. I am so excited.'

'That's wonderful,' said Richard. 'Florence Nightingale opened her school while I was in London. Her ideas have changed nursing and hospitals. She is quite a remarkable person.'

'You haven't met her?' asked Angharad.

'No, but I heard her speak about her hopes for the training school and hospital reform.'

Angharad, suitably impressed, said that she would love to meet her heroine.

'Have you heard about Betsi Cadwaladr, who was also a heroine of nursing?' asked Richard.

'I haven't, no,' said Angharad.

'Betsi came from around here. She left Bala and worked in service for many years before training as a nurse at Guy's Hospital in London. At the age of sixty-five, she joined the military nursing service and went to the Crimea. She worked with Florence Nightingale in Scutari, but they often disagreed over nursing practice.'

'In what way?' asked Angharad.

'Well, they were from different backgrounds, and Betsi was much older, of course. But Betsi also felt that some of the rules got in the way of urgent help for the injured soldiers and Florence was a stickler for procedures. They did have a lot of respect for one another, though.'

'I can see Betsi's point,' said Angharad.

'Betsi died a few years ago but she wrote her life story. I've got a copy of the book at home if you'd like to borrow it. She had a very interesting life – she was maid to a ship's captain for many years and travelled all over the world.'

'Oh yes please, I'd enjoy reading that. There are so few books about interesting women.'

'Nursing, and especially the training, is very hard. It's a tough life and you have to be very determined,' said Richard.

'I'm sure that it is, but the work must be rewarding. I want to do something useful and to achieve something with my life. I would like to be a doctor like you, but it's so unfair that women can't be doctors, so the next best thing is to be a nurse.'

Angharad's sheer enthusiasm made Richard smile.

She looked curiously at him. 'I am serious, you know.'

'I can tell that you are, and that you know what you want. I'm very impressed with your ambitions.'

'What other ambitions are there for a girl? Going into service? Pandering to the rich and idle, at their beck and call? No thank you very much.' Angharad pulled a face confirming her disgust with the very idea.

Richard looked at her and they both laughed.

Samuel Vaughan heard the laughter and looked over. He was surprised to see Richard with a young woman in a hotel, and they were apparently quite familiar with one another. It was not what he expected of a doctor and certainly not of a gentleman already betrothed.

Through the window, Angharad saw her mother returning to the hotel.

'I have to go now, and thank you for listening to me.'

'You are welcome. I am sure that you will secure a place at St Thomas' and that you'll become a very good nurse. If you need any further help then let me know. I'll let you have that book when I'm next in Corwen.'

Richard finished his lunch and left the hotel without seeing Mr Vaughan.

CHAPTER 5

Sir Clayton Davenport had taken over the Berwyn Hall estate, with its nine tenanted farms and river valley woodland, when his father had died twelve years earlier. He'd retired from the army and returned to his childhood home with his wife Margaret and their three children, Humphrey, Grant and Elizabeth. Humphrey, the eldest, died in the Crimea, and Grant was now away in the army.

In his fifties, Clayton had become the real country squire, with his tweed suit, plus fours and faithful gundog at his side. Despite also having a residence in London, he rarely used it and preferred rural life at Berwyn Hall. The house was both impressive and comfortable. A long avenue of trees led to the wide, symmetrical stone facade of the two-storey mansion. High windows with stone mullions stood either side of the arched central entrance. The gothic roofline was crowned with thirty-five tall chimneys behind pinnacled gables.

Sir Clayton was a fair man and readily agreed to Richard's request to attend the railway company's board meeting. The meeting took place at The Hand Inn and Richard made his case very well. Several board members agreed with Richard's business argument that safer working practices would result in fewer accidents and stoppages in work. The board voted in favour of a review of all incidents that had caused injuries. William had spoken against the proposal, but Richard had persuaded the meeting to his point of view. William tried hard to hide his annoyance.

A delighted Richard left the meeting and went for a drink. As he sipped his ale, Elin appeared with some food for a customer.

'I hoped that I might see you tonight,' said Richard. 'How is John since he left Ty Celyn?'

'He's recovering but I've told him that he's not fit for work yet. I finish work soon, so you can call in and see him if you like.'

'I'll walk back with you,' said Richard, 'as I have some news that will interest him.'

When Elin was done with work, Richard met her at the back of the hotel and told her about the meeting.

'I feel that I have achieved something tonight. Profits should not come before people's lives.'

'But you must feel that you do good every day,' said Elin. 'As a doctor, you're always helping people.'

'Sometimes, though, I feel that I am continually treating symptoms and not dealing with the real causes of illness and injury.'

'You are a good man, but it can't all be done at once. Enjoy your victories, like tonight.' Elin smiled at Richard. There was warmth in her eyes and loveliness in her face. Her allure troubled him.

At her lodgings, Elin passed Richard on the stairs as she ran up to see John. Richard was aware of her proximity as her clothes brushed against him.

'I'm back, John, and Dr Lloyd is here to see you.'

Richard followed her into a small room with a couple of chairs and a bed against the wall. A door behind the chairs led to an adjoining room. John asked Richard to sit down, while Elin perched on the side of the bed. Richard told John of the board's decision to review working practices.

'You've done well, and thank you for your efforts.' John hesitated, and Richard could sense that he wasn't convinced. 'Do you really think that things will change? The company's aim is to build the line as quickly as possible to get trains running and start making profits for the shareholders. It's only the government that can force better working conditions for the men, and they're with the bosses.'

'You may be right,' said Richard, 'but unless we stand up and try to improve things for ourselves, we shall certainly achieve nothing.'

They chatted on for a few minutes, after which Richard stood up to leave. Elin went outside with him. They stood at the roadside.

'Thank you again for everything you've done for John. He may not always show it, but he is grateful and so am I.'

Elin moved forward and kissed him. The kiss was intended for his cheek, but somehow, their lips touched. It was a fleeting moment that seemed much longer. Elin averted her eyes and Richard stared at her in surprise.

'I'm sorry,' said Elin, embarrassed by her spontaneity and misguided act of gratitude.

'No, the apology is mine,' said Richard. 'And you a married woman, too.'

'I'm not married,' said Elin.

'I just assumed that you and John were married.'

'John is my brother.'

Richard was taken aback and Elin laughed.

'I see,' said Richard, slowly absorbing this news.

'So you can kiss me back if you like,' said Elin, with a teasing smile.

'You may not be married, but I am promised to someone else,' he said quietly.

'Oh, I'm sorry – I didn't know,' said Elin, blushing.

As Richard made his way home, he tried to make sense of his feelings for Elin. The answer was not what he wanted and certainly not what he needed at this time. But he couldn't get Elin out of his mind.

***

William's mood had improved only slightly by the end of the meeting. He was annoyed with himself for losing the argument to Richard Lloyd so publicly. After most of the other board members had left the room, he took Mr Lucas, the assistant engineer, to one side.

'We'll talk further but take no action regarding the review. I'll decide what we do next for the board. There will be no hold-ups to the tunnel. I want work to continue as before, and we need to catch up on the recent delay.'

'Very good, sir,' said Lucas.

William then joined some of the other board members in the public area of the inn. Samuel Vaughan came over to speak to William.

'A good meeting, despite the doctor getting his way.'

'It will have little consequence. The board will get their report, but there will be no impact on the work programme. You are still going to invest in the Corwen to Bala line?'

'Most definitely, as I feel very committed to the venture now.' Vaughan paused and looked around to see if anyone could hear them. 'I have a rather sensitive matter to bring up with you. Am I correct in believing that Dr Lloyd and your cousin are engaged to be married?'

'Unfortunately, yes,' said William.

'I was in the Owain Glyndwr Hotel last week and I saw Dr Lloyd enjoying the company of a pretty young woman. They were on their own and clearly having a good time and enjoying lunch together.'

'Did you speak to Lloyd?' asked William. He was angry, but intrigued, by Richard's actions.

'No, and I don't think he noticed me. It was market day and the place was busy. It's probably nothing. It might even be his sister, but I thought you should know.'

'He doesn't have a sister. You thought that the two of them were acting in a way that looked as if they were more than just acquaintances?'

'They were jovial and familiar with one another, but I wouldn't say any more than that,' said Vaughan.

Whether Samuel's gossip had substance or not, William knew he could use this information to try and sour Sara's relationship with Richard. He was not the right man for her.

William decided that Sara would find the news more convincing if their aunt told her. Later that evening at Plas Gwyn, William told Aunt Grace that he would appreciate her advice.

'Samuel Vaughan told me that he saw Richard acting affectionately with a pretty girl in a Corwen hotel. They were alone and having a meal together. I feel that Sara should know about this. If we don't tell her, she might find out from someone else.'

William's exaggerated version of Vaughan's account of Richard and Angharad Edwards' innocent conversation greatly concerned Aunt Grace.

The following morning, Grace decided that Sara needed to know about Richard and the mysterious young woman. Her niece needed to talk to Richard and find out the truth. After breakfast, Grace and Sara were alone.

'Why are you telling me this? Do you believe that Richard is seeing someone else?' questioned Sara.

'No, I don't think that Richard would do such a thing. You know that I have a very high regard for him. But this story has been brought to our attention. We can't ignore it, and you need to know the truth.'

'Richard loves me. He would never cheat on me.'

'Speak to him about the incident. There will be a very good explanation for the situation. Put your mind at rest.'

Sara wrote a stark message to Richard:

'I need to see you immediately. Come to Plas Gwyn on receipt of this note.'

***

Richard was out on calls when Sara's letter was delivered. He did not return home until late afternoon. The brief and urgent command surprised him, and while riding over to Plas Gwyn, he puzzled over the possible reasons for his summons.

William saw Richard arrive and waited for him, impatiently, in the hall.

'What are you doing here?' he demanded.

'Sara wants to see me urgently. Is she alright?'

'I warned you, Lloyd, that if you ever hurt Sara, there would be consequences.'

Richard was now very concerned about Sara. He stared at William for a few seconds and then pushed by him and entered the drawing room. Aunt Grace acknowledged Richard and promptly left the room. William had followed Richard, but Grace took his arm and told him to leave Sara and Richard alone. Sara, looking very straight-faced, sat on a sofa with her arms folded.

'What is the matter?' Richard asked Sara. 'I came as soon as I read your note. I've been working all afternoon.'

'Sit down. I need to know what's going on,' said Sara.

Richard sat down, but she allowed him no time to speak.

'I'll get straight to the point. I've been told that you have been seen in public with a young woman and behaving in a way that is not becoming of someone who is engaged to be married.'

He looked blankly at Sara, but then his thoughts turned to Elin's kiss, the night before. Someone must have seen them. Sara noticed his hesitation.

'Look, if there is someone else then just tell me. And if not, then who was the woman you met and dined with in the Corwen hotel?'

'Corwen?' queried Richard. He then realised that she must be talking about the Edwards family. The young woman was Angharad, not Elin.

'I didn't dine with anyone at the Owain Glyndwr. Mr and Mrs Edwards and their daughter were finishing their lunch when I arrived at the hotel and they asked me to join them. I have been treating Mrs Edwards for a long-term illness. They had business to attend to and left their daughter with me for a few minutes. She wants to be a nurse and is planning to go to London, so needed some advice from me. That's it.'

'But I was told that you were acting improperly.'

'We may have laughed once or twice, but that's all. She wanted to know about the hospital.'

'You need to be more careful. You have caused me much embarrassment. Who else might have seen you and come to the same conclusion?'

'I cannot understand how anyone would come to that conclusion anyway. Who told you this? It was William, wasn't it?'

'It was Aunt Grace who told me.'

'Yes, but William told Grace, knowing it would cause trouble between us. He will not rest until he drives us apart. Don't you see that William has exaggerated all of this?'

Sara knew that Richard was right but didn't want to admit it.

On the way out, Richard saw William again.

'Complete misunderstanding; the girl's mother is a patient of mine. Anyway, you'll be delighted to learn that everything is fine again, between Sara and me.'

William removed his spectacles and almost immediately put them back. 'Sara is a fool for accepting your story. I don't trust you, Lloyd, and in time, neither will Sara. She will realise that you are a cheat as well as a penniless doctor, and she will end your tedious relationship.'

Richard got his horse and rode back to Ty Celyn. The skirmish with William was only a temporary victory. William was still a major irritant in his relationship with Sara.

CHAPTER 6

Ben Hopkins' gambling debts had got out of hand. He hadn't had a successful night at cards for some time. Dan Williams, the carter, had told him to pay up, and Jed James also wanted his money by the end of the week.

When Ben Hopkins had visited John Roberts at Ty Celyn, he had seen a cash box in an open drawer in Richard's surgery. It was where Richard kept his patients' payments. When Ben left Ty Celyn, he had realised that he and John had been alone in the house. Maybe the house was often unoccupied on Thursday afternoons. He decided to find out.

That Thursday, around noon, Ben went to Ty Celyn. As he walked in front of the house, he did not see Sian in an upstairs window. Sian saw him but thought no more about it. She had more important things on her mind.

Ben decided to wait a few minutes and was rewarded when he saw Sian hurry out of the back door and go down the lane.

Ben quietly opened the door. He had a quick look in the downstairs rooms and there was nobody around. He went to the doctor's surgery. The drawer containing the cash box was locked this time, but he had come prepared. He forced a crowbar above the drawer lock and cracked the wooden frame holding the drawer. The cash box was also locked, and he looked for the key. It was at the back of the second drawer. Ben urgently lifted the lid of the cash box and saw what he was after. He grabbed the money and put it in his pocket. He made his way to the back door, looked both ways and walked quickly back to the lane.

***

Sian looked forward to Thursdays and her secret outing. She headed down to the river, and her heart beat just that little bit faster when she saw Owen under the tree on the riverbank. This was their spot, and the water of the Dee ran especially fast just here. They could watch it rush and twist its way around the large stones in the river from an elevated position on the bank, quite secluded from the occasional passerby.

They were both nineteen years old and had met in chapel when Owen first came to Berwyn Hall as a servant. Sian was pretty, with dark hair that was not quite shoulder length. Owen was her first love, slim and tall, and she liked his kind eyes.

'How are you, *cariad*?' asked Owen, taking Sian in his arms. 'It seems such a long time since we were together.'

They kissed.

'I feel better for seeing you,' said Sian. 'More to the point, how are you getting on with the two witches?'

Sian referred to Lady Davenport and her housekeeper, Eve Lyons. Unfortunately, it was not Sir Clayton but his wife, Margaret, who controlled the domestic side of Berwyn Hall. Lady Margaret had very strict rules regarding the servants, and Eve Lyons, who had been at the hall for many years, enjoyed enforcing them.

'I love our time together, but I wish we could have longer. We seem to be snatching a couple of hours here or there. I long for a day out together, a whole day, perhaps going on the train to the seaside. Do you think we ever will?' asked Sian.

'Of course we will,' replied Owen, 'but it's just too risky now. The mistress would sack me if she found out that we were seeing one another. You know her strict rules about servants having sweethearts. I need to get a new job before we can tell anyone about us.'

'But we don't even work in the same house. It's ridiculous that Berwyn Hall wants to prevent us from being friends.'

'Anyway, let's enjoy the time we have.'

Owen put his arm around Sian and they kissed again. The sound of footsteps on the path below interrupted their moment. A man came into view. Hopkins was walking slowly and counting Richard's money. Sian and Owen remained silent. Although they were well hidden, they were close to the path.

Once he was gone, Sian spoke. 'I saw him earlier outside Ty Celyn. He was one of the men who brought the injured navvy to the house after the explosion. And he came to see him again a couple of days later.'

'He's come into some money for sure,' said Owen.

***

That evening, Jed was already in The Chain Bridge Inn when Ben arrived.

'Have you got my money yet?' asked Jed, sipping his tankard of ale. 'I want the debt paid by tomorrow night.'

'You'll get it, don't worry,' said Ben.

'You're the one who needs to worry, if you don't pay up.'

Two navvies came in and asked whether there was a card game that evening. One of the railwaymen was a miner working in Berwyn Tunnel. He reminded Ben that there would be a lot of blasting tomorrow and they would need plenty of powder. Ben confirmed that he had it in hand.

Jed listened to the conversation and asked Ben to sit with him at a table where they would not be overheard.

'I take it that you have access to the blasting powder,' said Jed.

Ben nodded. 'I have a key to the store and I control the supply of all the materials. Why?'

'I have a bit of business to put your way. You owe me almost two pounds. You can forget your debt if you get me some powder and fuses.'

'That could cost me my job,' said Ben.

'How will anyone find out? You said that you control it all.'

The landlord brought Ben his ale and the talking stopped for a minute. Ben thought again about Jed's offer. He could clear more of his debts if he didn't have to use any of the stolen money to pay him back.

'Look, I'm not bothered if you don't want to do this. I thought it would help you with your debts. But remember that I want paying tomorrow.'

'I'll take your offer,' said Ben. 'I'll get you what you want.'

***

Richard had worked late and arrived home at Ty Celyn just in time for supper. He went to the surgery to put his patients' receipts in the cash box. He saw the broken drawer and the empty cash box. Richard went to see Sian and asked whether there had been any visitors. She said that she hadn't seen anyone but that she had gone out for an hour earlier that afternoon.

The house was checked to see if anything else had been stolen or disturbed. Only the money from the cash box had been taken.

'I don't like this,' said Richard. 'Someone has targeted the cash box. They must have known that it was in that locked drawer. But how did they know?'

Sian remained quiet. She realised that she knew the answer and she wanted to tell him. But how could she tell him about Hopkins without revealing her furtive meetings with Owen? She became even more worried by Richard's next announcement:

'I shall inform Sergeant Parry in Corwen tomorrow morning. No doubt he will want to talk to all of us.'

'Me as well?' Sian asked anxiously.

Richard noticed her discomfort and asked why she was worried. Sian told him about Hopkins acting suspiciously, and that previously he had visited John Roberts in the surgery after his accident. Sian, blushing and hesitant, also explained to Richard about her fondness for Owen and the reason for their furtive meetings. Richard reassured her that no one outside the family need know about their friendship.

***

The following morning, Richard rode to Corwen. His first call was to Sergeant Parry. Parry, a lean, tall man in his thirties, listened with interest about the theft and Hopkins' suspicious behaviour. The local constabulary, formed only a few years earlier, dealt mainly with fairly routine matters like rate collection and road surveying. Most arrests concerned drunkenness and vagrancy, so the prospect of arresting a proper thief was a lot more interesting.

Sergeant Parry interviewed Sian later that morning. He then went to the engineer's office in Llangollen and asked if he could arrange for Ben Hopkins to be brought in. Mr Lucas, the assistant engineer, explained that Hopkins was in Berwyn but that he would get a message for him to be in the office at half past two.

Mr Lucas was inspecting progress with the new station buildings at Carrog that afternoon, so Sergeant Parry used his office to interview Ben Hopkins. Hopkins put on an air of confidence, but he was feeling worried.

The sergeant asked him where he was yesterday afternoon.

'At work, as usual,' said Hopkins.

'So, there will be navvies who will confirm that they saw you working at the railway, at all times, between noon and three yesterday?'

'No, I had to go and see my boss after midday, but I was back around half past two.'

That allowed plenty of time to get to the doctor's house, steal the money and return to work. And it fitted the time period when Sian was out of the house.

'So, you came here then, to see Mr Lucas. Why?'

'I needed time off work as my father is ill. But Mr Lucas wasn't here and the office was closed. It was a wasted journey.'

Hopkins prayed that Lucas had been out yesterday afternoon.

'I don't think that you came here,' Parry said. 'You went to Ty Celyn, stole the money and then went back to work. You were seen outside Ty Celyn, and on the river path, counting the money.'

Ben Hopkins laughed. It was too nervous a laugh to be convincing. 'I have no idea what you are talking about.'

'I'll tell you what I am talking about. Yesterday afternoon, money was stolen from the doctor's house.'

'I know nothing about any money.'

'I have more enquiries to make, but I shall see you again tomorrow.'

Ben Hopkins went straight to the Crow Castle Inn. He had some hard thinking to do.

When Mr Lucas returned from Carrog, he told Sergeant Parry that he had been in his office all yesterday afternoon. He had not seen Ben Hopkins.

CHAPTER 7

It was Saturday morning, and the early post had been delivered to Plas Gwyn. William sat in a high-backed chair in his study, an elegant room dominated by a large oak desk with an inlaid leather top. He read the board report he had commissioned from an old associate, a retired railway engineer. William smiled to himself. The forty-page report confirmed his view that there were no safety issues to address, and that the Llangollen and Corwen Railway Company adhered to sound, accepted practice in railway construction. This conclusion was of little surprise; it was what William had asked his associate to write. The forty pages backed up the conclusion with expertise and industry knowledge. It was a convincing read, assuming that the board members even bothered to study it. William looked forward to the next board meeting for his vindication.

Most board members had little involvement with the building of the railway apart from participation in meetings. William, however, took an active interest in operational matters. He saw it as his right to protect his investment and safeguard future profits and dividends.

Sara had also received some post that morning. She sat at her dressing table in her bedroom, fascinated with the agents' descriptions of various expensive properties for sale. However, these were not properties in the Dee Valley. Every month, Sara received details of prestigious houses for sale in London. She imagined Richard and herself living in the luxurious, three-storey townhouses in Kensington and Belgravia. She had asked the property agents to send her the information, to prepare for the day that they would move to London.

At first, Sara was realistic about the homes that they might be able to afford and looked at properties convenient for the hospitals at which Richard might be working. However, as the weeks and months went by, she realised that this was not going to happen anytime soon, so she allowed herself to dream a bit bigger. Living in those houses might be a dream, but she believed that one day she and Richard would make it happen.

Sara didn't tell anyone about her property mailings and always read the particulars in the privacy of her bedroom and kept them in her wardrobe. However, Aunt Grace had discovered a couple of house details that Sara had left on her dressing table. Grace felt sorry for her niece. She knew how desperate Sara was to marry Richard and start a new life in London, but Grace decided not to embarrass Sara by raising the matter with her.

Elizabeth Davenport visited Sara that afternoon. They had been friends long before their engagements to Evan and Richard. However, their friendship had become even more special because of their relationships with the brothers. Elizabeth and Sara could be mistaken for sisters. Both were of a similar height with slim figures. Sara's blonde hair was fairer than Elizabeth's, but they both wore their hair in plaits at the back. They even acted like sisters, talking incessantly, linking arms and laughing at the same things. Elizabeth in particular could tell when her friend was in the slightest way unhappy.

'What's the matter?' Elizabeth asked her. 'You're not as cheerful as usual. You seem to have things on your mind.'

'I'm sorry, but I'm fine. I am so pleased that you are here.'

Sara took her friend's arm as they walked through the garden.

'How are things with Richard?' Elizabeth asked. 'I noticed that you were both a bit tense the other day when Father asked about your wedding plans.'

'I'm tired of waiting for Richard to realise that London is the answer to our problems. William constantly tells me that I could do so much better than marrying a poor doctor who has no future. He tells me to give him up and find a husband with money. I want Richard to prove William wrong. He could be a huge success as a hospital surgeon.'

'Do you love Richard, or the life that he will give you in London?'

'I love both. He is handsome and kind. I know what I want, but because I am a woman, I am unable to achieve my ambitions. Richard will give me that power and the life that I want.'

'Can't Richard give you that if you stay here? He is so committed to staying in Wales. Evan says that he will not be happy in London.'

'Nonsense. He lived in London before and seemed perfectly happy. Richard can't give me the life I need if we stay here. I want London society, a house that people will envy, and a husband who is an eminent surgeon. I want to do something with my life. I don't want to be a country doctor's wife in sleepy Berwyn.'

'So what are you going to do?'

'Richard must come to his senses. His practice is going nowhere. If he wants to marry me, then London is the only way forward.'

Elizabeth didn't know what else to say. Her best friend and her future brother-in-law, both people she loved dearly, were at loggerheads and she could not see a solution for them.

***

That evening, Richard dined at Plas Gwyn. After dinner, Sara took Richard to a quiet room so that they could be on their own.

'I have something to show you.' Sara pulled out one of the house descriptions that she had received that morning. 'Just look at this house. Isn't it perfect for us?'

Richard took the sheet of paper and read the London address. He shook his head in disbelief.

'Go on, read it. It would be wonderful for us. It has a huge hall and a dining room that would be ideal for entertaining. Only five bedrooms, but that would be enough, don't you think? This is what we could have if you were a surgeon in London. I want a house like this.' She paused for a response.

Richard read the words on the paper but he did not take in any meaning from them. His mind was full of other thoughts. Did Sara not understand his wish to stay in Berwyn, or was she trying to browbeat him into submission regarding London?

'I'm sorry, but it doesn't matter how nice that house is, we're not going to London,' he said eventually. 'My mind is set on my practice, and I wouldn't be happy if we left Berwyn. We both could have a wonderful life here. Just give me time to save some more money and we'll buy a lovely house in the Dee Valley. You can choose it.'

Sara stood up, snatched the property details from his hand and threw them to the floor. Her eyes flashed with anger.

'Time! I've given you too much time already. I shall be an old maid before we can afford to buy a house anywhere. It's London that will provide us both with an income to enjoy life. How do I persuade you that this is our only way? You are hopeless and stubborn. I hate you.'

Sara raised her hand, but Richard grabbed it before she could slap him. She struggled to free her arm from Richard's grip.

'Let me go! How dare you hold me like that! You're hurting my arm.'

Sara's raised voice alerted William and Grace, and they came running into the room.

'What is going on?' demanded William, looking at Richard's crude restraint of his cousin.

'He's hurting me!' Sara cried. 'Get him away from me.'

Richard let go of Sara's arm. William asked Richard to come with him, and reluctantly, Richard followed William to his study.

'I have no desire to know what that was all about, but I am vexed to see my cousin so upset. It is not like her to get angry, so I can only assume that you have acted inappropriately towards her.'

'You assume wrongly,' replied Richard, who was now angry with both Sara and William. 'We disagree on a fundamental part of our future lives together, and that is distressing to both of us. I hope to resolve the matter, but you will appreciate that this is between Sara and me, not you.'

'Sara has no father, and I take an interest in her life and happiness.'

'I repeat that this is a matter between Sara and me. I think it is time that I was leaving. I shall see Sara on my way out.'

'I don't think that is a good idea. Please do leave the house, but you will not bother Sara again tonight. I'll escort you to the door.'

'I would prefer to say goodnight to Sara.'

William ignored his wish.

'Before you leave, do you know what this is?' William picked up the railway safety report that he had received that morning.

Richard shook his head.

'It is a comprehensive report on the construction of the Llangollen and Corwen railway. It looks at all our working practices. It says that we comply with all standards in the industry. The report will go to the board at its next meeting. It gives the company a clean bill of health. The members will be pleased, and they will no doubt query the fuss that you made about the accident.'

Fists clenched, Richard moved towards William.

'Calm yourself, man,' said William, 'you must learn to control your anger. Now, the door, if you would be so good. I'll ring for a servant to show you to your horse.'

'Don't worry, I know where the stables are,' said Richard.

***

The next day, at Ty Celyn, Richard was ready to leave for church. His father and Evan had already left the house, but Richard waited for Sara. She frequently accompanied Richard to the morning service at Berwyn Church. Following the events of the night before, he didn't expect her but decided to wait anyway until the last possible minute. There was no sign of her carriage, and Richard hastily made his way to the old church. He wondered whether there was any future for them, now. They had argued many times before, but last night had been the worst yet.

Richard arrived at the little church just as the first hymn was starting. He looked across at Evan and

Elizabeth. For the first time, he envied his brother's happiness. Evan and Elizabeth wanted similar things from life, and there was every chance that they would achieve them together. It made Richard wonder whether love alone was enough to ensure a happy marriage.

Nevertheless, that evening Richard wrote a note to Sara. He told her that he had missed her at church that morning and their walk by the river. He asked if they could meet soon.

He awaited her reply.

CHAPTER 8

Mr Lucas' confirmation that he had been in his office all afternoon and had not seen Hopkins was the conclusive information that Sergeant Parry needed. Ben Hopkins had lied and he no longer had an alibi for the crime. Sian's evidence was sufficient to make an arrest. Parry and the local constable went to Ben's lodgings. The landlady told them that she had not seen him and that he was often out until late. Parry decided that they would return the following morning to arrest him. Ben spent the night hiding in Berwyn Tunnel.

On Saturday mornings, Ben, as the gaffer, collected the week's wages from the engineer's office and paid the men at the end of the day's shift. He picked up the wages as usual and walked back to Berwyn. He unlocked the door to a trackside hut and removed some blasting powder and fuses.

Ben crossed the main road and headed up the Glyn Ceiriog lane. He passed Dan Williams' cottage, noticing his cart in the yard.

A few minutes later, Ben stopped alongside a dry-stone wall. He looked around to make sure he was alone, then removed a few of the top stones and slid the wages bag inside the wall. He replaced the top stones to conceal the bag, which contained about fifty pounds.

Arriving at Jed James' farm, he kept away from the house and went into the barn. After about twenty minutes, the farmhouse door opened and Jed walked across the yard. Ben watched him through a narrow gap in the door. The barn door swung open and Jed turned around.

'You've done it then. I had my doubts when you came here first thing this morning,' said Jed.

'I've done the easy bit. When they realise that I've taken the wages, every man on the railway will be looking for me. Are you still prepared to hide me up here?'

'If you've got the blasting powder that you promised, you can stay up here for a few days until things quieten down in the valley. I'll take you to the hut.'

They went to a small, disused quarry surrounded by scrub woodland that was part of the James' land. Above the old quarry, there was a windowless, stone hut. It had been used to store blasting powder before the quarry closed. Jed pushed the door open. There was a straw mattress that just fitted alongside the wall.

'It's dry and the straw came from the barn this morning,' said Jed. 'There's bread and water in the corner.'

***

The navvies and miners were waiting at Berwyn for their weekly wages. After another half hour passed, John Roberts and four others decided to walk to the office in Llangollen. They wanted to know what had happened to Ben Hopkins and their pay.

Sergeant Parry was in the office enquiring about Ben Hopkins' whereabouts. Parry and his constable had called at Hopkins' lodgings to again find his room empty. Mr Lucas and Parry heard John Roberts and the other men outside the office. When they realised that the navvies were also looking for Hopkins, they feared the worst.

'He can't have gone far,' said Parry. 'We'll organise a manhunt.'

'If I find him, I'll kill him,' shouted an angry John Roberts, who was still very short of money after his accident.

'Let's all stay calm,' said the policeman. 'I need to alert the railway station, canal wharf and the coaching inns first. He's not going to get far.'

By late afternoon there were almost thirty men combing the town and countryside. However, as night fell with no sign of Hopkins, the search was abandoned until the morning.

***

Ben Hopkins had a restless night. He was glad when the first light of dawn came under the door of the hut, and he could forget about trying to sleep. Ben took the bucket to the stream that ran through the old quarry and freshened his face with the cold water. He had only been back in the hut for a few minutes when he became aware of movement outside.

The door was pushed open. It was Jed with food and news. He told Ben that he was the talk of The Chain Bridge Inn last night and that an even bigger search was planned for today. He told him to stay in the quarry and not to go down to the farm or anywhere near the Glyn Ceiriog road.

John Roberts and a couple of navvies had been assigned the Glyn Ceiriog road as their search area for the afternoon. Sergeant Parry had instructed them to make enquiries at all cottages and farms and to search any outbuildings. They had been out for almost two hours when they arrived at the James' farm. Jed saw them cross the yard to the house.

He called out from the barn. 'What do you want?'

'We're looking for the thief who stole our wages. Have you seen any strangers?' said John.

'Nobody ever comes up here.'

'Do you mind if we have a look in the farm buildings?'

'Please yourself, but I've been in them today already.'

'Have you any other buildings on your land?'

Jed shook his head. He watched John Roberts and his companions leave the farm. Ben remained a free man for another night.

The following morning, Jed brought Ben some more food and news. He showed him a reward notice.

'These are all over the town. You have a price on your head. You're a wanted man.'

Ben took the piece of paper. 'Five pounds,' he said. 'I'll give you that if you don't turn me in.'

'I'm not going to turn you in. There were men at the farm yesterday asking about you. If I wanted the reward, I could have told them where you were. You'd have been on your way to gaol inside of ten minutes. We have a deal.'

Ben didn't trust Jed. He had intended to stay another night, but he now wanted to make his move. Ireland was to be his destination. He knew a former navvy who had gone home to western Ireland following a railway injury. He could help out on his small farm until he decided what to do.

Ben needed to get to Holyhead for the crossing to Ireland. He didn't want to risk the local railway stations, so he had to get to one further away.

Once Jed was gone, Ben slipped out of the quarry hut and closed the door behind him. He avoided the James' farmhouse and went through the wood. After ten minutes, he stopped and saw the Glyn Ceiriog lane some twenty yards in front of him. He kept cover under the trees and continued down the hillside.

Dan Williams' house lay at the end of a row of six. It had a large yard to the side and a stable at the back. There was no sign of Dan, and the stable was empty. Ben settled down at the back of the stable wall, hidden behind a stack of hay.

It was early evening when Ben heard the horse and cart pull into Dan's yard. After a few minutes, the stable door opened and Dan brought the mare in for her well-earned rest and feed.

'Hello Dan.' Ben appeared from behind the hay.

'Are you trying to frighten me to death? Half of the county was out looking for you yesterday. They searched my yard.'

'I have money for you.'

Ben held out the money he owed Dan.

'Well, I didn't expect to see that again. There's a few men who are short of their money, thanks to you.'

'Yes, I'm sorry, but I was desperate. Look, Dan, I have a job for you if you'll help me. I need to get to a railway station at least twenty miles from here. Can you take me on your covered cart tomorrow?'

Dan thought for a minute or so. Ben waited for a response that seemed to take forever.

'It'll cost you. I'll be helping a criminal, and I'll be in gaol too if we're caught. I do a run to Llandudno on Tuesdays and can take you to Llandudno Junction, if that's any use to you. Where are you heading?'

'Liverpool,' Ben lied. 'So what time do you want me here?'

'It's too risky coming here. You might be seen. I'll meet you on the track outside Berwyn Tunnel at five o'clock in the morning. You'll pay me ten pounds before you get in the cart.'

'I'll pay you five pounds when we meet, and another five pounds at Llandudno Junction.'

'I'll see you tomorrow morning.'

When night fell, Ben left the stable and went up the lane. He retrieved the moneybag from the wall and put it inside his jacket. He spent the night in the tunnel.

At four-thirty, Ben walked back to the tunnel entrance and waited for Dan. He appeared just before five o'clock.

'Let's go,' said Dan.

'Where's the cart?'

'It's on the road near the new station.' Dan paused, squinting at something over Ben's shoulder. 'What's that down the tunnel?'

Ben turned round to see where Dan was pointing and felt a massive blow across the back of his head. He fell face down on the track-bed. He never felt the second strike of the metal bar.

Dan bent down to pull open Ben's jacket and found the moneybag. The bag contained the wages in individual brown envelopes. Dan stuffed them in his pockets and dropped the bag. He headed back to his cottage, where he hid the money and changed his bloodstained clothes. Within the hour, he was heading for Llandudno, as he did every Tuesday morning at that time.

***

Almost an hour later, John Roberts was walking to the tunnel and thinking about the rent that hadn't been paid. It was only his second week back at work since his accident. Elin had already increased her shifts at The Hand Inn and couldn't do any more.

John was the first worker to arrive at the tunnel entrance, where he saw Hopkins' body. He knelt at his side and felt for a pulse. Ben was still alive but only just. As a couple of navvies appeared on the scene, John picked up the metal bar that lay on Ben's leg.

The navvies stopped and looked at him. They saw John standing over Ben with the bloodstained weapon in his hand. Ben's blood was on his arms and on his trousers where he had knelt alongside him. Suddenly, John realised why they were staring at him. He threw down the bar.

'He's alive,' he shouted. 'I'm trying to help him. Get the doctor!'

When Richard arrived, there were several workers around Ben Hopkins. Richard told them to move back. The faint pulse that John had detected earlier was no more. He rode to Corwen to inform Sergeant Parry of the apparent murder.

Mr Lucas met Parry at Berwyn. The two men walked over to the body, and the policeman inspected Ben's injuries.

'It is as Dr Lloyd told me. Two heavy strikes to the head, presumably by this bar,' said Parry. 'I'll need to talk to each of the navvies who saw Hopkins before he died. Who found him?'

'I'm told that John Roberts was here first,' replied Lucas.

Parry turned to John and looked him up and down. 'I remember you, Mr Roberts. You helped with the search for Hopkins at the weekend. You are no friend of his, are you?'

'He stole our wages. None of us would count him as a friend.'

'You were very angry though. You threatened to kill him if you found him. It looks as if you did find him in the end.'

'When I found Ben, he had already been attacked. I tried to help him.'

Parry didn't believe a word of it.

He then spoke to the two navvies who had been next on the scene. They told the sergeant what they had witnessed. They confirmed John's dislike of Hopkins but neither felt that he had murdered him. However, Parry put this down to workers' solidarity, rather than a vote of innocence.

Sergeant Parry arrested John Roberts on suspicion of the murder of Ben Hopkins and took him to Corwen police office.

CHAPTER 9

Sian opened the front door at Ty Celyn to see Elin Roberts looking worried and tired. She had been working at The Hand Inn since six that morning, and at midday, Mr Lucas had told her about John's arrest. He said that John had killed Ben Hopkins, but she couldn't believe that he could do such an awful thing. Then she remembered how angry John had been when he spoke about Hopkins and the theft of the wages. Elin didn't know what to do, until Richard came to mind. He had been so kind to them. She went to see him as soon as she finished work.

Sian took Elin to Richard's surgery, where he had been writing up some notes.

'Will you help me, please? I need to make sense of what's happened.' Elin's voice was choked with emotion, and tears came to her eyes, as she struggled to tell him about John's arrest.

'Of course I will. Don't cry. We shall go to Corwen in the morning and see John and Sergeant Parry.' Richard put his arms around Elin to comfort her. Again, he sensed her warmth and allure. She hugged him, too, and felt the strength in his arms and his kiss on her forehead.

'Thank you; you have given me some hope. All I could see this afternoon was my brother going to the gallows.'

'I don't suppose you have eaten yet. Why don't you have some supper here and stay the night? Then we'll be ready to go to Corwen in the morning.'

After supper, Richard and his father Edward were in the parlour, making small talk to try and keep Elin's mind off her worries.

'I have some writing to do later,' said Richard.

'Your entry has gone in for the eisteddfod, hasn't it?' said Edward.

'My piece for the National went in a few weeks ago. I'm working now on an essay for the local eisteddfod in Corwen. Goronwy Tudor asked if I'd enter, and I don't want to let him down.'

'What's the subject?' asked his father.

'Emigration and the language. I'm writing about the proposed settlement in Patagonia.'

'I've heard about Patagonia,' said Elin. 'There's someone back home in Rhuddlan who is thinking about going there. He has been promised a lot of land so he can have his own farm. Are you going to the National Eisteddfod this year?'

'It's in Llandudno in August. I'll probably stay for a night.'

'I'm sorry to trouble you with taking me to Corwen tomorrow, and losing a day's work too. I hope it won't harm any of your patients.'

'It's no trouble, but I do need to call on Ann Thomas at Tyn y Rhos in the morning. That's on the way to Corwen and will take no more than an hour. She is very ill. There are no other calls to make and I'll soon catch up during the week. You are my priority tomorrow.'

Richard's good intentions regarding his writing came to nothing that evening. His thoughts were elsewhere. Elin was relying on him to prove her brother's innocence. He could do everything humanly possible to help her but knew there was a very good chance that he might fail. There may be no evidence to prove John's innocence, and he may even be guilty. He shared Elin's fear of the gallows for her brother.

***

It was a sunny and fresh June day when Richard and Elin rode in the gig towards Corwen. Richard made general, light conversation but Elin was not in the mood to chat. After about a mile they turned off the main road for Tyn y Rhos. Elin wanted to stay in the gig, but Jac Thomas persuaded her to come inside, while Richard attended to Ann in the bedroom.

'You have a lovely house,' said Elin.

'I built it myself, with a bit of help from family and friends.'

'Did it take you very long to build?'

'Let me think now. It must have been about eight hours.'

He waited for Elin's surprised reaction and laughed. 'This house started life as a *caban unnos*. It was just one room, made from whatever we could lay our hands on – turf, wood, straw and bracken. It had to be built in one night on common land. You started building at sunset, and providing there was a fire in the hearth and smoke coming out of the chimney before sunrise, then the cabin was yours.'

'But how did you light a fire without burning it all down?'

'The chimney was made of hazelwood covered in clay, and we had a neat stone hearth.'

'Were there a lot of homes built in this way?' asked Elin.

'Not so many now, but in the past many were built on the common land in the hills. It was a recognised custom that the builder could stay in the house. It was the only way that a poor man might put a roof over his head. I have access to the common land for grazing, and over time have cultivated some land of my own for growing food. I've added to the one room over the years, building in stone and slate, and there is nothing really left of the original cabin now.'

Richard joined them as Jac was finishing his story.

'You and Ann have done well to build this farm from nothing,' he said. 'I have great respect for your determination over the years. It has not been easy for you.'

'And now we have the worry of the enclosure of the common land,' said Jac. 'I feel very sorry for the farmers who are losing their land and homes because of the enclosures. I have heard of two farm evictions this summer, and not so far away either. It seems so wrong that the common land can be taken away by the big landowners. Men are losing their life's work at a stroke and there seems little they can do about it. I am praying that we shall not be affected.'

'You have a fine farm here and have worked hard to achieve it. You do not deserve this additional worry.'

'I haven't mentioned any of this to Ann – she has enough to fear already. How did you find her this morning?'

'She is doing well and tells me she's eating better now.'

'She eats like a bird,' said Jac.

'Small portions as often as she can manage are fine. I know it's difficult, but encourage her to do what she can.'

'I will. Thank you, doctor.'

Richard and Elin left the little farm and continued on to Corwen.

***

They met Sergeant Parry at the police office. Elin asked him what evidence he had to arrest her brother. Despite her deep despair and distress for John's situation, she remained calm and collected.

'It is well known that he didn't like Hopkins,' Parry explained. 'I heard him making threats against the man and saying that he would kill him.'

'Hopkins had stolen the men's wages and feelings were running very high,' said Richard. 'He didn't mean that he would really kill him.'

'I believe that he was prepared to kill Hopkins.'

'I saw John yesterday and his only concern was to get help for Hopkins,' said Richard. 'He showed care for the man, not anger and hate.'

'Perhaps it was just guilt for what he had done, or concern about the consequences. Witnesses have told me that they found Mr Roberts alone with the victim, holding the murder weapon, his clothes and hands stained with blood. Mr Roberts was at the scene of the murder and he has a motive for the crime. He was also known to be short of money, although the stolen wages have not yet been found.'

Elin looked at Richard. His obvious concern did nothing to raise her hopes. She asked to see her brother.

John came into the room, with the constable behind him. John looked tired and drawn but he managed a smile for Richard and his sister. He had felt abandoned in the cell overnight and was relieved to see a friendly face. Elin tried to embrace her brother, but the constable put his hand out to stop her.

'The sergeant has told us his case for your arrest and says that he has both evidence and motive,' said Richard.

'I know, but the evidence is based on the fact that I happened to be the one who found Ben. Whoever had been first to find him would have done what I did and therefore be the suspect. As for motive, every miner and everyone he owed money to had a motive.'

'We don't think that you did it,' interrupted Elin.

'Being in that cell last night and unable to sleep, I've had time to think. The big question is: where's the money? Whoever killed Ben must have taken the stolen wages. Ben didn't have the money, nor have I. There was an empty bag on the trackside near his body.'

'You say that he owed men money. I assume through gambling debts?' asked Richard.

'He played cards regularly and was on a long losing run. He'd asked me for a loan. He owed a lot of money. I think that could be the motive for his death. He was planning to run away without settling his debts. Someone that he owed money to took the stolen wages from him, and then killed him.'

'Do you know his drinking and gambling partners?'

'There are two navvies that he played cards with. They might know something. You can probably find them in The Chain Bridge Inn, about midday.'

'I'll see you in the morning and let you know how we get on.' Elin looked at Richard, hoping he would come with her.

'I'll bring you into Corwen,' he told her, then turned to John. 'We'll both see you in the morning.'

***

On the journey back to Berwyn, Elin asked Richard about Sara and their engagement.

'We've been engaged for two and a half years,' he said.

'Are you happy?' She caught the look he gave her, and hastily added, 'Oh, I'm sorry, I didn't mean to pry.'

'I don't mind talking about it. I love Sara.'

'Loving someone doesn't always mean you're happy.'

'That's true. We don't agree on things that we need to sort out before we can be married.'

He told her about Sara's insistence that they should live in London and his desire to stay here. Elin could see that just talking about his dilemma made Richard sad.

'It sounds as if you're reaching a point where one of you will have to make a decision about your future,' she said. 'It seems as if neither of you is going to back down, as you both want quite different things from life.'

'Perhaps, but we don't want to separate.'

'You can't force someone to live a life that makes them unhappy.'

'You're right, of course. Is there anyone special in your life?'

'There isn't anyone now, but I have loved. It was some time ago.'

'Did he love you?'

'Yes, I believe so.'

'So why did it end?'

There was a pause and he took his eyes off the road and looked at Elin. She was thoughtful, and those thoughts were somewhere else, a long distance away. After a few moments, she turned to Richard and forced the faintest of smiles. At that instant he wanted so much to put his arms around her. She was an enigma, strong and yet vulnerable, honest but sometimes reticent. He was fascinated by her.

Richard looked back at the road. 'We're in Berwyn,' he announced. 'Let's go to The Chain Bridge Inn and see if those navvies are there.'

At the inn, the landlord pointed them out, and Richard and Elin went over.

'I've already told the sergeant all that I know,' said one.

'We want to know about Ben Hopkins' debts and who he owed money to,' said Richard.

'I don't know anything about that,' said the other.

'Who else played cards with you and Ben?' asked Elin.

'Ben was a friend, and we don't discuss our friends with strangers.'

When Elin left the inn, her spirit was at its lowest that day.

'If no one is going to tell us about Ben Hopkins' enemies then we are wasting our time.'

'Don't give up,' Richard told her. 'We have another man to see. He owes me a favour. Come on.'

CHAPTER 10

Richard and Elin left The Chain Bridge Inn and headed into the hills to the James' farm. Jed was in the yard. Richard asked after his mother.

'Come and see for yourself,' said Jed.

Mrs James appeared in the doorway. 'I'm feeling well, doctor, thanks to you. What can we do for you?'

Richard explained how Elin's brother had been wrongly arrested for the death of Ben Hopkins. He hoped that Jed might have some information that would help them.

'I don't help the law catch men that I drink with,' said Jed.

'We're not the law. Sergeant Parry has got an innocent man locked up in Corwen. Telling us the names of the men who were pressing Hopkins for their money is not accusing them of murder.'

'I don't know,' said Jed, hesitating.

'Please, Jed. Elin's brother is going to hang unless we can find the real killer. You promised me that if I ever needed anything, I only had to ask. I'm not asking you to name Hopkins' murderer, just the men who might have a motive or have information that might help us.'

'Help him if you can, Jed,' said Mrs James.

Jed looked at his mother, who was still standing at the door.

He sighed and looked back to Richard. 'You saved Mam's life. I meant it when I made you that promise. I owe you far more than a couple of names.' Jed also didn't want anyone to suspect him.

'I was told that Hopkins owed several men money,' he said, 'but there were two men that Hopkins owed a lot of money. The first is Dan Williams. He can be a violent man. You must be careful.'

The second man was one of the navvies that they had already spoken to at the Chain Bridge. Jed told them where they could find Dan Williams.

Richard took the gig back to Ty Celyn and they walked to Dan's home.

There was no sign of the cart in the yard and the stable was empty. Richard tried the back door; it opened.

'What if Williams comes back?' asked Elin, as they went inside.

'We'll hear the cart in the yard. We'll have time to get out.'

Richard and Elin looked around. They searched the drawers of the old oak dresser and inside the cupboards. They were about to go upstairs when Richard went back to the fireplace. There was a wooden box next to the grate, part filled with kindling, but down the side was some brown paper. Pulling some of the paper out of the box Richard realised they were brown envelopes with names and numbers written on them. Richard showed them to Elin. She recognised the small, square envelopes as those that her brother brought home with his wages. Richard hugged her.

'I think we've got what we need. Williams has taken the money out of the envelopes but thankfully, didn't burn them. I wonder where he's hidden the money.'

'Shall we take them as evidence in case he burns them when he comes home?' asked Elin.

'We'll take a few just in case, but Sergeant Parry should see these where we found them.'

He led Elin upstairs and entered a bedroom. A bed, positioned against a wall, was unmade from the night before. Clothes lay in a heap on the floor at the end of the bed. He bent down to have a closer look when he heard the sound of a horse and cart pull into the yard below.

'This was going too well. Let's hope he takes the horse to the stable. That should give us time to slip out,' said Richard.

'What if he comes straight into the house?' asked Elin.

'Get under the bed. I'll watch what he does in the yard.'

Almost immediately they heard the back door open. Richard bent down and whispered to Elin to move towards the wall. He joined her, and they lay together, motionless, looking up at the underside of the wooden-framed bed. Richard held Elin's hand. The back door closed, and there was movement downstairs. Richard prayed that Williams stayed downstairs.

The stairs creaked.

The footsteps approached the bedroom. Richard saw a man's feet enter the room. Elin held her breath. She was glad that Richard lay beside her and that she couldn't see what was happening. The man went over to the pile of clothes. Richard saw Williams gather them up, and heard him return downstairs. Richard tightened his hold on Elin's hand. She looked at him, and his smile made her realise that she could breathe normally again.

'Let's wait until we hear him go out the door,' whispered Richard. 'The floor creaks, and we can't make any noise.'

'Did you see what he came into the room for?' asked Elin.

'The pile of clothes that were probably the ones he was wearing yesterday. He's getting rid of the evidence.'

The outside door closed and Richard and Elin felt able to leave their hiding place. Richard stood at the side of the window and looked down into the yard. He saw Williams come out of the stable and then climb up onto the cart. He drove the cart down the lane towards the main road.

'He's gone. Come on, let's get out of here,' said Richard. Elin took his hand as they went downstairs.

Richard and Elin rushed back to Ty Celyn. He asked Elin to stay with Sian while he rode to Corwen to inform Parry.

The sergeant was impressed when Richard showed him the wages envelopes. He wanted to get to Williams' house and speak to the man himself.

When he arrived, Dan was still absent, and Parry was keen to find the stolen money. While he started to search, Richard went to the stables. Hidden amongst the hay, he found Dan's clothes. The shirt was bloodstained. Sergeant Parry went upstairs to search the two bedrooms. Richard heard a shout. He rushed upstairs to find Parry looking very pleased. He was counting the money that he had found inside the chimney breast.

Almost an hour after the discovery of the money, Dan Williams arrived home to find Sergeant Parry at the back door. Dan's first thought was to run. Turning round, he saw two constables blocking his exit in the lane. He had no alternative but to face the sergeant.

'A constable will attend to your horse, and I need you to answer some questions, Mr Williams,' said Parry.

Dan Williams shrugged and stepped into his house. Parry followed him through.

'Can you tell me where you obtained these?' asked the sergeant, pointing to the wages envelopes on the table.

Dan looked at them, his brain working overtime. He also saw the bloodstained clothes.

'I found them in the lane yesterday. And it's dog's blood on the shirt. The cart wheel caught the poor animal and I had to check whether it could be saved.'

Parry stared at him. 'I don't believe you. You attacked Hopkins outside the tunnel with an iron bar. You then removed the stolen money and left him to die.'

'I don't have any stolen money.' His confidence was wavering. Parry moved the shirt to reveal the stolen wages.

'Please explain then why I've just found this money hidden upstairs in your bedroom. It's a similar amount to that stolen by Hopkins from the railway.'

Dan knew that the game was up but he had to maintain his pretence of innocence. He said that the money was his winnings from playing cards.

'We'll talk further at Corwen police office. Daniel Williams, I am arresting you on suspicion of the murder of Ben Hopkins. Constables, take him away.'

Richard had been in the adjoining room and heard everything. Parry told him that John Roberts would be released tomorrow morning.

'You have done some good work here today,' said Parry. 'Williams was clever. He arranged to meet Hopkins on the railway line so the finger would be pointed firmly at one of the navvies. John Roberts was in the wrong place at the wrong time.'

Arriving home, Richard went to find Elin. She was on her own in the parlour. His smile told her everything she needed to know.

'So John really is free to go. I can't believe it.'

'We'll go and collect him tomorrow.'

'I don't know what to say. You have saved my brother's life twice. *Thank you* is not enough.'

'You played your part too. We make a good team, and I've enjoyed being with you.'

'Even hiding under the bed together?'

'Especially being under the bed with you,' said Richard with a broad smile.

Elin moved towards Richard. Her face was serious now. She closed her eyes and kissed him. This was no accidental kiss as had happened outside her lodgings. Elin wanted this so much. Richard held her in his arms and they continued to kiss. She felt so safe in his embrace. But Elin was the first to break away.

'I'm sorry, that was wrong,' she said. 'I just wanted to tell you how grateful I am for what you have done. I should go now.'

'Don't apologise, Elin.'

'But you are engaged to be married and this isn't right.'

'Please stay, Elin.'

They fell silent and pensive about those brief but beautiful moments. It was more than a kiss of gratitude and they both knew that.

Their thoughts were interrupted by Sian letting them know that supper was ready.

Sian also told Richard that there was a letter for him. It was from Sara. She had been so annoyed with Richard after the events of Saturday evening that she had deliberately delayed her reply to Richard's note. After almost three days, she relented and curtly wrote:

'Come and see me tonight. S.'

It was too late now to get a message to Sara. It was also too late to ride over to Plas Gwyn. He decided he would face the music tomorrow.

***

Richard and Elin's journey to Corwen in the morning was uneventful, and while the conversation was relaxed, there was no further mention of the kiss. John Roberts was pleased to see them, a free man once again.

CHAPTER 11

After Richard had taken Elin and John back to Llangollen, he went to Plas Gwyn. He hoped that William was out; he could do without his sarcasm this morning. The maid asked Richard to wait in the drawing room and told him that Miss Sara wouldn't be long. To Richard's relief, she also confirmed that William wasn't home.

Some twenty minutes passed before Sara, in a flowing red gown, swept into the drawing room and sat down opposite him.

'I'm sorry to have kept you waiting. It's so boring to sit and wait for someone you're expecting, isn't it? I was waiting for you all yesterday evening.'

Richard had expected a cold reception.

'I'm sorry, Sara. I left the house before your note was delivered and didn't return home until late.'

'Well, you've not exactly rushed over this morning either, have you? I have been expecting you since breakfast.'

'I had an urgent visit to make in Corwen. This is the earliest I could get here. I have missed you and have been desperate to see you.'

'Well, you're here now, and I suppose this is a consequence of being engaged to a doctor. Your work can be a matter of life and death, when all is said and done.

'Now, I want to talk about Saturday night. How dare you get cross when I showed you the details for that house? I am entitled to have ambitions. We are to be married one day, and you have no right to dismiss my ideas.'

'I know, and I should have given you the courtesy of listening to you.'

'But the worst thing,' Sara continued, 'was leaving on Saturday evening without even saying goodbye. I was very upset.'

'I can assure you that my sudden departure was not down to me. I wanted to see you, but William stopped me and told me to leave immediately. I didn't like it, but I had no alternative.'

'William didn't tell me,' said Sara, warming to Richard again.

Hoping the worst of the inquisition was over, he asked Sara whether she would like to have a day out on Saturday.

'If the weather is good, we could take the gig over to Rhuthun and have lunch. On the way back, we could call in at the cottage and spend some time together, just you and me. What do you think?'

'I think that would be lovely.'

'You don't mind going to Berllan then?' asked Richard.

'I always enjoy spending time there with you, with no interruptions, no family getting in the way – especially my cousin.' She smiled. 'I know that I was rude about the cottage the other day.'

'You called it a hovel,' said Richard.

'I know, but it's a dear cottage really and we've had some lovely times there. It was when you were suggesting that we should go and live there. It's far too small for that.'

'That's settled then. We'll have a good day out,' said Richard.

***

The weather was fine on Saturday, with sunshine and a blue sky. Richard was delighted when he opened the bedroom curtains. After breakfast, he got the horse and gig ready and set off for Plas Gwyn.

Sara was all smiles when Richard arrived. He helped her onto the gig and admired her long blue velvet dress as he settled her onto the seat. The dress was a good choice as, even on a fine day, the Horseshoe Pass between Llangollen and Rhuthun could be very breezy. Sara also had a warm cape with a white fur collar and muff. She would not need the blankets that Richard had provided.

One of the strongest horses had been chosen to pull the gig, as the road was very steep in places. The view from the pass was splendid, and on such a clear day they could see for miles over the hills and down into the valley.

As planned, they arrived in Rhuthun for lunch and then took a walk around the town and its fine old buildings. Sara took a fancy to some blue leather gloves in a shop window, saying they would match her new dress. Richard took her into the shop and bought them for her. The day was going so well, and they were happy together again.

It was late afternoon when Richard drove the gig into the yard at Ty tan y Berllan. They used to visit the cottage quite frequently, but not so often recently. Richard helped Sara down from the gig. Still holding her around the waist, he kissed her, and she put her arms around him.

'I love you, Sara.'

'I love you too, but you know that. All I want is to marry you and for us to be together. We've spent too much time apart in recent months.'

'That is exactly what I want as well. I've got something here which I want to show you.' Richard leaned over behind the seat of the gig and pulled out some papers.

'What's that?' asked Sara, excited about anything connected to a possible wedding.

'Come in the house and I'll show you.'

Richard laid the papers on the table. He had collected them yesterday from a surveyor and draughtsman in Corwen. They were the plans for a large house including a drawing room, dining room and four bedrooms. Sara looked puzzled.

'It looks nice.' She hesitated. 'But what is it, where is it?'

'You are in it,' said Richard. 'It's a new Berllan. I'll have it extended, and it'll be more than twice the size of the existing building. Look, this is the old part, and all this at the side is new. It's only a first draft and you can change the design and choose all the furnishings to your own taste. I'll get a loan to do it.'

Richard's obvious enthusiasm with his idea was not reflected in Sara's expression.

'You still do not understand, do you? The house looks lovely, but it wouldn't matter if you had designed a palace for me – it's in the wrong place. I don't want to live in the Dee Valley anymore. I want a new lifestyle, a new social life. I want this for both of us. After all the discussions that we've had, I cannot believe that you really thought that this was the answer. Have you not listened to me at all?'

Richard was thrown by her total rejection of his plans. He hesitated as he tried to regain his composure. 'Of course I have. You said that you liked Berllan but that it was too small. I thought that this might be a compromise.'

'But it's not in London, and that's the point,' she said a bit more calmly. 'I know that you would like to stay here but I am convinced that we need to move. We are both young and have our future ahead of us. When you qualified, people said that you could become one of the finest young surgeons in the capital. I remember your colleague, James Morton, telling me that you were destined for a top position. But that was two years ago, and your reputation as the most promising surgeon of your year will be forgotten, and your opportunity will be lost. An excellent career is at stake, and the risk of losing it is greater as each year goes by. There will be others taking what could have been yours. James has done very well for himself. It may already be too late.'

Richard was listening carefully. Sara was right that he would be forgotten if he did not return to surgery soon.

As he had not disputed her argument, Sara continued presenting the case that she had been working on for several days:

'When I talk of going to London, I don't mean that we would go forever. I'm thinking of perhaps ten years, during which we can enjoy our young lives in the capital of the world. It would be very exciting. Thanks to the railway we could holiday at Berllan whenever we wanted a break from the city. And then, when we have finally had our fill of London, we can return to live in the valley.'

Sara sat down on the small two-seat sofa and asked him to join her.

'It would be the best of both worlds,' she said, and leant against him, resting her head on his shoulder.

He turned and kissed her. 'I love you, and I promise that I'll think about everything that you have said,' he told her.

'If you love me, then you will marry me and give me what I want, and what we both need.'

Richard didn't answer. He kissed her again. Richard put his arms around her and felt the deep velvet of her tightly fitting dress. Sara then pulled away, sat bolt upright and stared at him.

'Well, are you going to give me what I want?' she said, now with no hint of affection.

Richard was taken aback. 'I meant what I said. I will think again about London, but you know that here is where my heart is.'

'Your heart belongs to me. Could you live without me?'

'I don't think I could.'

'I know that you couldn't. You know what to do then, don't you? You can't have me. You won't kiss me or touch me again until we set a date for our marriage and you have a job in London.'

Richard felt her coldness. Sara stood up and walked over to the table. She picked up her new leather gloves and put them on.

'You can take me back to Plas Gwyn now. Give me my cape.'

'Come on, Sara, there is no need for this.' Richard reached out for her hand. As he did so, he felt her other gloved hand slap him hard across the face. His shock contrasted with the calmness in Sara's face as she smiled at him.

'I said that you are not allowed to touch me, not even my hand.'

'Are we not going to see one another?' asked a confused Richard.

'We'll go to church together and you will come to dinner at Plas Gwyn when I invite you. But until you agree to give me what I want, there will be no further contact of any sort between us. One day you will thank me for this. Now take me home.'

It was a silent ride in the gig back to Llangollen.

CHAPTER 12

The following days were very busy, and Richard was glad to be fully occupied with work. He didn't tell anyone what had happened with Sara. Normally, he would confide in Evan, but he couldn't bring himself to talk about it. How could such a lovely day turn so sour? Although he still loved Sara, he now wondered how well he really knew her. Patients' problems became a welcome distraction. One such patient was Mrs Price.

Mrs Price had been widowed for just over a year. Her late husband had been the miller at Llangollen corn mill. The water mill stood on the bank of the river, almost directly opposite the site of the new railway station. Mrs Price had taken over the running of the mill with an employee, Tom, doing the physical work. The loss of her husband and the worry of running the mill had taken its toll, and Richard had become concerned about her health. A month ago, she had fallen and spent a cold night on the stone floor before Tom had found her in the morning. Richard had visited her regularly since the fall.

'How are you today, Mrs Price?' he asked.

'I've been a little better since your last visit, doctor. The medicine has helped. But I had very little sleep last night. To be truthful, I didn't sleep at all.'

'Are you still worried about the mill? Some time ago, we talked about you selling the business.'

Mrs Price sat down and tears came to her eyes.

'I decided to sell it. But I've had little interest and only one offer, which was less than I had expected. I don't know whether to accept it or wait for something better. But if there isn't a better offer then I'll lose that buyer, and be left with the worry of running the mill.'

'What does your advisor say about the offer you've received?'

'He's told me that the mill and the business are worth more.'

'Well, there you are then. Perhaps it's better to wait and see what else happens. I know it's difficult, but try not to worry about the mill. A better offer is probably just round the corner.'

'I do need a higher price. I shall have to get somewhere else to live. Mr Griffiths-Ellis' offer is not enough. He says it's not worth any more as the buildings need repairs and the mill is not making enough money. I explained to him that the business suffered due to Mr Price's ill health, but it will pick up again with the right man in charge.'

Richard's interest level and his eyebrows were raised by the mention of the name of the potential purchaser.

'Do you mean Mr William Griffiths-Ellis of Plas Gwyn?'

'Yes, do you know him? Is he a fair man?'

'He is a good businessman. I suggest that you wait and see if another buyer comes forward, or whether Mr Griffiths-Ellis increases his offer.'

'But in his letter it says that the offer will only remain on the table for two days.'

'I think that he is trying to get you to make a hasty decision. Mr Griffiths-Ellis is after the lowest price that he has to pay. You asked me whether he is fair. Let's just say that it's not a fair price. I think that you will find that his offer will stay open and that he may well increase it.'

Mrs Price thanked Richard for his advice. She felt a little more confident now about calling William's bluff over the offer.

That evening, after supper, Richard told Evan and his father, about his visit to Mrs Price, and William's attempts to buy the corn mill on the cheap. Edward explained that the mill had belonged to William's grandfather. William had spent a lot of his early childhood with his grandparents at the mill. Staying with them and playing around the mill had been a happy time for him. Edward thought William probably wanted to return the mill to family ownership.

'I was right to tell Mrs Price to reject William's offer then,' said Richard. 'William will offer more, if he wants it for personal reasons.'

'What condition is the mill in?' asked Evan.

'William told Mrs Price that the mill buildings were run down and in need of repair. But then he would say that, wouldn't he?'

'And what do you know of the business? Is it profitable?'

'I don't know. Are you interested in buying the mill?'

'I might be,' said Evan. 'It depends on the investment needed. But it could be an asset for our business. We could process our own corn and have an additional income, aside from the farm.'

Edward looked concerned. 'I don't doubt your business reasoning, but I tell you now that if you buy it from under William's nose, then it will cause trouble. You don't want to start married life with conflict between the families, Richard.'

It's already too late to avoid that, Richard thought to himself.

'I'd like to see the mill for myself and then decide,' said Evan. 'It may not be the right investment anyway.'

***

His father's warning did not dissuade Evan. The brothers visited Mrs Price at the mill the following afternoon. She asked Tom to show them around and said that she would get the accounts book ready for Evan to look over.

'What do you think?' asked Mrs Price on their return. 'Let's discuss it over a cup of tea.'

'Thank you,' said Evan. 'It's a sound building but does need some work carried out.'

'That is what Mr Griffiths-Ellis told me too. But I do think that it is worth more.'

'So do I, Mrs Price. I shall look at the accounts and see if I can better his offer.'

Richard left after tea while Evan stayed at the mill house to study the accounts. After half an hour, Evan told Mrs Price that subject to the bank agreeing a loan, he would make an offer, higher than William's. Mrs Price was delighted. Evan told her not to let William know that he was the buyer.

***

Richard had left the mill to visit a patient who lived near the railway station. As he got near, he became aware of a commotion and people shouting. He ran into the station and saw a man sitting on the platform in great pain. Merryman Christmas was slowly pouring a jug of water over the man's head and face. A group of people had gathered round.

'What has happened?' asked Richard putting his doctor's bag down and leaning over to see the injured man.

'The engine's boiler burst and the stoker got caught by the steam,' said Merryman. 'I'm hoping the water will cool his skin.'

'I told him to get some butter,' said one of the onlookers, obviously annoyed that his advice had been ignored.

'You have done the right thing,' Richard told Merryman. 'We need plenty of water to run over the scalded skin. Butter or anything greasy is the worst thing you could use.'

The onlooker wished he had kept quiet.

Richard asked for more water. The stoker looked at Richard, clearly relieved that a doctor had arrived so quickly after the accident.

'I was lucky,' said the stoker. 'I had turned away to leave the footplate, otherwise it would have been far worse for me.'

'I sent for Dr Bevan about ten minutes ago,' said Merryman.

Dr Bevan lived in Abbey Road and was the nearest doctor to the station. Richard continued to trickle the water over the scalded skin of the stoker. A few minutes later, Bevan arrived.

'Thank goodness you are here, Lloyd,' he said. 'I was with a patient when the lad called but came as quickly as I could. I hate to think of the damage to the skin if you had not been here.'

'We have Mr Christmas to thank for that,' said Richard. 'He started applying the water immediately after the accident. He is the hero of the moment.'

Merryman looked pleased.

Dr Bevan was in his late fifties and was well-regarded as a doctor and a respected member of the town and valley community. He had tried to obtain the practice that Richard had bought two years earlier. The competition to purchase the practice had meant that Richard paid over the odds for the opportunity to fulfil his ambitions.

Dr Bevan harboured no grudge that Richard had frustrated his chances to grow his practice. He was a kind man who accepted that you didn't always win every competition or deal. He did not view it as success or failure. It was simply life's way.

'When the boilers explode, they release such high-pressure steam that the scalding is often worse than a fire burn or that caused by boiling water,' said Dr Bevan. 'Fortunately, this has not affected too much of the skin.'

'Thank you, doctor,' said the stoker.

'I'll leave you now,' said Richard. 'I have a patient to visit.'

'Yes, of course,' replied Bevan. 'I'll carry on here. We must get together one of these evenings for dinner,' he added before Richard left.

***

Richard returned home just in time for supper. His father and Evan were discussing the corn mill. Evan told him that he intended to make an offer for the property and business. Edward remained unconvinced that the mill was a good idea. However, Evan now ran the farm, and Edward would not stand in the way of his son's plans.

Evan said that he would be going to the bank in the morning, to secure a loan. He'd then instruct their lawyer to make the formal offer and handle the conveyance.

***

A few days later, William called on Mrs Price.

'I am surprised that you have not replied to my letter, Mrs Price,' he told her. 'You are aware that my very fair offer was only open for two days and has therefore expired.'

William paused to gauge the widow's response.

'Indeed, it has expired, Mr Griffiths-Ellis,' replied Mrs Price, without any of the concern anticipated by William.

'Well, I am pleased to be able to tell you that I'm prepared to keep my offer open, if you need more time to consider your situation.'

'That is very kind of you. I have considered my situation very carefully and have decided not to sell you the mill.'

William had not expected this. He had been prepared for a feeble request from Mrs Price for an increased offer, and he might have given a little ground on that. But to be rejected outright was a complete surprise.

'Look, Mrs Price, I might be able to let you have a little more money, but as I have explained, the mill needs investment.'

'I do understand that. However, I have sold it to someone who offered a proper price for my mill.'

'Who has offered you a higher price?' demanded William. His gentle approach had evaporated.

'I'm unable to disclose the name of the buyer,' replied Mrs Price. 'I thank you for your interest, but I don't think that there is any more to say. Will you see yourself to the door, please?'

***

Back at Plas Gwyn, William was in a foul mood. He angrily told Sara and Aunt Grace what had happened. They had little sympathy for him.

'Why did you offer such a low price?' asked Sara. 'Did you not think to go back sooner to Mrs Price when she didn't accept your offer?'

'I didn't know that anyone else was interested in buying the mill. I deliberately left it a few days to show that I was not desperate to buy the property. That's how business is done.'

'Or how business is not done, in this case. Have you offered to better the new purchaser's offer? Who is he?'

'She refused to tell me. I don't know what he offered, but Mrs Price said that it reflected the mill's value, and she is happy with that. I'll find out who the purchaser is in due course.'

'Have you a plan then?' asked Sara.

'The embryo of a plan,' said William, 'which will be developed as soon as I know who is buying the mill.'

CHAPTER 13

Sian met Owen in their usual place, hidden from the footpath, their sweet talk muffled by the sound of the river.

'We shouldn't have to hide away like this,' she said.

'I know, and things will be different one day, but we need to be careful for now. When I leave Berwyn Hall and get a job somewhere else, then we'll be free to do whatever we want. Come here, *cariad*.'

Owen kissed his sweetheart.

'I've missed you so much, Sian. I live for our moments together. You deserve so much better, and I promise that once I'm free from the hall, we'll do all the things that you want.'

'Are you sure that you'd be dismissed if they found out about us? The Lloyds don't mind me seeing you.'

'You've told Edward Lloyd about us?'

'Well, I had to tell Richard, after the theft of the money, but they're all fine about it. I'm much happier that it's in the open.'

'That's a big risk. Sir Clayton and Edward are neighbours and will talk. The families will be united too, when Evan marries Miss Elizabeth.'

'Edward won't say anything. I've asked him not to.'

In his concern about Edward Lloyd telling Sir Clayton about their relationship, Owen had forgotten about the need for hushed voices.

'Owen Phillips, is that you up there? And who have you got with you?' asked a stern voice. Owen recognised it straight away.

Sian looked puzzled, but seeing his reaction, she knew the situation wasn't good.

'No one, Miss Lyons,' Owen called back. 'I was resting in the fresh air and listening to the sound of the river.'

'I heard you and a girl talking. Get down here now, both of you, if you please.'

Owen came down to the path, followed by Sian. They emerged to see the housekeeper, arms akimbo, blocking the path. Eve Lyons was in her late thirties, tall and not unattractive, except that nobody ever saw her smile. She always wore a long black dress with a high collar and long sleeves. A wide belt around her corseted waist accentuated her height and formidable appearance.

'And who might you be?' she asked Sian.

'Sian is a good friend of mine,' said Owen.

'I can see that,' said Miss Lyons. 'Good friends always hide in the bushes together.' She stared at Owen and Sian, who looked down at the path like naughty children. 'I want to see you in my room at three o'clock sharp, Phillips. Do you understand?'

'Yes, Miss Lyons.'

She turned and walked down the path towards Berwyn Hall. With her back to the shocked young couple, Eve Lyons actually smiled.

***

At five to three, Owen stood outside the door to Miss Lyons' room. He hesitated for a minute, asking himself whether he should knock on the door now or wait until the precise hour. He looked at his pocket watch again and knocked on the door.

'Enter,' commanded Eve Lyons.

Owen went into the housekeeper's office and sitting room. Miss Lyons sat at her desk, facing into the room.

'Stand there, Phillips,' she ordered, pointing at the other side of the desk. 'When you were appointed, it was made clear to you that relationships with young women were not permitted while in the employ of Lady Davenport. Have you forgotten that?'

'No, Miss Lyons.'

'Well then, do you no longer wish to work at Berwyn Hall?'

'No, Miss Lyons, but Sian is just a friend. We are not engaged or anything like that.'

'Your behaviour by the river with that young woman is disreputable and if it was witnessed, would affect the good name and standing of Berwyn Hall, and Sir Clayton and Lady Davenport.'

'We were not doing anything that would affect Berwyn Hall.'

'It worries me that you do not understand my justifiable concerns, Phillips. Perhaps I do need to dismiss you. I was hoping to avoid doing that, as you have been a good servant in other respects. You do realise that if I dismiss you, then it would be without any reference, and you would find it impossible to find further work in service?'

This was Owen's worst nightmare. While he intended to leave Berwyn Hall, he still needed a reference for his next job. The only glimmer of hope was that Miss Lyons had said that she didn't wish to dismiss him.

'I am sorry, Miss Lyons, I don't want any embarrassment for the hall. I wish to carry on working here and will do whatever you want—'

Miss Lyons interrupted him. 'Yes, Phillips, you will do whatever I want, if you wish to keep your job. You must agree that your behaviour was unacceptable and promise me that you will not see that girl again.'

Eve Lyons paused and stared at Owen. There was no emotion in her face. She was waiting for his reaction.

He stayed silent.

'Well, it's the girl or your job. I have been very fair with you, Phillips. You are being offered a second chance.'

'Thank you, Miss Lyons. I wish to keep my job.'

'Good. Now you may see her one more time to tell her your decision, but after that there will be no more contact.'

Owen walked along the river path where he and Sian had met for the last three months. Despite the risks and obstacles put in their way, it had been the happiest period in his life. He had lied to Miss Lyons about his feelings for Sian. They'd been friends at first but he loved her now. He did not know how he could live without her. He felt empty inside and desolate.

Sian opened the back door and saw Owen.

'Let's walk down the lane and talk,' she said, taking his hand.

Owen told her what had happened in Miss Lyons' office. Sian squeezed his hand for moral support.

'Well, we shall just have to stay apart until you find a new job,' she said. 'It will be hard, but it won't be forever. We need to stay strong.'

'That's what I thought at first. But I'm not going to stop seeing you. Her rules are cruel and wrong. She forced me to lie when I said that I won't see you again.'

'We'll have to be very careful not to be caught,' said Sian.

'I'll find new meeting places for us, further away from Berwyn Hall. Perhaps for the next week we should not meet at all, as she will be watching my every move. But we can beat Miss Lyons.'

***

It was late in the evening and Richard was alone in the parlour. Eventually, Evan returned from Berwyn Hall where he had dined with Elizabeth and her parents.

'Did you have a good evening at the hall?' asked Richard.

'Yes, apart from Elizabeth's mother. Have you heard that she and her housekeeper have banned Owen from seeing Sian?'

'No, that's news to me. Sian hasn't said anything.'

'Lady Davenport boasted how she would not permit such behaviour from her young servants. She would not have the good name of Berwyn Hall brought into question. I told her that she was wrong to stop them from meeting one another. She then said that this was none of my business. Elizabeth did remind her that as Sian was employed at Ty Celyn, I had every right to make my views known.'

Richard shook his head in disbelief.

Evan continued. 'I sometimes wonder what sort of family I'm marrying into. You must feel the same about William Griffiths-Ellis. At least he's only Sara's cousin. Lady Davenport is going to be my mother-in-law. As you know, I've never got on with Elizabeth's brother, Grant, either but at least he's away in the army.'

'You can't choose your family, but you and Elizabeth get on well together,' Richard told him. 'You make a good couple and will support one another when you are married. Sara and I have big problems, and matters have got a lot worse in recent days.'

'What's happened?'

Richard told him about their day out to Rhuthun and what happened afterwards at Berllan. He explained how Sara's actions had been very upsetting, causing him to reflect on their relationship and whether it could be saved.

'I have been thinking about her idea of going back to London to develop my career and then returning to North Wales after a few years. Perhaps it's the only solution for both of us.'

'Do you think that she will want to come back, after gaining the society life that she wants in London? Do you trust her to keep to her word? If she treats you like this now, what will life be like when you are married and she has got what she wanted?'

'I have had similar thoughts, but she says that she loves me.'

'If she really loved you, she would support your need to be a successful doctor in Berwyn. She knows that you want to live here and would be unhappy back in the city.'

'If I really loved her, I'd give her what she wants in London.'

'Well, maybe that's it. You both want something else that's just as important to you. Sara is going to be miserable if you make her stay here. Your love and longing, your *hiraeth*, for your homeland will make you unhappy in London.'

Richard always valued Evan's wise and frank opinions. His brother knew and understood him better than anyone. Evan had confirmed his own view that a significant decision had to be made.

'I am at a crossroads in my life,' he said, 'and whichever road I take will have major consequences.'

'Sara's behaviour already shows signs that things aren't right between you,' said Evan. 'You're in love with Sara, and the problem is that love prevents you from seeing things clearly.'

'I know what I have to do,' Richard said gravely. 'In truth I have known for some time, but I couldn't bring myself to accept it. I shall visit Sara and let her know my decision.'

Richard wrote a note to Sara saying that he would visit her on Friday evening after dinner.

CHAPTER 14

At the workhouse infirmary, Richard examined young Bob Morgan, who complained of a sore throat and headache. Richard's first thought was that he had a cold. However, his thoughts changed dramatically after a closer inspection. The boy was running a high temperature and had a swollen tongue and red blotches on his chest. Richard feared the worst; the symptoms pointed to scarlet fever.

'How long have you been feeling ill?' Richard asked the boy.

'Two days, but I didn't have any red spots until this morning.'

'That's good. Is there anyone else who has a sore throat or spots?'

'Ben Davies said he wasn't feeling well.'

'Mrs Jones, will you please go and find Ben for me? I need to examine him as well. Before you leave the infirmary, wash your hands thoroughly, please.'

Ben Davies also had a high temperature and sore throat. Richard went to see Enoch Evans.

'I believe we have at least two cases of scarlet fever. I should like to speak to the children in the schoolroom as soon as possible, to check whether there are any others feeling ill.'

'How ill are the two boys?'

'Thankfully it's at an early stage, but we must isolate them from the other children and the patients in the infirmary. If we are not careful, it will spread very quickly.'

In the schoolroom, Richard told the children about the two boys and their symptoms. He asked the children whether any of them were feeling ill. To Richard's relief only one hand went up. He told the boy to come with him and reminded the rest of the children that if they felt poorly, they must tell their teacher or Mrs Jones in the infirmary, straight away.

The infirmary had two wards for the sick and infirm, one for the men and the other for women. There were only five women and three men in the wards, so Richard asked Mr Evans to arrange for a screen to be put up in the women's room and for the men to be moved to beds at one end of that room. This freed up the men's ward to use as an isolation room for patients with scarlet fever. There were only three cases so far and Richard prayed that it would remain that way. However, he had to be prepared for more. The next few days would be critical.

The following morning, Richard arrived at the workhouse infirmary just before nine o'clock. He was pleased to see no more beds occupied in the temporary fever ward.

'Good morning, nurse. How are the three children doing?'

'The rash has got worse and they had a fitful sleep,' said Ann.

Ann was working shifts on the fever ward with just one other nurse, Mrs Thomas. They were sleeping temporarily at the infirmary, to reduce the risk of the fever spreading.

Richard examined the boys. Their temperatures were still very high and they all now showed signs of the red rash. Enoch Evans appeared at the entrance to the ward.

'Don't come in. I'll come over to you,' said Richard. 'We have to be so careful. The fever must be contained within this room, and we must not let it affect other parts of the workhouse or get out into the town. I don't want to scare anyone, but if we do not manage this effectively, we could have an epidemic on our hands.'

Enoch Evans stared over his spectacles at Richard, clearly alarmed at the doctor's warning. He realised that this could damage his reputation if the workhouse infected the town – and cause him a lot more work, too. As an afterthought, he asked, 'How are the children?'

'The fever is progressing as I would expect. If they are strong, they have a fighting chance. If they are still with us in ten days or so, then they will survive. Ann Jones is making sure that they have plenty of water to drink. Will you instruct the kitchen to provide them with a good meaty broth? They have little appetite, and eating will be painful because of their sore throats, but we must keep their strength up. There isn't any nourishment in the usual breakfast gruel and porridge at supper.'

'Is there no cure then?'

'We must let the fever take its course and hope that there are no complications which could affect the heart.'

Trying to stay optimistic for the benefit of the nurses and patients, Richard did his round of the other ward. He examined David Lewis and asked whether his chest felt any better.

'Not too bad today.' He wheezed. 'That is, until I laugh. The good news is that I have nothing much to laugh about. The only benefit of being ill is that I don't have to pick oakum every day. My thumbs have a chance to recover.'

As an older inmate, David Lewis was excused the very hard labour of breaking stone and instead had to unravel lengths of rope; the resultant fibres were known as oakum and used by the navy. The work was long, tedious and painful on the hands, often causing his fingers to bleed.

The nurse came over to Richard and told him that Ann Jones needed him in the fever ward.

Ann looked concerned. She was talking to a woman who was very flushed and unwell. Richard came over.

'This is Mrs Morgan, doctor. She is Bob's mother. I thought it best that you saw her straight away.'

Richard examined Mrs Morgan. She had all the symptoms of scarlet fever.

He turned to Ann and said, 'Please go immediately to Mr Evans and tell him to arrange for screens to be put up. We need to separate the fever room into male and female sections.'

***

On Thursday, before Richard went to the workhouse infirmary, he had some urgent calls to make in Llangollen. However, while he was visiting those patients, he was unaware of a gathering storm at the workhouse.

Bob Morgan, the first boy to fall victim to scarlet fever, had developed pneumonia during the night and was gravely ill. Ann Jones had sat up with him, and she did what she could.

Just after half past nine, the schoolteacher appeared at the ward with two girls. Ann Jones left Bob Morgan's bedside and went over to her.

'The doctor needs to examine these girls,' said the teacher. 'They have all the signs that he warned us about.'

Ann took the little girls' hands. There was little doubt that these were two new cases of scarlet fever.

'How long have you been feeling ill?' asked Ann.

They thought for a moment and then one answered. 'About two days, I think.'

'Why didn't you come here straight away? The doctor told you that you must tell us if you felt unwell.'

The girls were tearful. 'Are we in trouble, miss?'

'No, you're not in trouble, but you are going to have to stay here with me for a few days. You can have the two beds over there next to Mrs Morgan. I'll come over to see you in a few minutes.'

Ann asked a nurse to tell the master that there appeared to be two new cases and Bob Morgan was not showing any signs of improvement.

Enoch Evans, a worried man, came to see Ann immediately.

'Where's Dr Lloyd?'

'He hasn't arrived yet,' said Ann.

'He should be here now. We are going to lose a child if he doesn't get here soon. I'll send someone up to Berwyn to find him.'

At Ty Celyn, the messenger was informed by Sian that the doctor was attending to patients in Llangollen, but would be going to the workhouse by midday. He arrived back to inform an anxious master.

Richard arrived at the workhouse later that morning completely unaware that the outbreak of scarlet fever had become a crisis. Evans saw him arrive.

'Where have you been?' He accosted Richard in the corridor leading to the infirmary. 'We have a boy who is dying and two new cases. I sent a man to find you this morning.'

'I have been with patients since half past eight this morning,' said Richard, trying to remain calm amidst the panic. 'I told you that this was always a possibility. We have done our best to control the spread of the disease. Let me get on and examine the children.'

Richard saw Bob first.

'It's pneumonia. How long has he been like this?'

'Since ten o'clock last night,' replied Ann.

'He is tough then,' said Richard, 'and you have taken good care of him. If he keeps fighting, then he has a chance. I'll stay with him tonight; you must get some sleep.'

They went to see the girls, and Richard confirmed two new cases of scarlet fever. He asked them gently why they had not come to see him sooner. Neither of them wanted to speak but when pressed, the older girl hesitantly mumbled, 'We were frightened. They said that if we came here then we would die. No one comes out of the 'firmary alive, they said. So we hoped we would get better.'

Richard looked at the two sad, little children. They were a pitiful sight. They had nothing, and now even their short lives were at risk.

'I shall do everything that I can to make you better.'

Richard told Ann that he was going to check all the children in the workhouse.

'I pray that there will be no more cases, but I'm not taking any chances. I shall examine them in their schoolroom because they are frightened to enter the infirmary. Tomorrow morning I shall check all the adult inmates. I assumed that people would come to me if they were feeling unwell. A mistake that I shall have to live with.'

Two hours later he had completed the examination of all the children. No others showed any symptoms. He informed Evans that things seemed under control again.

Evans had a particular and personal reason to feel relieved. As medical officer, Richard had a responsibility to inform Mr Vaughan, as Chairman of the Union Board, of any serious medical issues. This included an outbreak of any contagious diseases. When the first case was diagnosed, Richard had asked Evans to report the outbreak to Mr Vaughan as they were to meet later that evening. He had agreed to do this but then forgot to mention it to the chairman. Evans had sent him a note two days later but had not clarified that he was at fault for not notifying him earlier. Evans had been worried that if there were any deaths then an investigation would be inevitable and his mistake would be discovered. He did not tell Richard about his error.

Richard spent the night in the infirmary. He sat with Bob Morgan, watching for any change in the boy's condition. Bob's breathing seemed less laboured.

Richard got up and walked round to check on the other patients. When he returned to Bob's bed, the boy had awakened and looked confused. Richard examined Bob and there were some positive signs of recovery. *Thank the Lord,* Richard thought to himself. *The boy might be over the worst.*

CHAPTER 15

Richard left Corwen just before midday and rode back to Ty Celyn. It had been raining, and the freshness of the air was just what he needed after his night at the infirmary. As he got closer to Berwyn, he could only think about the evening ahead, and seeing Sara. He planned to arrive at Plas Gwyn after they had finished dinner. He needed to talk to her privately, with no interruptions from the rest of the family. The garden would be the best place.

At Plas Gwyn, William was reading his newspaper while Grace and Sara were sitting talking. They all looked over to Richard as he entered the room.

'You've missed a fine dinner tonight, Lloyd. Perfectly cooked pheasant and a good wine,' declared William in his assertive manner.

'Work commitments prevailed, I'm afraid. I trust that I find everyone well,' replied Richard.

'It's good to see you,' said Grace. 'We have missed you at Plas Gwyn these past two weeks.'

'That's kind, but I have been very busy. If only people didn't get ill, I would have an easier life.'

'But an even poorer life too, I dare say,' said William.

'And what brings you here this evening?' asked Sara.

'I need to speak with you,' said Richard, 'and I wondered whether we could go to the garden as it's such a pleasant evening.'

'Let's go to the garden then,' said Sara.

After a few minutes of idle conversation about various garden blooms, Richard stopped on the path by the pool and the fountain.

'I have always been truthful with you. When I asked you to marry me, I did believe that one day we would marry and spend our lives happily together. It is now clear to me that we cannot give one another that happiness. If we move to London, then I shall resent not living the life that I want. If I make you stay here, then I shall make you unhappy. I am not prepared to do that.'

'And I am not prepared to let that happen for all the reasons that we have discussed,' interrupted Sara. 'These reasons are as much for your benefit as mine. I cannot understand why you do not see my argument. It is so obviously the right thing to do.'

'I have carefully considered all the things that you have said. There is a small part of me that would like to resurrect my career as a hospital surgeon, but it is nothing compared to my lifelong ambition to be a doctor in this valley.'

They fell silent for a moment or two staring at the fountain. Richard suggested that they sit down on a seat at the side of the pool.

'Is there any way that you could be happy here as my wife? If there is anything I can do, then please tell me.'

Sara did not answer Richard's question. For a long time, she had ruled out staying in the valley. As far as she was concerned, it was not an option, and no longer to be discussed.

She didn't realise the importance of this moment, but for him, this was the last chance to save their relationship and the engagement.

'Your so-called lifelong ambition is a false obsession,' she said. 'What's worse is that it will turn into a nightmare for you when you get bored with the humdrum life that you have created. A boring job with tedious people and without the woman you love. And yet, you could have everything. I am not giving up on you, but I'm not giving in to your false ambition either.'

Richard hesitated. He knew that the moment had come. With reluctance, he said the words that he had to say: 'I'm sorry, but I am not leaving Berwyn. Therefore, we must end our engagement. Even though I have never stopped loving you, our marriage would be incompatible.'

Sara looked at Richard. Her immediate thoughts quickly turned from anguish to anger.

'Oh, you think that you are very clever. All these nice words, and then you play the trump card, threatening to end our engagement. I am not marrying you and staying in this valley.'

'I know, and that is why our engagement must end. You can of course maintain your standing and good name by announcing that you have decided that we no longer intend to marry. You can determine any reasonable grounds for your decision, providing it will not damage my professional reputation.'

'But this is your decision, and you have clearly worked all this out in fine detail. I shall not announce anything. As far as I am concerned, we are still engaged.'

'Our engagement is over,' said Richard. His tone of voice was firmer now. 'You have to come to terms with it, hard as that will be. I love you, but we must part.'

'I shall not accept your decision. We've been engaged for over two years, and you plan to end it in two minutes, without consulting me first?'

'You and I have been struggling with this matter for months. I thought that we could sort out our differences. I have considered your views and your wishes, but I cannot give up what I need and believe in.'

'So, you believe that you don't need me then? You are wrong, and I shall prove you wrong. You will regret this day.'

Richard realised that he could not convince her of their sad situation. Not tonight, not with all this anger in her.

'Please think about what I have said. It is the only way forward that allows us to both get on with our lives. I shall call on you again in a couple of days.'

'Just go. Don't go back through the house. Leave by the garden gate for the stables. You must think again about your foolish decision and then beg me to have you back.'

'Goodnight, Sara,' said Richard.

Sara said nothing.

He rode down the drive and away from Plas Gwyn. Sara's reaction to the ending of their engagement had surprised him. He had not expected the outright rejection of his decision.

Richard arrived home and stabled his horse. He decided to walk down to the river and The Chain Bridge Inn. The evening was still warm, and he sat outside on a bench and sipped his ale, listening to the rush of the river. He pondered what he should do next. Sara had made it clear that she had no intention of discussing the ending of their engagement. There was no point in visiting her again. He would only raise her expectations that he was there to apologise and to return to how things were.

Richard walked partway across the old chain bridge. He paused to look down at the river and the turbulent white water tumbling over the rocks. As night fell, the light from the oil lamps appeared through the windows of the inn. He could feel the loss and sadness as a sickening pain. It was as if the gushing water below was surging through his body.

***

At Plas Gwyn, Sara also felt pain, but it was not because she had lost Richard. She still believed that he would come back to her. No, Sara's pain was born of anger. She had convinced herself that Richard's proposal to end their engagement was merely a threat, a bluff to force her to stay in Berwyn. Sara didn't believe Richard and therefore didn't tell anyone at Plas Gwyn what had happened in the garden that evening.

In the morning, Richard wrote a short letter to Sara, telling her that it needed to be made public that their engagement was over. They could say that they'd both realised they wanted different things from life. He also repeated his offer that Sara could declare that she had ended their betrothal.

Sara took the unopened letter to her room. She expected that the letter would be apologetic, a plea for forgiveness, and contain a request to see her.

Then she read it. Her mouth dropped open after the first line, where Richard confirmed that there had to be a public declaration that their engagement had ended. For the first time, she wondered whether she had really got this so wrong. Richard was not bluffing, and he was not trying to force her to stay in the valley. She ran to the drawing room to find Aunt Grace.

As she started to talk to her aunt, her voice failed and tears followed. She managed to say that 'he no longer wants us to be married' and then thrust the letter into Grace's hand.

'Look. Read it.'

Grace read the note and looked up at her niece.

'Oh, my poor dear. Is this what he came to talk to you about? What has happened?'

'I didn't believe him,' Sara sobbed. 'I thought he was trying to trick me into staying in Wales. Perhaps he still is; do you think he is?'

'No, Richard would not play such a game. I am sure that, even now, he has the best of intentions. Richard is facing up to a difficult situation, and I'm sure that he is distressed, too.'

'I don't know what to think or do,' Sara said. 'I just want things to be right again. I do love him.'

'I know you do. You don't have to do anything now. Be gentle with yourself for a few days. You will then know what to say to Richard.'

Sara followed her aunt's advice and didn't respond immediately to Richard's letter. She also told Grace not to say anything to William until she had decided what she was going to do. Sara knew that his reaction would be angry and overly protective, and unhelpful to her in trying to get things straight in her mind.

***

Every morning since sending the letter to Sara, Richard had anticipated a reply. But it didn't arrive. By the evening of the fourth day, he felt in purgatory, waiting for Sara's judgement. He began to wonder whether she had even received the letter. Surely, she would have replied by now. Had she taken ill? Perhaps the letter was too curt and she had suffered a terrible shock? Richard decided to wait another two days and if he still hadn't heard from her, then he would visit Plas Gwyn.

At last, Richard received a reply. She had kept him waiting for five days. He took the letter into the parlour to read it without interruption.

My dearest Richard,

I am sorry for the delay in replying but I am sure that you will know that I have been in quite a state of shock since I received your letter. It has made me ill. Thank God for Aunt Grace who has been here for me. I've not been able to tell William this awful news yet.

I still cannot believe that you have decided to end our engagement and our relationship. It is a stupid decision that will devastate our lives. You do not appreciate what we have and what you have chosen to throw away. One day, I fear that you will realise all this, but it will be too late for us.

Anyway, as I have said, this is your decision and yours alone. You should therefore stand by it and own it alone. There is no question of it being "a shared, mutual decision" as I neither share it, nor agree with it. Similarly, whilst I appreciate your well-meaning motives towards me in giving me the option of ending our betrothal and saving face, I have no wish to do this. It is your decision, and if I am asked to explain our position to family, friends and acquaintances, then that is what I shall say.

So, dearest Richard, I suppose that this is the end for us? How sad that is, and so unnecessary. I should sign off by wishing you happiness and that you find love with someone else. But I can't because it would be a lie. We both know that we had found true love together.

Your loving fiancée,
Sara

Richard read the letter twice. He knew how she felt all too well; he'd felt the same reluctance before deciding to end the relationship. Sara's letter made him question all over again whether he had done the right thing. There was no doubt that they had found love, and perhaps he would live to regret throwing it away. But the fact remained that neither of them had been happy in recent times and neither wanted to pursue the other's chosen lifestyle. Marriage would be a folly under such circumstances.

But even at this late stage, when their engagement was in its final throes, Sara had thrown a lifeline: '*I suppose that this is the end for us?*' She had temptingly opened the door again and posed the question that Richard did not want to revisit.

Yet it was another part of the letter that impacted him the most. In a practical sense, rather than emotionally. Sara had told him that he should stand by his decision and own it alone. Richard decided to do just that.

He wrote a firm but kind letter back to Sara. He said that he agreed with everything that she had written, except that his decision was in both their best interests. There had been no doubting their love for one another, but their happiness would have proven elusive. He wished her well for the future and signed off simply with "Richard".

***

Sara had hoped that her question about whether this was the end for them would make Richard reflect and reconsider. It was her last throw of the dice. Richard's reply was therefore a bitter blow. Aunt Grace, as always, was there to comfort her and to say that this pain would fade in time.

Sara had still not told William that Richard had ended their engagement. She had maintained a vain hope that she could avoid the announcement.

When she had regained control of her tears, she went to see William in his study. He looked up from his desk.

'How are you?' he asked.

'I have had better days. Richard has ended our engagement.'

William was genuinely surprised, but he feigned his anger. 'What? What reasons has he given for this insult?'

'He says that we are no longer suited. He does not want us to be married.' Sara's voice wavered as she became aware of the reality of what she had said. She turned her head away from her cousin so he couldn't see her tears.

William went over to her.

'I'm fine, William. Thank you.'

'You must be deeply hurt after this shock,' he said. 'It will take time for you to recover, but you must remember that I am here for you. Anything you need or want me to do for you, then tell me.' He put his arm around Sara's shoulder and drew her closer towards him. 'Richard Lloyd will pay for his treatment of you. It is a breach of promise, and I shall speak to our lawyer to see what can be done.'

'No, William, please no. I don't want Richard to think that I need redress in some way. It's too soon to talk of such things.'

'I'm sorry, you are right, it is much too soon. There will be plenty of time to discuss what you want to do.'

After Sara left his study, William walked over to the window with the broadest of smiles. Richard Lloyd was out of his family, and he needed to ensure that there was no way back for him. He would see the lawyer in the morning. He had to be prepared for when Sara was ready to punish Lloyd for jilting her.

CHAPTER 16

As Sara had made it clear that she didn't want any involvement in the announcement of their separation, Richard took sole responsibility for the task. Over the next few days, he told family, friends and associates that they were no longer betrothed. Most people were sympathetic.

It was only after Richard had informed everyone that he felt the full impact of his decision. He didn't regret what he had done, but the cold reality of not having Sara in his life still hurt.

He also received sad news from the workhouse infirmary. Poor little Bob Morgan had suffered further complications and had passed away. Richard had not been there when he died. While there was nothing more that he could have done for the boy, he felt he had let him down.

***

Apart from her family, Sara had not told anyone about the situation. Elizabeth Davenport visited her to see how she was coping.

'Elizabeth, how wonderful to see you,' Sara greeted her friend. 'Please, have some tea.'

'You seem fine, considering what you've been through,' said Elizabeth. 'I was worried that I would find you very emotional and upset. I am pleased, of course, to find you so well.'

'I have been angry and sad, but I have to get on with my life. Seeing you is a real tonic. Anyway, I have this feeling that he will come back to me.'

Elizabeth looked surprised. 'Would you have him back?'

'Oh yes. I still love him and he still loves me. Of course, I would make him suffer for what he has done, but eventually I would take him back. Anyway, I don't want to talk about Richard. I want to hear about your wedding plans. I hope that I am still getting an invitation?' Sara smiled and sipped her tea.

'You are my oldest friend and your name will be the first on my guest list. Father will also be inviting William.'

'Thank you – I am so relieved. I was worried that Evan would not want us there. Richard is his best man after all.' Sara stood up and put her teacup on the table. 'William is very angry with Richard for ending our engagement. He says that Richard has humiliated me and insulted our family. He wants me to take Richard to court for breach of promise, but I don't want to do that. For some reason, he is also angry with Evan and their father.'

On hearing all this, Elizabeth's concern was only slightly reduced by the fact that the wedding was still several weeks away. That would hopefully be enough time for William's fury with the Lloyd family to subside.

William had not told Sara the real cause of his outrage: he had discovered that it was the Lloyd family who had bought the corn mill. Samuel Vaughan had informed him, and they were meeting later that day.

Elizabeth left Plas Gwyn just before Vaughan arrived to see William. He was shown to William's study, and the two men got down to business. Evan had bought the mill on a long lease with the freehold owned by a property company called North Wales

Land Holdings. Samuel Vaughan had his hand in several local businesses, including this property company, where he was a director. The company had been informed that the lease had been transferred from Mrs Price to Edward Lloyd and sons, of Ty Celyn.

'They have done this deliberately to upset and annoy me,' said William, 'and what's more, damn them, they have succeeded.'

'You know more about the personal aspects of this matter, but the mill could be just a good investment for the Lloyds,' Vaughan told him. 'It was bought below the market value of the property and the business has potential for growth.'

'Edward Lloyd knows our historic connections with the mill and that I would have wanted it back in the family. If the Lloyds want trouble, then they have got it. What can you do to help me?'

'North Wales Land Holdings can increase the rent. There is a ground rent payable on the mill. As it hasn't been increased for several years, a large increase could be justified. They won't realise that you are behind this; neither will my name be on any correspondence.'

'That is a good start to my campaign against the Lloyds. I will own that mill before Christmas.' Behind his desk, William smiled. 'I also intend to teach Richard Lloyd a severe lesson for his treatment of Sara.'

***

The scarlet fever outbreak at the workhouse continued to concern Richard. He had scarcely recovered from the sadness of Bob Morgan's death when Bob's mother also passed away. Mrs Morgan, aged only thirty-five, had been a frail woman, a widow for the last five years. Illness, poor housing and a hard life had taken their toll.

The workhouse had sapped her dwindling resilience, but she had persevered for the sake of her children. Her two surviving children, a brother and sister both under ten years old, were now orphans.

Samuel Vaughan entered the master's office where Richard sat talking to Enoch Evans about Mrs Morgan and her family.

'I need an update on the scarlet fever situation,' said Vaughan.

'I'm glad to say that we've had no new cases for two weeks,' replied Richard.

'That's good, but we have had six cases in total and two deaths. Furthermore, you don't seem to have followed proper procedures. You should have informed me personally as Chairman of the Board of Guardians that we had a contagious disease in the workhouse.'

'I apologise for that, but I did take immediate steps to inform you.' Richard looked at Enoch Evans, expecting him to explain what had happened. Evans offered no words of support or an admission that he was to blame.

'Your apology is accepted, but it was nevertheless a failure to follow set procedures and I have no alternative but to reprimand you for this failure. I was also concerned to learn that as the disease reached its peak, you were not present at the infirmary and could not be found.'

'Is a reprimand really necessary?' said Richard, staring at Vaughan in incredulity. 'I was looking after other patients in Llangollen that morning, and you must know that, in recent weeks, I have spent most of my time here in the infirmary.'

'You did not follow established procedures and as such a reprimand is appropriate,' said Samuel Vaughan.

He nodded to Richard and Enoch Evans and walked out of the room.

'Thank you for your support,' said Richard sarcastically to Evans, and he shook his head in disbelief as he left the office.

***

That evening, Richard went to The Hand Inn hoping that Elin might be at work. It had been almost six weeks since he had last seen her, and she knew nothing about his separation from Sara or the tragic scarlet fever incidents at the workhouse. His mood immediately improved as she walked through with some food for a customer.

'How are you, Elin?'

'Well, thank you. It's lovely to see you. I'll come and talk in a few minutes.'

Five minutes later, she returned to Richard.

'I have asked the landlord if I can have a break now as it's fairly quiet. Are you meeting anyone here tonight?'

'Yes, you – I needed to see you. Let's go to that table over there. A lot has happened since I last saw you.'

Richard told Elin about Sara's intense behaviour and that they had reached the end of their road together.

'I'm not surprised. On the way back from Corwen, you told me your concerns. You've made the right decision for both of you.'

'I'm sure that I have, too, but we did love one another.'

'Sara's idea of love is strange. It's twisted and selfish. Is that love? For me, love is about giving and caring for one another. All you have told me about Sara are threats and slaps.'

'Lately, that has been true, but it was different in the beginning.'

Elin smiled sympathetically, and was about to say something, when someone at the bar caught her attention. 'Listen, I shall have to go back to work soon. The landlord has looked at his watch and then at me, twice now.' Elin laughed.

Disappointed that their time together had been so brief, Richard forced a smile. 'We have other things to talk about and need more time. Would you like to go for a walk, perhaps on Sunday?'

'Yes, of course, that would be lovely. Enid, who also works here at The Hand, and her fiancé, often go for a walk on Sunday afternoons. We could join them.'

'I'll call round for you at two o'clock then.'

'I'll look forward to it. Remember, you are a free man now. You must find someone who will make you a good wife.'

And with that last remark, Elin stood up and smiled. Richard wondered whether Elin intended herself as that good wife.

And yes, he *was* a free man now.

Chapter 17

Sian and Owen had met secretly in various places over the past month. Owen would always arrive first and wait for Sian. On this occasion, he had arranged to meet her in a back-street tavern in Llangollen. It was a place that wouldn't be used by anyone from Berwyn Hall, and where they could sit, talk and hold hands.

'Any luck with finding your new job, yet?' asked Sian.

'There's a footman's job going at Chirk Castle.'

'I expect that a lot of people will want the job. It's further for us to travel to see one another too, isn't it?'

'Chirk isn't so far away. Anyway, I haven't got it yet.'

A woman appeared in the doorway to the dimly lit tavern. The bright sunlight only allowed her silhouette to be seen, and her face was temporarily obscured. Sian gasped as she looked at the tall, slim figure.

'What's the matter?' asked Owen.

As the woman came into the room and the door closed, Sian saw her face. She breathed a sigh of relief.

'I thought she was Eve Lyons,' she whispered. 'I swear that my heart stopped for a moment.'

'I have something that will make you smile,' said Owen as he took two railway tickets from his jacket pocket and put them on the table. 'Two excursion tickets for Rhyl this Saturday, as I know that you want to go to the seaside.'

Sian jumped up to hug Owen. 'I love you. I love you so much,' she told him excitedly.

Some of the other people in the tavern looked over to the couple and smiled and raised a glass to them. As she sat down, Sian looked serious.

'But is it safe? What if someone sees us and tells Berwyn Hall?'

'We were unlucky when Eve Lyons heard us at the river. Anyway, I happen to know that she is visiting her sister in Chester, so we don't have to worry about bumping into her on the promenade. Nobody from Berwyn Hall will be going to Rhyl that day.'

'I can't wait – a real outing to the seaside for just you and me.'

***

Saturday morning finally arrived, and Sian and Owen were at Llangollen Station. Owen went to ask about the time of the return train, as it was a special excursion. As Sian stood looking at the notices on the wall, Merryman saw her and came over to talk.

'I don't know if you remember me, but I left you a note for the doctor, a few weeks ago. Thank you for giving it to him.'

'Not at all,' said Sian. 'I am the housekeeper at Ty Celyn but I also manage Dr Lloyd's messages and appointments for him.'

'You're young to be a housekeeper.'

'My mother used to be the housekeeper and I was a general servant, but when she died, the Lloyds asked me to take over. Mam had taught me all I needed to know.'

Owen came back from the ticket office and Sian introduced him.

'I'm pleased to meet you, Owen,' said Merryman. 'I hope that you have a good day in Rhyl.'

It was more than a good day in Rhyl. Sian had looked forward to a day at the seaside with Owen for months. She linked arms with her Owen as they walked on the front and paddled in the waves. She didn't have to look over her shoulder to see if anyone recognised them. They could relax and chat, and even kiss on the beach if nobody was looking. Sian felt free.

Owen bought her a brooch that she had fancied in a shop window. He told her it would be a souvenir of their first real day out together. She said that this day would live in her memory forever.

***

After church on Sunday morning, Richard went to Llangollen to see Elin. They met Enid and her fiancé on Llangollen Bridge. Their walk would take them up the hill to Castell Dinas Bran, the castle ruins that looked over the town. Richard and Elin followed a few yards behind Enid and her fiancé.

'I haven't been up here before,' said Elin.

'As we get higher, the views are very good, and from the castle itself they are magnificent,' said Richard. 'We're lucky that it's a fine, clear day. I am glad that we are having an afternoon out together. I have so much to tell you. But how are you and John?'

'John is fit now and able to work normally in the tunnel. He didn't complain, but I know that he struggled when he first went back to work. The heavy work made him very tired, and he was clearly in pain – it was too soon after the accident, but we needed the money.'

'Are you still working all the hours God sends at The Hand?'

Elin laughed. 'Most of the hours He sends, but I manage to have two days off every fortnight to go home to Rhuddlan to see my family. That is important for me.'

'Just the family, or perhaps you now have a young man back home?' Richard asked cautiously.

'I have no time for that, not anymore.'

Richard wasn't sure whether she meant that she was too busy or whether the idea was abhorrent to her.

'What did you want to tell me?' asked Elin.

Richard wanted to say how much he thought of her, and how he hoped that they could become more than good friends. But he knew that the time was not right.

Instead, he told her about his difficulties at the infirmary with the scarlet fever outbreak and the reprimand from the chairman.

'It seems very unfair,' said Elin. 'Why didn't you tell the chairman that you had been let down by this man, Evans?'

'I thought Evans would do the decent thing and admit his mistake. And then the moment had gone, and there seemed little point to cause him trouble as well.'

'You are too good, Richard.'

'Too stupid, more like.'

'I see what you mean about the views from here,' said Elin as she paused to get her breath back and take in the scenery.

She asked him about the castle. Richard told her that it was built by a Welsh prince, Gruffudd, six hundred years ago, so it was a Welsh castle, not a Norman one like Conwy. King Edward did eventually capture it, but Gruffudd's sons had set fire to the castle so it would be of no use to him.

'I expect Gruffudd's family were tired of the climb up the hill every time they came home. I'm not surprised that Edward didn't want it either.'

Elin huffed and puffed, as if to show the effort needed to scale the hill, and Richard laughed.

'You're probably right, but it was a magnificent castle.'

When the four walkers reached the ruins, they sat on the grass next to the two large arches which had once held the windows in the castle hall. Richard bought some refreshments and the two girls chatted about people at work. Enid decided to head back to Llangollen, but Richard suggested to Elin that they stay for a few more minutes and look around the castle remains. They found a quiet spot, well away from other visitors.

'I have enjoyed being with you this afternoon,' he told her. 'I would like us to go out again, if you would like to.'

'It's been a lovely day. Next time, though, we'll have an easier walk—perhaps by the river?'

'Good idea,' said Richard, delighted that there would be a 'next time'. 'We could walk along the river by the Horseshoe Falls and then return to Ty Celyn for a meal. How does that sound?'

'Are you sure? I don't want to be a nuisance.'

'You will never be a nuisance to me.'

Richard looked into her eyes, smiled and gently put his hands on her waist. Elin moved closer to him, and Richard let his lips lightly caress hers before he kissed her.

'I have dreamt of this moment since we kissed at Ty Celyn but I didn't believe that we would ever kiss again,' she said.

'I was attracted to you from the day that you walked into my life. I thought that you were married to John, so it never crossed my mind that this might happen.'

'And you were to be married to Sara,' added Elin.

'That is the past. You are here now, and I hope in the future, too.'

They kissed again and then began to make their way down the hill. Richard looked back at the mysterious castle ruins. The ancient ghosts of Dinas Bran kept their secrets in those dark walls. Richard's hopes for the future were now linked to this mystical place where many lovers had dallied over the centuries.

***

As Richard and Elin walked back, hand in hand, to Llangollen, a train pulled into the station. One of the passengers was Eve Lyons, returning from the visit to her sister in Chester. Merryman opened the carriage door and helped Miss Lyons down from the train. He took her case and asked whether she needed further transport to be arranged.

'No thank you, porter, I am being met by the carriage from Berwyn Hall. I am the housekeeper.'

'Very good, madam. You are the second housekeeper from Berwyn that I've spoken to in the last day or two.'

'That is unusual. Who was the other one?' asked Eve Lyons.

'The young woman from Ty Celyn was here yesterday morning. I'm sure that Sian is her name.'

'The housekeeper role at Berwyn Hall is a much more responsible job than at a farmhouse like Ty Celyn.'

'I expect it is. It's a bit like comparing my job as foreman porter at Llangollen to that of the foreman at Waterloo,' said Merryman.

Eve Lyons was more interested in finding out about Sian's business at the station than the porter's occupational comparisons.

'Was Sian on her own yesterday?' she asked.

'I believe that she had a young man with her.'

'What did he look like?'

'Very tall with dark hair.'

'Was he called Owen?'

'I think he was.'

'Thank you, porter, you have been most helpful. Do you recall where they were going?'

'Rhyl, madam, for a happy day at the seaside.'

CHAPTER 18

Owen had the task of cleaning the shoes on Monday mornings. He was downstairs in the boot room, brushing the dirt off Sir Clayton's boots, when he heard the clicking of Miss Lyons' heels on the stone floor.

'Good morning, miss. How was your time in Chester?'

'Good morning, Phillips. I want to see you in my room at three o'clock this afternoon.'

Owen waited for her to say more, but she just looked at him with the shoe brush in his hand.

'Why do you wish to see me?' he asked eventually.

'I shall tell you this afternoon in my room,' she said and turned to walk out. 'I enjoyed seeing my sister in Chester, thank you. Did you have a good time in Rhyl?'

Owen couldn't believe what Eve Lyons had just said, and his worries began. What did she know about Rhyl? Did she know that Sian was with him? How did she find out?

His mental anguish continued for the next five hours until, at three o'clock, he knocked on Miss Lyons' door. He was told to enter the room. Eve Lyons stood at the side of her desk, and sitting behind it was Lady Davenport, empress of Berwyn Hall. Owen stood in front of them as directed. Their severe expressions told him everything. It was Lady Davenport who spoke first.

'Miss Lyons tells me that you spent Saturday in Rhyl with the young housekeeper from Ty Celyn. Several weeks ago, after being caught in an improper and compromising situation with this young woman, you made a formal promise not to see her again. You understood that the alternative to this undertaking would be instant dismissal. Is it true that you have seen this woman again despite your promise not to?'

Owen considered for a moment whether to deny the allegation, but he realised there was little point. They obviously knew the truth, and Lady Davenport's involvement showed how seriously they viewed the situation.

'Yes, it's true that Sian and I went to Rhyl on Saturday. Months ago, Sian had asked me to take her on an outing to the seaside, and I promised that I would do it one day. I'm sorry that I broke my promise to Miss Lyons, but I had already promised Sian her day out, you see.'

'Are you saying that a day at the seaside was more important than your employment at Berwyn Hall?' asked Eve Lyons.

'No, of course not.'

'You have admitted that you deceived us regarding your ongoing relationship with this girl,' said Lady Davenport. 'You have broken your promise to Miss Lyons and risked the good reputation of this house.'

'I've done nothing wrong.'

'I am not here to argue with you, Phillips. I have better things to do,' said Lady Davenport. 'You rudely interrupted me before I could say that I want you dismissed from Berwyn Hall. You will leave immediately. Furthermore, your behaviour leads me to the decision that Miss Lyons cannot provide any references for you, regarding future employment.'

'But that's unfair! My work has always been good, and you've never had any reason to criticise what I've done. That means that I shan't work in service again.'

'Being in service requires high standards of behaviour and morality. Any future employer would require Miss Lyons to confirm that you would meet those standards, and she clearly couldn't do that. She may, however, provide you with a written record confirming your employment at Berwyn Hall. If you wish such a testimonial then you must ask Miss Lyons for that favour.'

Owen looked at the floor. He wanted to leave Eve Lyons and her room but knew that he needed that written statement for any chance of getting a job. His voice couldn't hide his pent-up emotion as he asked her for the statement regarding his employment.

Eve Lyons produced a note from her drawer and handed it to Owen. There were just two lines. The first one confirmed the dates that he had worked at Berwyn Hall and the second line said that his work had been acceptable. She had already signed it.

'It will not get you the job of footman at Chirk Castle,' said Eve. 'I had a letter from the butler at Chirk this morning saying that you might be considered for employment, although he queried your experience. I have replied saying that I could not recommend you.'

A mixture of anger and hurt choked Owen. He said nothing but left the room and collected his belongings. Five minutes later, he walked down the drive with his case. He didn't turn around for a last look at the hall. If he had, he might have seen Eve Lyons at the window, watching his sad figure depart.

On leaving the grounds, Owen stopped and put down his case. He had nowhere to go, no job and no roof over his head for the night. As he walked alongside the river, he came to the secluded spot where Sian and he used to meet. He went up the bank and put his case against a tree. He broke down some bracken and laid it out on the ground, his bed for the night ahead.

Owen then went to tell Sian the sorry events of his day.

She was in the kitchen beginning to prepare the evening meal. When Owen told her what had happened, she sat down and wept. He knelt beside her and held her in his arms.

Still sobbing, Sian turned to Owen. 'It's so unfair, and you did it for me. If I hadn't gone on about a day at the seaside you wouldn't have lost the job. It's my fault. I'm so sorry.'

Owen took her hand. 'It's not your fault at all. We love one another, and we're not going to be kept apart by anyone. If we hadn't been seen together last Saturday, we would have been caught on another day. It was going to happen. I shall find another job.'

'Where are you going to sleep tonight?' asked Sian.

'Don't worry, I have a bed that will do for a couple of nights while I sort something out.'

'I can let you have some food. The meal will be ready in an hour and you can have it here in the back kitchen. The Lloyds won't mind.'

'I can't stay for a meal, but some cold food to take back would be welcome. Thank you.'

Sian wrapped up some bread and cheese.

'Have you got enough money? I have some if you need it.'

'I have enough for now.' Owen jingled some coins in his pocket.

They kissed at the back door, and Sian made him promise to come and see her tomorrow. Owen then made his way down the path. He reached into his pocket and took out the copper coins. He had five pennies and one farthing, to his name. He had spent all that he had on the train excursion tickets and the day out in Rhyl.

He found his den for the night.

Heavy rain woke him in the small hours, drenching the bracken he had arranged as a mattress.

Owen awakened to a sunny morning. The rain had stopped. He had a change of clothes in his case and was pleased to have a dry shirt next to his skin. He put the wet clothes to dry on a tree.

The last of Sian's bread and cheese was eaten for breakfast, and then Owen set out. He called at each farm asking whether there was any work available. He had no luck. By mid-afternoon, he arrived at Ty Celyn.

'I was just thinking about you,' said Sian as she showed him in. 'And in truth, I have hardly thought about anything else all day. How have you got on?'

'I have lost count of the farms I've visited,' Owen replied, 'but nobody is hiring a labourer today. Where there might be a job, they need someone with experience. It was the same at the slate works and at the railway. There's no work, even at the inns.'

'It's early days,' said Sian, 'and you might have better luck tomorrow. Have you eaten?'

'Not since breakfast.'

'Come into the kitchen and I'll get you some food.'

Owen was pleased to sit down at the table while Sian put some ham and bread and butter on a plate. Owen devoured the food. He said that he had some more places to try before evening and that he would go to Corwen in the morning. Sian wrapped up some ham, cheese and bread for him. Owen kissed her and he went on his way.

His last call was as fruitless as the rest, and as he made his way back to the riverbank, it started to rain. The clothes that he had put on the tree to dry were soaked again, and the damp bracken provided no comfort. He felt desolate, and this was only the end of the first day.

***

Sian had not seen Owen for two days and was worried about him. She had not expected him the previous day as he was looking for work in Corwen, but it was now almost five o'clock in the afternoon.

Sian didn't even know where he had been sleeping. She desperately wanted her sweetheart to appear at the door.

***

Richard had gone to meet Elin at the end of her shift. Arriving at The Hand, he saw her waiting in the yard. He helped her onto the seat of the gig and then climbed up beside her.

'It's the National Eisteddfod in two weeks' time,' he said. 'I've been asked to speak in a discussion about the proposed Patagonian settlement. The essay I wrote on emigration and the Welsh language has come to people's attention.'

'I would love to hear your talk.'

Richard thought for a moment. 'You could come with me on the train to Llandudno, see the events in the pavilion, and after the debate we'd travel home. That would be on the Wednesday.'

'But you're going to stay in Llandudno, and I'd spoil your plans.'

'I would much prefer a day with you than staying overnight in Llandudno on my own.'

'Are you sure? I really would like that.'

Elin leaned over and kissed him on the cheek and then rested her head on his shoulder as he drove back to Berwyn.

Before supper, Richard and Elin went for their walk along the river. They stopped to look at the rushing water. There had been several thunderstorms over the last three days and the heavy rainfall in the hills had caused the river level to rise. Above the sound of the torrent, Richard heard someone coughing. It came from above the path. Richard could see that someone had been coming and going up the bank and had flattened the long grass.

He called out to the hidden person but received no response except another bout of coughing. He went to investigate and found Owen lying on the drenched bracken. He was semiconscious and shaking uncontrollably. Richard, shocked and horrified, put his hand over Owen's forehead. It was hot with fever. Richard asked Elin to go back to Ty Celyn and ask Evan to help carry Owen home.

Sian was in the kitchen when she heard the commotion in the hall and came out to see what was going on.

'Owen!' she shouted as she saw her love with his eyes half closed and clothes and skin wet from sweat and rain. '*Cariad*, what has happened to you?'

There was no reaction from Owen.

'It looks like he has been sleeping in the open and has caught a chill,' said Richard. 'We'll get him to bed in the surgery and I'll give him a full examination.'

'I want to be with him,' said Sian, crying.

Elin tried to comfort her.

Richard's examination confirmed that Owen had a chill with a fever. His temperature was very high and he was delirious.

'He'll be alright, won't he?' Sian asked anxiously. 'I can't lose him. This is Berwyn Hall's fault. The two witches have done this.'

'He is very ill, but the fever will subside,' said Richard.

Sian explained how he had been dismissed without references on Monday and had been looking for work. 'He told me that he had somewhere to sleep.'

'Well, he will have a dry bed tonight.'

Elin made supper at Ty Celyn that evening.

'I invite you for a quiet walk and a meal, and you end up making supper,' said Richard. 'This is not how I planned it. I'm sorry.'

'Don't be silly, that poor boy needed your help. I hate to think what might have happened if we had not walked by and heard him coughing.'

After supper, Evan took Elin back to her lodgings. Richard attended to Owen, but there had been no improvement. His fever still raged with his delirious muttering and frequent coughing.

Richard prayed that he would make it through the night.

CHAPTER 19

The morning brought little change for Owen. Over breakfast, Richard told his father that the next twenty-four hours would be critical. Edward said that he would go to Berwyn Hall to tell Sir Clayton what had happened to Owen, and the consequences of Lady Margaret's actions.

Edward walked up the long avenue of trees to Berwyn Hall. He was greeted by a servant and invited to wait in the great hall. He sat beneath a portrait of Lady Margaret, painted when she was barely twenty years old and was a very beautiful young woman. Looking up at the warm, smiling face, he wondered where that lovely apparition had gone.

A couple of minutes later, Sir Clayton appeared.

'My dear Edward, how good it is to see you. Come into the library. Would you like a sherry?'

'Too early for me, Clayton.' Edward had known Sir Clayton since they were boys, so he never addressed him formally.

'Yes, you're right. Eleven o'clock is just about respectable, but nine-thirty is a bit desperate really. Damn it.' He laughed. 'What brings you here so early?'

Edward told Clayton about Owen's sad story.

'I want to know why Owen was dismissed,' he finished. 'You must know that Berwyn Hall has a reputation for its harsh staff practices?'

'That's a bit strong,' said Sir Clayton. His earlier jovial attitude had turned serious. 'You know that I have nothing to do with the running of the house or servant matters. That is very much Margaret's responsibility, and she does have a strong view on the behaviour of young male servants.'

'But why? It's bad enough when the big houses prevent relationships between their own staff, but Sian is not even employed by the hall. It doesn't make sense.'

'Sometimes things don't,' said Sir Clayton, and he paused in thought for a few moments. 'I'll tell you in strictest confidence, as Margaret cannot know I told you. You're an old friend and I trust you.

'As you are aware, the death of Humphrey in the Crimea, eight years ago now, affected us both very badly. Margaret didn't want him to join the army, but Humphrey persuaded me to sign his papers and I managed to get him a commission. Margaret has never forgiven me since he died in action. The loss of her firstborn son caused her such devastating grief. She is consumed with the thought that he died so young and saw such little life. She hurts whenever she sees other young men living the life that she feels Humphrey should have had. I suppose it is a form of jealousy, but it is also a pain that she cannot control. She cannot bear to think about young men enjoying themselves, especially in the company of women. Thank God we still have Grant, who Margaret lives for now, but she also has fears about his future in the army.'

Edward considered what he had been told. 'I still don't agree with Margaret's actions, but I do understand. I am sorry, Clayton.'

'I'm sorry too. I cannot change her. In the past I have stepped in and tried to intervene, but she will not relent. She is aided and abetted by Eve Lyons, who has emotional scars of her own. Apparently, she was betrothed for several years and then deserted at the altar. They are a formidable partnership, believe me.'

'What does Margaret make of Evan's forthcoming marriage with Elizabeth?' asked Edward, who was becoming increasingly concerned about the state of mind of his son's future mother-in-law.

'She wants Elizabeth to be happy, and she can see that Evan makes her very happy, so there will be no problems. When Evan becomes part of our family, I shall explain to him about Margaret's behaviour and illness.'

Edward nodded. He could see the look of resignation in his friend's eyes as he spoke about his wife. 'I came here to ask you to consider giving Owen his job back, but I can see now that is impossible.'

'Yes, but I shall provide him with a proper reference.'

'Let's hope that he lives,' said Edward.

***

At supper that evening, Edward told Richard and Evan about his visit to Sir Clayton and his offer to provide Owen with a reference. He respected Clayton's confidences regarding Margaret.

Edward had been thinking about Owen's future after his hopeful recovery and asked Evan about the possibility of finding useful employment for him at Ty Celyn, as an estate apprentice. He could gain hands-on experience on the farm and at the corn mill. Evan openly welcomed the idea but kept his concerns to himself about the costs of another employee.

Later, after their father had gone to bed, Richard and Evan were sat in the parlour. Richard was preparing his talk for the eisteddfod debate and Evan was studying a letter that he had received about the corn mill. The contents did not become any better on a further reading. He interrupted his brother's work on Patagonia.

'I'm concerned about the mill. I've had a letter from the freeholder telling me that the annual ground rent is being raised. It's a big increase and it's due next month.'

'How can they justify that?' asked Richard. 'Do you have the right to challenge the rise?'

'The letter says that there has been no increase for several years. I sought legal advice this morning and was told that under the terms of the lease there is no limit to the rise. The law would expect that any increase should be reasonable, but that would be up to a court to decide. I have asked for a letter to be sent to North Wales Land Holdings saying that we object to the increase, and that the proposed rent is excessive. We'll see what they have to say, but I'm not very hopeful.'

'I expect that a challenge in court would be very expensive.'

'Expensive and probably unsuccessful,' replied Evan. 'I cannot risk that sort of money. I'll just have to pay the bill next month. But the rent increase might be the least of our problems. We are losing customers. A longstanding customer has moved his business to another mill. Another client told me today that he is also going elsewhere. We are already under capacity and need to get new business, not lose existing customers.'

'Will the modernisations to the mill have to wait?'

'I have taken out a loan to fund the essential repairs and improvements, but everything else will be on hold. The whole thing is a mess, and there is something not right about it either. Losing one customer might just be unfortunate, but losing two in a matter of a fortnight is not a coincidence. I need to find out why and where they have moved their business. I expect that will be easier said than done.'

***

The following morning, Sian was smiling again. The fever had broken during the night and Owen awakened as the sun rose. The delirium had gone, and Richard confirmed that his temperature had returned to normal. He polished off his breakfast like a man who had not eaten for five days.

'I cannot believe that it's only a week since we went to Rhyl,' said Sian. 'What a week we've had. I thought I had lost you when Richard and Evan brought you here.'

Evan came into the surgery and told Owen about the offer of a job on the estate, and also Sir Clayton's promise of a reference. It was now Owen's turn to smile.

'I can't thank you enough,' said Owen as he took Evan's hand in gratitude. 'I'd welcome the chance to learn new skills and do something different. The job is perfect for me.'

'Good, and there is a bed for you in the stable loft. You can start work as soon as Richard says that you are well enough.'

CHAPTER 20

Elizabeth hadn't visited Sara for over three weeks. Sara, delighted to see her friend, linked her arm and they went into the garden at Plas Gwyn.

'We'll be alone here, and you can update me on everything that is going on at Berwyn Hall, especially the wedding preparations.'

'And I want to know what you have been doing,' said Elizabeth.

'I've not done much since you were here last. I have been a bit bored, to tell you the truth.'

'Why didn't you come over to see me at the hall? We could have gone out for a walk.'

'I don't know. Well, yes I do. It's too close to Ty Celyn, and I didn't want to bump into Richard or Evan. Richard hasn't been in touch with me. Perhaps he has met someone else, but surely it would be too soon for that to have happened.'

Elizabeth quickly looked away from Sara. She spoke hastily about the weather.

Sara noticed her friend's unease and stared at her.

'He has met someone else, hasn't he?' she said.

Elizabeth hesitated. 'I think they're only friends.'

'Come on, Elizabeth, you must know more than that. You're engaged to Evan. Who is she?'

'It's not my business to talk about them. I cannot say anymore.'

'Who is she?' Sara asked in a firmer voice. 'I will find out, so you may as well tell me. You are my dearest and oldest friend, surely it is right that I find out from you and not from idle gossip.'

'I suppose so, but I really don't know much. Evan doesn't talk about it to me and I haven't seen Richard for ages. As far as I know, Richard and Elin are only friends.'

'Elin. How long has he known this Elin?'

Elizabeth hesitated again.

'Did Richard know her when I was engaged to him?' Sara pressed.

'I believe they met some time ago,' admitted Elizabeth.

'William was right,' said Sara. 'Richard has broken his promise to me for another woman.' Her voice faltered as she took in the news.

'I'm sure that Richard hasn't betrayed you.' Elizabeth tried to comfort Sara, who was now crying in her arms. Her visit had been well-intentioned, but now she wished that she had never gone.

After Elizabeth had left Plas Gwyn, Sara calmed herself and went to see William. He was in his study, but when he saw her, he put down his pen and pushed the papers to one side of his desk to demonstrate his full attention.

'Sit down. What can I do for you?' asked William.

Sara closed the study door and sat down opposite William.

'When Richard ended our engagement, you said that I should sue for breach of promise.'

William looked even more interested. 'I did indeed.'

'I didn't want to do that then, as I secretly hoped that Richard would come back to me, but now I do want him to pay for what he did.'

'What has changed?'

'Elizabeth has told me that he is seeing another woman and she thinks that it started while he was still engaged to me.'

'I am so sorry for you, but surely you must realise now that you are better off without him. I'll get on to my solicitor straight away, and we can get his advice on the matter. I'm no expert but I'd be surprised if this news doesn't help your case significantly.'

'I thought that too.'

Sara stood up and kissed her cousin on his cheek. When she had left his study, his utter delight shone through. He'd already spoken to the lawyer; Sara had a good case.

***

The next day, the solicitor's brougham was brought to a halt outside Plas Gwyn. The driver opened the carriage door and Albert Mason stepped down with his briefcase. He was shown into the drawing room, where William and Sara were already seated.

'I hope that you have some good news for Sara,' said William.

'From the information provided by you, William, we appear to have a sound argument for bringing a case against Dr Lloyd. That is the good news. The bad news is that these cases are very unpredictable. I need a few more facts from you before we can make a proper assessment of your chances.'

Albert Mason asked Sara about the length of her engagement to Richard and whether he had remained faithful to her over that time. He also wanted to know about any costs that she had incurred as a result of the engagement, and whether Richard had the ability to pay damages. The lawyer noted her responses.

'I now have to ask you a very personal question but an important one nevertheless. Did you and Dr Lloyd enjoy sexual relations during your engagement?'

Sara looked aghast at Mason and then at William. She stood up, clearly agitated.

'I am not prepared to answer that. I don't want my reputation called into question now, or in any court, if we decide to proceed with a case.'

'I do understand, Miss Griffiths-Ellis. I shall put down in my notes that you did not. I must explain, however, why I asked you that question. If you had sexual relations during your engagement then that might demonstrate a higher degree of commitment by you both to one another. It is also likely to result in higher damages because of a loss of reputation and virtue on your behalf.'

'Richard ended the engagement and therefore broke his promise to marry me. Surely that is the crux of the matter?'

'Indeed it is, but as I said earlier, these cases are very unpredictable and especially concerning the level of damages.'

Mason explained that the cases were decided by a court jury not a judge, and were very dependent on the lawyers' presentations. The court would see any private correspondence between the two parties, and he would need to know whether any letters or other written evidence existed that may affect the case.

'So, the intimate details of our engagement might be shared with a jury of strangers?'

'They might be, but it will depend on what evidence Dr Lloyd's lawyer might present to the court. These cases can become malicious and distressing, and you need to consider that when deciding your course of action.'

William had remained quiet but was becoming concerned that Sara appeared less convinced about pursuing this action.

'You would brief your lawyer about what you want to have disclosed,' he told her.

'Dr Lloyd may well decide to settle out of court,' said Mason, 'and most gentlemen will make that offer. You could expect an offer of up to a hundred pounds for an out-of-court settlement. You would get an admission from the man that he has wronged you.'

'And what sort of figure could Sara expect if the case goes to court?' asked William.

'Well, that is the greatest uncertainty. One hundred pounds is common but any amount up to, say, a thousand is possible. But all of this is dependent on whether the lawyer wins the jury over to her cause.'

'I am not prepared to subject myself to any humiliation or embarrassment on the whim of a jury, which favours a doctor over me,' said Sara. 'The risk is not worth it.'

The lawyer pointed out that the odds were in favour of the woman. On average, nine out of ten women who claimed for breach of promise received some form of damages, often out of court.

'I am not going to decide today,' said Sara after a further moment or two of thought. 'I am unsure whether taking this matter forward will do me much good.'

'You are doing the right thing, Miss Griffiths-Ellis, as you need to be certain that you want to pursue the matter.'

William looked disappointed but concurred with Mason.

Sara quickly clarified her position. 'Oh, I do want to pursue the matter, and I want to make sure that Richard admits his mistake and wrongdoing, and pays for what he has done to me. But I'm not prepared to risk my reputation, not at any price. I, therefore, need to think about it further.'

'Very good, Miss Griffiths-Ellis,' said Mason with a slight bow of the head. 'Is there anything else you need to know, or anything I can do for you, at the present time?'

'Yes, I think so. You asked me whether Richard had been faithful to me, and I told you about a girl called

Elin. I need to know who this Elin is, and what sort of a relationship Richard has with her. I've been told that they are just friends, but if it is more than that then I need to know whether it was going on while we were engaged. Can you find out?'

'I can employ a private inquiry agent to look into it for us. If you decide to proceed with a case then it may provide valuable information.'

'Thank you, Mr Mason.'

William showed the solicitor outside to his waiting brougham.

'I would like you to get on with the investigation as soon as possible,' William told him, 'and I would view proof of a relationship between Dr Lloyd and the woman called Elin as a very positive outcome. Do you understand?'

'Yes, of course,' replied Albert Mason.

'I take it that you are very keen that Sara proceeds with a case.'

'It is imperative that Sara sues Dr Lloyd for breach of promise,' William replied.

'I understand fully, and you may leave it with me,' said Mason.

CHAPTER 21

Merryman Christmas had asked Richard to visit. His youngest son, Gareth, was in bed and feeling unwell.

'So, what is the matter with Gareth?' asked Richard.

'He came home from school yesterday very weepy and took himself off to bed without any supper,' Mary explained. 'It's not like him – he'll never miss a meal. Then this morning he told me that he had a headache and felt sick and did not want to get up and go to school.'

Richard and Mary went upstairs to see Gareth. The boy flinched away as Richard examined him.

'Have you a pain in your back or at the top of your legs?' Richard asked.

'No, I'm fine, doctor.'

Richard looked dubiously at the boy. 'Come on – let's have a look anyway.'

He lifted the boy's shirt to see a nasty cut at the base of his back, followed by welts and bruising on his bottom and the top of his leg.

'Who did this to you?' asked Richard, trying to hide his shock at such an ugly sight.

Gareth hesitated, and then murmured, 'Mr Morris caned me.'

Mary was fighting back the tears as she looked down at her son, so marked and in obvious pain. Merryman had come up the stairs to find out what was going on.

'Why, boy? What have you done to deserve this?'

'Nothing, Dad. I was just the last with the board. Mr Morris is the new teacher, and we're not allowed to speak Welsh now.'

'What do you mean?' asked his mother.

'I have heard of it being used in other schools, but not here,' said Richard. 'It's a punishment for speaking Welsh at school. A wooden board saying 'Welsh Not' is hung around the neck of a child who has been heard speaking Welsh. That child can pass it on to another that he catches speaking Welsh in the schoolyard. The last child wearing it at the end of the school day is caned by the teacher.'

Mary was weeping now.

'It is outrageous, and this caning has been especially brutal and vicious,' said Richard, looking at Gareth's injuries. 'I do not understand how teachers can inflict such pain on children.'

'I'm going to see the headmaster about this,' said Merryman. 'I don't suppose you could come as well? You can back me up, actually, on the injuries that Mr Morris has caused.'

'No, Dad, it will only make things worse,' Gareth pleaded. 'Please don't go.'

'Your father is right,' Richard said. 'The school needs to be warned that this is unacceptable. Mr Morris cannot be allowed to do this again to you, or any other child. I shall go with your father.'

Richard dressed the boy's wounds. He and Merryman then made their way to the school.

As it was the end of the school day, most of the children had left. One little girl stood by the school door. As Richard got closer, he could see that she was crying. A large wooden board hung from her neck. In big letters, the words 'Welsh Not' had been painted.

Richard knelt beside the girl and spoke softly to her in Welsh.

'Don't cry. I am going to remove this board now and then you can go home to your mam.'

'No, you can't do that,' she told him. 'I shall be in even more trouble with Mr Morris. Only he can take it off as I was the last one to speak Welsh.'

'You will not be in trouble. Tell him that Dr Lloyd took it and gave it to the headmaster. I'm going to see him now.'

Richard removed the board and put his arms around the girl.

'Go home now, and don't worry.'

She ran out of the school gate, and Richard and Merryman went into the school.

The headmaster was alone in the main classroom. Richard slammed the board on his desk.

'I have just removed this monstrosity from the neck of a girl who was about to be punished by your Mr Morris. I have sent her home. I did not want to see any more injuries inflicted on defenceless children.'

Merryman went on to explain to him why Gareth had not been in school that day. Richard confirmed the severity of the beating and said that Mr Morris should be held to account for his actions.

'I shall speak with Mr Morris and ensure that he exercises more control over his punishments in future,' said the headmaster, looking very uncomfortable.

'Why are you allowing him to punish the children for speaking Welsh?' asked Richard. 'We are all Welsh speakers, and I am proud of our language. Aren't you?'

'He persuaded me to use the Welsh Not because in his previous school it had improved the pupils' use of English. I am sure you would agree that is important.'

'Yes, but not at the expense of injuring and humiliating the children, and letting them think that the Welsh language is worthless.'

Richard's anger grew. 'To beat a child so severely that he needs medical attention is an abomination and a perversion. I think that Morris is using the Welsh Not as an excuse to cane his pupils. I was subjected to a brutal teacher when I was at school. He got away with it, but I shall be damned if someone does that to one of my patients and is not reprimanded.'

'I am sure that is not the case, Dr Lloyd, but as I say, I will speak with Mr Morris urgently. I'm very sorry, Mr Christmas, about your son's experience. It will not happen again.'

Merryman thanked the headmaster. When they had left the school, he turned to Richard.

'Duw, you did a good job back there, standing up for the children.'

'I think that I was also standing up for myself, even if it was almost twenty years late,' said Richard. 'I was unable to do it then, just as Gareth and that little girl are helpless today.'

***

Richard was pleased that he had arranged to meet Elin that evening for supper at the Waterloo Inn. He met her at her lodgings and they walked the short distance there together. He had been shocked by the brutality of the schoolmaster, and the chance to relax in Elin's company was just what he needed. They ordered their meals.

'Is Owen fully recovered from his fever?' asked Elin.

'He moves into the stable loft tonight and starts work on the farm tomorrow morning. Evan's offer of a job and accommodation at Ty Celyn has aided his recovery more than any medicine. The lad's got hope again and he can see a future for Sian and himself.'

'I'm very pleased. It was lucky that we found him in time.'

'How has your day been?' asked Richard.

'Oh, as usual at The Hand, you know. I'm looking forward to going to Llandudno with you. It'll be something new, and a whole day together as well.'

'A week today, we'll be there' said Richard, 'and it cannot come soon enough.'

CHAPTER 22

The next morning broke with a beautiful sunrise and a pink-red sky. After breakfast, Richard set off for Corwen, and his first call was at the workhouse. In Enoch Evans' office, he was told that an inmate, Mary Jenkins, had died yesterday evening in the infirmary. There was a suggestion of an overdose. Ann Jones had been nursing the patient.

Ann was summoned to the master's office to discuss the situation with Richard and Enoch Evans.

'We need to know more about the death of Mary Jenkins,' said Evans.

Ann Jones frowned and looked at the floor. Richard asked her how Mary had been yesterday, and what medicine she had received.

'Mary had a lot of pain and she said that it was getting worse,' said Ann. 'The medicine wasn't helping her. I gave her a dose at around six o'clock. When I checked her at nine o'clock, she had died.'

'Some of the inmates have said that Mary and you were often seen arguing and shouting at one another. Why was that?' asked Evans.

'She wanted more medicine, Master. She would shout at me when I told her she couldn't have it.'

'As the morphine dose didn't seem to be working and Mary was demanding more, did you increase the amount of medicine to help ease her pain?' asked Richard.

Ann was quiet for a moment. Richard prompted her for a reply.

'She was suffering. I might have given her a little more to help with the pain.' Ann looked down at the floor again.

'I've heard enough to involve Sergeant Parry,' said Evans.

'Surely not,' said Ann, visibly shocked. 'I've done nothing wrong.'

'We'll let the police decide about that,' said Evans, staring at Ann over his spectacles.

Richard escorted Ann out of the room and quietly told her not to worry. It did nothing to abate her fears.

An hour later the sergeant joined the interrogation.

'How long have you known Mary Jenkins?' asked Sergeant Parry.

'Most of my life, I suppose,' answered Ann. 'We became friends with Mary and her husband when we lived in Cerrig.'

'What happened to end your friendship? I have been told that you and Mary argued a lot.'

'We had trouble with Mary's family.'

'Yes, but what happened to cause the trouble between you and Mary?'

Ann paused for a few moments.

'I'd rather not say. It was a family matter, personal you see, and it was a long time ago. Soon afterwards, my husband got work in a quarry near Llangollen and we moved there. I didn't see Mary again until six months ago when she came here.'

'Perhaps so, but I understand that you had a big argument on the evening that she died. If you don't tell me the reason then I have to assume that it was serious enough for you to want to harm her.'

Ann said that the arguments in the infirmary were about Mary's demands for morphine and nothing to do with the past.

'Tell me about Mary's medicine. Did you give her the medicine on the day that she died, and how much did she have?'

'I gave her the medicine that Dr Lloyd had provided, both morning and night, just as he told me.'

Sergeant Parry looked at Richard.

'It was a solution of morphine to relieve the pain in her legs,' he explained.

'Dangerous medicine then, doctor?'

'Yes, if an excessive dose is given.'

'What was the dose that you gave Mary, Mrs Jones?'

'Two spoons, morning and night.'

'You mean one spoonful. The dose was one spoonful, two times a day,' said Richard.

'No, you said two, doctor.'

Richard excused himself from the room and went to the infirmary. He returned, holding Mary Jenkins' medicine bottle.

'This is the morphine that you were giving Mary Jenkins. What does it say on the label?' asked Richard.

'I always remember what you tell me. I don't need labels.'

'But it says quite clearly one spoonful to be taken twice daily.'

'I can't read,' said Ann, looking down at the floor and feeling very sheepish. 'That's why I have to remember what you tell me.'

'Why didn't you say that you couldn't read? I could have marked the labels in some way. We could have avoided this dangerous risk.'

Ann repeated again that there was no need, as she always remembered what he told her. Richard, with increasing annoyance, told her that quite clearly she had not remembered.

Parry cut in. 'On the evening that Mary died, you told Dr Lloyd and Mr Evans that you gave her an additional dose of morphine. How much did you give her? Tell me what happened.'

'I gave her two spoons of medicine at about six o'clock. Two hours later she was still in great pain and demanding more. She was crying with the pain. I gave her another two spoons and she finally fell asleep.'

'Well, asleep or dead, it is clear that you gave her too much morphine, but the questions are: firstly, did that kill her, and secondly, was it a mistake or did you deliberately intend to kill her?'

'I have told you that it was a mistake and it wasn't my fault,' said Ann, with tears in her eyes.

Parry said that they would have a break and asked Ann to return at two o'clock. She left the room without saying a word.

'Would the overdose have killed Mary?' Parry asked Richard.

'Mary was frail, so it might have affected her heart'.

Parry said that he wanted to interview someone who had witnessed the arguments between Mary and Ann. Evans suggested Nurse Thomas.

Sergeant Parry asked Mrs Thomas whether she knew what the arguments were about. Mrs Thomas said that she had heard them shouting at one another, but she didn't know why.

'I remember Ann saying, "I can't do that" and Mary shouting back, "You will, or else." After the last argument, I heard her shout, "You'll be sorry if you don't get it now."'

'Do you know what Mary wanted?'

'Ann told me that she wanted morphine.'

'Did Mary ever ask you to get her morphine?'

'Once or twice at the beginning,' said Mrs Thomas, 'but she never argued when I told her that it wasn't possible.'

'Thank you, Mrs Thomas; you have been most helpful.'

'It's interesting that Mary continued to demand the morphine from Mrs Jones and not Mrs Thomas,' said Parry, once she had left the room. 'It suggests that Mary knew something about Mrs Jones that was a threat to her.'

Ann Jones returned at two o'clock. Sergeant Parry spoke to her.

'I am of the opinion that Mrs Jenkins knew something that would be very hurtful to you. She was threatening to tell people your secrets unless you gave her extra doses of morphine. If you don't tell me the truth, then I have to believe that the consequences of what Mary knew were a motive for you to kill her.'

'I can't tell you any more.' Ann sobbed. 'But I promise you that I didn't hurt Mary. Please believe me.'

'You, therefore, give me no alternative. I am charging you with the suspected murder of Mrs Mary Jenkins.'

On Monday, Ann appeared in front of the magistrate, where Sergeant Parry asked for her to be remanded in custody, to enable further evidence to be gathered. The magistrate granted the sergeant one week and told Ann that she would be taken to Rhuthun gaol on remand, on suspicion of murder. Ann left court still pleading her innocence.

The following day, Richard returned to the workhouse mortuary to carry out an autopsy on Mary Jenkins, as requested by Parry. The sergeant continued his investigations for any evidence that might provide the motive for Ann Jones' actions.

CHAPTER 23

Richard and Elin had arranged to meet at the railway station, and he arrived a few minutes early to get the train tickets for Llandudno. Merryman greeted him in a particularly jovial mood. He had received some good news; he was to stand in for the stationmaster, who had taken ill. Richard offered his congratulations and said that it was a good opportunity for him.

Richard bought the train tickets and went to the station entrance where he met Elin.

'I hope I'm not late – the train looks ready to go,' said Elin.

A moment later the engine let out a blast of steam and Elin jumped in surprise. They looked at one another and laughed.

In the carriage, they sat together, with Elin by the window. There was another blast of steam and then the train started to move. Elin looked out of the window and then back at Richard with a happy smile. He took her hand and held it discreetly between them.

Arriving in Llandudno, they went for a walk on the seafront, and then made their way to the eisteddfod pavilion where the main proceedings were taking place. The large, octagonal pavilion had been specially designed for the occasion, and as they got nearer, Elin saw a flag flying above it with the words 'Welcome to the Temple of Genius' in Welsh. She was even more amazed when they entered the auditorium. The huge space, with room for five thousand people, was decorated with evergreens and flags with patriotic proverbs. The interior was illuminated with gaslights. Elin had never seen such a place, and she tried to take it all in as they took their seats.

Following a speech by the eisteddfod's president, the various competitions took place. Elin loved the competition for the best tenor singer. After the poetry competitions, there followed the adjudication of the essays.

'Now I'll find out whether I've been successful,' whispered Richard to Elin.

'Good luck,' she spoke softly in his ear.

The adjudicator praised Richard's essay, but he didn't win a prize.

'I'm sure that your work was the best,' said Elin, 'and I would have given you first prize.'

'Thank you, but there's always next year.'

The highlight was, without doubt, a grand concert that brought the day's proceedings to an end. The concert attracted an audience of almost 3,500 people. Afterwards, as Elin and Richard filed out of the pavilion, Richard took her hand so that they would not be parted amongst the huge crowd.

***

Richard's talk took place in the National Schoolroom. It formed part of a debate where someone first spoke in support of the proposed settlement in Patagonia, and then Richard was invited to express his concerns about the venture. Elin sat in the audience next to Goronwy Tudor from Corwen, who had helped organise the event.

Both speakers were good and made their case well, but it was clear that the audience preferred what the first speaker had to say in favour of the new settlement. The chairman asked if there were any questions.

A man at the front put his hand up.

'Dr Lloyd, I am disappointed at your apparent dismissal of the brave adventurers who plan to emigrate to create a new Wales. We should encourage the new settlers and praise them. God bless them and Michael Jones.'

Richard stood up to answer. 'I do not dismiss their bravery which, of course, should be praised. We have to remember though why this new colony, a new Wales, is being created. It is to safeguard the future of the Welsh language and our culture. That aim is to be commended, but in my opinion, it is not the answer for the language or our way of life. It has to be fought for and protected here in Wales. We need to be proud of our language, encourage the children to speak it at all times, including in school. The use of the 'Welsh Not' to punish children caught speaking Welsh in school has to be ended. The language should not just be one for the home or the chapel, it should be used in business and education, and have the same legal standing as English.'

One or two in the audience offered support for Richard's answer but others had not been persuaded.

Someone called out, 'English is the language of the Empire. How can Welsh have equal standing? Our children need the English language to get on in this modern world. You are out of date, Dr Lloyd. Do you want our sons to be second-class citizens or to be successful?'

'I want them to be successful Welshmen and to follow their aspirations and chosen careers. Of course, they need English but that should not be at the expense of their Welsh heritage. I said that English and Welsh should have equal standing. Good schooling should ensure that our sons and daughters are proficient in both.'

The chairman intervened and returned the discussion to the issue of Patagonia.

'You raised an interesting point about the native peoples of Patagonia, Dr Lloyd. Are they really threatened by our people?'

'I am sure that our settlers will respect their land and customs. But isn't it ironic that Welsh people who fear that their language and culture in Wales are threatened by newcomers could effectively be doing the same thing to the nomadic tribes of Patagonia?'

'I believe,' continued the chairman, 'that Patagonia is sparsely populated and there will be plenty of land for everyone to live peaceably.'

'I wish the settlers and the natives every good fortune. However, we need to do much more to ensure that the language thrives in Wales and that responsibility rests with the great and good of the eisteddfod world to pressure the politicians, educationalists and business leaders to give the language the status it needs. Otherwise, it will be lost to our children.'

There was applause from the audience, recognising Richard's stoic attempts to get his points across. The chairman thanked the speakers and hoped that the discussions would continue into the evening. Richard rejoined Elin and Goronwy in the audience.

'I think that you made a very good case,' said Goronwy.

'Some think that the language is old fashioned in our modern world. They see it as fit for just the hearth and the tavern. We need to change that view, but it will take time,' said Richard.

Many members of the audience wanted to talk to Richard about his views. The time slipped by, and when Richard looked at his watch, he realised that the last train was due to leave shortly.

Richard and Elin rushed to the station only to find that it had left five minutes earlier.

'We'll have to stay over in Llandudno,' said Elin, 'and catch the first train in the morning.'

'Llandudno is extremely busy because of the eisteddfod,' said Richard. 'We'll struggle to find rooms.'

'We could sit on a bench on the seafront,' said Elin.

Richard took Elin's hand and they walked towards an inn on the corner of the street. He enquired about any vacancies, but the inn was full. It was the same story at other hotels and inns until Richard finally had some news for Elin.

'They only have one room available, but apparently it is a large room,' said Richard. 'I have said that we shall take it. We'll have to say that we are married.'

The room was very large with a double bed at one end and a couple of comfy chairs on the other side. Richard told Elin that she should have the bed and he would be fine with a chair.

Downstairs, the hotel was busy but Richard got a table and ordered some food. He apologised to Elin for missing the train.

She smiled. 'We have an evening together in Llandudno, and I'm on a late shift tomorrow. There's no need to be sorry.'

They ate their meals and went up to their room.

'You must be tired after a busy day,' said Richard.

'I'm not tired and I don't want the day to end yet. Let's sit and talk some more before sleep.'

It was dark now, and in the candlelight, Elin looked even more enchanting. Their conversation ceased as they looked into one another's eyes. They kissed. She closed her eyes and put her arms around him.

'I love you, Elin.'

'I love you too,' said Elin. 'I think I'll go to bed now.'

'I'll go outside while you undress.'

'There's no need, and I'll sleep as I am.' Elin removed her long skirt and got into bed. 'Don't try to sleep in the chair. There's plenty of room for both of us in here.' She pulled the bed covers back and patted the mattress.

'Honestly, I shall be fine in the chair.'

'I'm feeling cold, Richard; I think it was the sea breezes when we were looking for a room. I need you to keep me warm.'

Richard got into bed. Elin had her back to him, and he put his arms around her. She snuggled backwards into him.

'I feel warmer already. Thank you.'

'Turn around, *cariad*, and look at me,' said Richard.

Elin turned and smiled at him. Richard touched her face and hair and kissed her. They continued to kiss and caress passionately.

Elin sensed his hands move down her body. Richard became aware of her sudden tension. The smile had gone and her face was stressed. He stopped immediately.

'I'm sorry, Richard. I can't do any more.'

'I shouldn't have rushed you. It wasn't fair to take advantage of the situation. I'm sorry.'

'I wanted this as much as you, but I just couldn't.' Elin's words faltered and a tear came to her eyes.

‘Don’t cry, *cariad*. It wasn’t the right time for us.’

‘No, Richard, that’s the problem. It’s not right and can’t ever be right.’

Richard kissed her good night. He left a candle burning and watched her from a chair on the other side of the room. Every now and then, there was a muffled sobbing from the bed. Elin was crying in her sleep. Richard, perplexed, tried to sleep but he saw every hour until four in the morning. Then, as he stirred from yet another doze, he knew what he had to do. Reassured by his plan, he fell into a deep sleep. Richard awoke with a jolt and for a moment wondered where he was. He looked across at the bed, which was neatly made and empty. Elin had left. There was a note on the table saying that she had gone for the train.

Richard left the hotel and ran towards the station. There was no sign of Elin on the platform, and Richard sank onto a bench, head in his hands.

***

Richard arrived back in Llangollen just before eleven o’clock, when Elin would be about to start work at The Hand. The landlord told him she was busy upstairs cleaning rooms, and Richard left her a message. Elin had told the landlord that she didn’t want to speak to Richard.

Richard returned later that evening. Elin had almost finished her shift, and she found Richard waiting near the back door. He said that he’d walk home with her.

As they walked towards the bridge, Elin said, ‘I’m sorry for leaving you this morning but I couldn’t face you. I was embarrassed about the night before. I didn’t know what to say.’

'I am the one who should apologise. I was in the wrong.'

'You didn't do anything wrong,' said Elin.

At the bridge, they stopped to look down at the river. Richard turned to Elin and held her hands.

'I upset you and that is unforgivable,' he said. 'It happened because I love you so much, but that is no excuse. I respect you, and what almost happened would have dishonoured you. I only want to love you in that way when we are man and wife. Will you marry me, Elin?'

Elin stared at Richard in disbelief. Richard feared her reply.

'I don't deserve your love or respect,' she said. 'I'm a servant and a maid. I could never be a doctor's wife. We have become friends through unusual situations. In normal times we wouldn't have met, never mind fallen in love.'

'But we have fallen in love, and we want to spend our lives together.'

The couple turned away and, resting their hands on the bridge wall, they pensively watched the white water below. Richard wanted desperately for Elin to say she'd marry him, but it was in hope rather than expectation.

Elin saw a small log caught amongst the rocks in the river. It twisted and turned in the continuous torrent but could not free itself of its hard restraints. *Such is life,* she thought to herself.

Eventually, Richard took Elin's hand and they walked on in silence, soon arriving at her lodgings.

'We're here already,' said Richard, 'and we've so much more to talk about.'

'I'm sorry, but I don't think we do,' replied Elin with a heavy heart. 'We both need to move on. I owe you so much for saving John's life and being the best friend that anyone could wish for. But we cannot have that friendship now, and it has to end here. I cannot marry you, Richard.'

Elin kissed Richard on the cheek, turned to open the door and went inside. Richard stood and stared at the closed door. On the other side, Elin slumped at the foot of the stairs and wept. He could not hear her sobbing.

***

The following day, Richard still couldn't understand why Elin had rejected him. He needed to see her again.

It was early evening and Richard sat in The Hand with a glass of ale, waiting for Elin to finish work. She had agreed to talk to him after her shift. He was relieved that she was at least prepared to sit and talk. Last night, things had appeared very final.

After a fairly long wait, Elin came to his table.

'I have thought about us and not much else since last night,' said Richard. 'I accept that it's too soon to talk about marriage. But we are good together and we make one another happy. We cannot lose that.'

Elin let Richard take her hand and she spoke softly.

'I never thought that you would ask me to marry you.'

'I love you and want to spend my life with you. I know that we would be happy together.'

'We come from different worlds, and while that might not seem important to you, it will be to other people in your society. They look down on people like me. I am of the lower class and should not move in their circles. It has happened to me in the past, and it will not happen again.'

'We would not have anything to do with such people. Our family has always treated everyone with respect, regardless of their background.'

'Your family is wonderful but isn't typical. It's impossible to avoid people's prejudice and I can't see any future for us. I love you, too, but it wouldn't work. You ended your engagement with Sara because you knew neither of you would be happy. I am doing the same for us now, even though it hurts so much.'

Elin's strength had held up well but was fading fast.

'This is goodbye. I shall always remember you, and be grateful for your friendship. Goodbye, Richard, and thank you.'

Elin stood up and walked away from Richard.

'Elin, please don't go,' he pleaded.

But she was gone. He remained at the table for a moment or two and then went to look for her. Elin was nowhere to be found.

Feeling nothing but completely lost in life, he went home.

CHAPTER 24

Ann Jones had spent four nights in Rhuthun gaol. She was due back in court on Monday, when she would be forced to explain everything about Mary. She knew that she had to swear on the Bible that she would tell the court the truth. The consequences could be dreadful.

Her thoughts about the trial were interrupted by the warder.

'You have a visitor, Mrs Jones.'

Ann was led to a small room with a table and two chairs. A smartly dressed gentleman stood up and introduced himself.

'I am Mr John Probert. I am a solicitor and I have been instructed to act for you in court.'

'I don't understand, sir. Who's instructed you? Because I have no money to pay for your services. There must be a mistake.'

'There has not been a mistake. Shall we say that I have been sent here by a well-wisher? Someone is very concerned about you and is happy to pay my costs.'

Ann was baffled at this unexpected turn of events, but also relieved that she had someone to support her.

'Yesterday I saw Mr Enoch Evans at the workhouse and he was very helpful in explaining your case. But now I need to hear about it from you. Can you please tell me exactly what happened on the night that Mary Jenkins died?' asked Mr Probert.

Ann repeated what she had told Sergeant Parry.

'Are you sure that the doctor told you that the dose was two spoonfuls of morphine? Perhaps you forgot and assumed that it was two?'

'I think so, sir. I cannot read and therefore I always pay very careful attention to what the doctor says.'

'Mrs Jones, you have to be certain about this. At court you may be asked about the confusion regarding the dose. It's very important for your case. Remember that you are accused of murder. Even if you have any doubts, you must say that the doctor instructed two spoonfuls.'

'I will, sir. Thank you.'

'Mr Evans said that Parry believes that Mary Jenkins had a hold over you and that is the motive for murder. Did she threaten to speak about something from the past that would hurt you?'

Ann did not reply.

'The magistrate may ask you about this and you'll have to answer his question. What are you going to say? If I am to help you, I need to know what has passed between you and Mary Jenkins. I can then prepare the best way for us to deal with it. Do you understand?'

'Yes, sir.'

Slowly, Ann started to tell Probert her story. 'It was about twenty years ago, when Mary and I both lived in Cerrig. My daughter was sixteen and had become friendly with Mary's youngest son, who was about a year older than her.'

Ann paused, struggling to continue.

'He made her with child. I'm sorry, but this is still painful for me. We expected Mary's family to do the right thing. That there would be a marriage, you know. They refused to accept that he had anything to do with it. They accused her of lying about the father.

My husband was so angry that he tried to make their son tell the truth and admit that he was the father. The son was stubborn and rude to him. My husband lost his temper and hit him several times. He was very badly hurt.'

'So what happened next?'

'The boy recovered, and Mary told me that unless we moved away, she would tell the police about the attack on her son. So we went to Llangollen, where nobody knew us.'

'And what about your daughter and the baby?' asked Probert.

'We decided to bring up the baby as if it was mine. My daughter went into service and later married and went to America. The baby is now nineteen years old.'

'Does she know about her true parents?'

'No, and that's what I'm worried about. I don't want her shamed. She worked hard at school and is now a governess to a family in a big house near Wrexham. I don't want them to find out that I am in the workhouse, or that I lied to my granddaughter about her real parents. And no one must know that her grandfather almost killed her real father.'

'I assume then, that Mary was threatening to tell people of this.'

'Yes, unless I gave her the morphine. I did give in sometimes and let her have an extra dose of the medicine, but she always wanted more.'

'Only you and Mary know what happened. Mary is dead and can do you no harm now. If the court asks about this, we don't need to tell the whole story. We will not lie, but we'll leave out anything that may damage your family's reputation. Where possible, I shall address the court.'

Even though Ann still had the ordeal of the court hearing on Monday, she was relieved that her secrets would not be revealed and that the lawyer would present her case.

***

The court was full for Ann Jones' hearing. The local press were in attendance, and the reporters anticipated a good story. The rumours of morphine poisoning had kept the gossips busy over the last few days. Sergeant Parry talked to Richard about his surprise that Mr Probert was defending Ann Jones. Lawyers, and especially Probert, usually only represented richer clients and in the higher courts.

The court was called to account and the magistrate opened proceedings. Sergeant Parry made his case regarding the death of Mary Jenkins and the excessive dose of morphine given by Ann Jones. He also told the court about the arguments and quarrels in the workhouse between the two women.

The magistrate asked Richard about Mary's medical history and the post-mortem report. Richard said that the autopsy showed that she was a frail woman with severe deterioration of her internal organs.

'Did the morphine contribute to her death?' asked the magistrate.

'Not necessarily,' replied Richard, 'as the medicine had only been administered for a short time and the deceased's organs had been damaged over a considerable period, probably through an excessive use of alcohol.'

'Are you saying that Mary Jenkins died of natural causes?'

'The autopsy is inconclusive, but it is very possible that she did die naturally, probably of heart failure.'

'Thank you, Dr Lloyd,' said the magistrate. 'Mr Probert, what do you have to say in defence of Mrs Jones?'

'Mrs Ann Jones is a fine, upright woman who has fallen on hard times,' said Probert. 'At the workhouse she wanted to help those who were sick and accepted the duties of a nurse and orderly in the infirmary. Dr Lloyd, the medical officer, has said that she is a hardworking and caring nurse.

'On the night of Mrs Jenkins' death, the patient experienced agonising pain, as the evening medication had not been effective. I suggest that Mrs Jones did what any caring nurse would do in that situation. She provided a further dose to try to help her patient's suffering and distress.'

'What concerns me,' said the magistrate, 'is that Sergeant Parry has told us that Ann Jones had fierce arguments with Mrs Jenkins, including on the day of her death. This leads me to believe that she may have had cause to harm her.'

'There were many quarrels, but these were always started by Mrs Jenkins. She frequently put my client in a difficult situation by demanding extra morphine. My client constantly refused her demands, and this was the cause of the arguments.

'Furthermore, I put it to you that if my client had wanted to cause harm to Mrs Jenkins then she would have given her the additional morphine in order to accelerate her death. Ann Jones refused to do this. She chose the more difficult course of action that resulted in arguments with the patient. Ann Jones caused no harm to her patient. She continued to care for Mrs Jenkins despite her belligerent behaviour.'

'Yes, I can see your point,' said the magistrate, 'but by Ann Jones' own admission she gave the deceased twice the prescribed dose of morphine. She is hardly blameless in this sad case, and I'm not sure that you can claim that she caused no harm to her patient.'

John Probert smiled with a look of inward satisfaction. The magistrate had agreed with the points that he had made in Ann's defence and had provided him with the perfect opening to call the doctor's involvement into question.

'I apologise, as I should have said *no serious harm to the patient*. Her actions quite clearly did not kill Mrs Jenkins. Dr Lloyd has earlier confirmed that fact. However, I have one very serious concern regarding Dr Lloyd's prescription of morphine.'

Probert paused for dramatic effect. The magistrate asked him to continue.

'Mrs Jones is very clear that Dr Lloyd told her to administer twice the correct dose. He told her to give the deceased two spoonfuls of the morphine solution, not one. As Mrs Jones cannot read or write, she is extremely careful to listen to his instructions. She has never made a mistake in administering the recommended dose, and I don't believe that she has in this case either. I believe that Dr Lloyd gave the wrong instructions to an untrained nurse who could not read. I call that gross negligence on his part. Ann Jones is innocent. If anyone here should be held responsible for the death of Mary Jenkins, then it is Dr Richard Lloyd.'

John Probert sat down to a shocked courtroom. Richard stared at the lawyer, trying to take in what had just happened. Even the magistrate was struck silent for a few moments. There was a hushed level of conversation, and the local press reporters busily wrote down the key phrases from Probert's attack on Richard. Then the magistrate addressed the court.

'The purpose of this hearing,' said the magistrate, 'is to appraise the facts of the matter and determine whether there is a case for the higher court to consider.'

He paused for a few seconds and then looked directly at Ann.

'There are no grounds to send you for trial. You are free to go.'

The magistrate then focussed on John Probert.

'We are not here to consider Dr Lloyd's actions in this matter, and in any case, there is no evidence that Mrs Jenkins died as a consequence of anyone's actions. In all probability, she died of natural causes.'

Probert looked over to where the press were seated and smiled. His client would be just as pleased with the outcome as Ann Jones.

CHAPTER 25

The following morning, Richard received a letter from solicitor Albert Mason. The letter explained that Mason was acting on behalf of Miss Sara Griffiths-Ellis of Plas Gwyn, who intended to sue him for breach of promise relating to his ending of their engagement.

'Damn lawyers,' muttered Richard to himself, throwing the letter onto the table. 'I had enough of Probert in court yesterday. What have I done to deserve all of this?'

Richard had patient visits in Llangollen that morning, and he decided to call on Sara to ask her to be reasonable and drop the threat of legal action.

'I knew that you would come to me,' she said with a smile.

'I didn't know that you hated me so much. Surely, there is no need for the solicitor's letter?'

Sara took his hands in hers.

'I don't want to sue you for breach of promise. I want you back.'

'Well, I'm glad that you don't want to sue me.'

Sara turned away from him and sat down on the sofa.

'Come and sit with me. We have a lot to talk about and I have missed you. Have you thought any more about looking to new horizons?'

'You mean moving to London?' asked Richard.

'I suppose I do. I have something here that might make you consider it again.'

Sara removed a letter from behind a cushion on the sofa.

'Please don't be cross with me, but I wrote to Mr Barton at your old hospital and asked whether there was any possibility of you regaining a position there. I have his reply here. He says that he would have you back tomorrow and would expect someone with your talent to be a senior surgeon within two years.'

Richard looked at Sara, at a loss for words. So Sara continued her justification for her actions.

'It's a lovely letter. I always liked Mr Barton when we met him socially in London, and I know he liked me too. I didn't think it would do any harm to write and find out whether there was a good chance of you returning. So now we know. Here, you read the letter.'

Richard took the letter from Sara and started to read it. She moved even closer to him on the sofa and leaned against him so that she could also look at the letter. He turned his head towards her, their faces almost touching.

'You shouldn't have written to Mr Barton. It was none of your business,' he said.

'I told you not to be cross with me,' said Sara with a pout, before another smile crept onto her lips. She kissed him on the cheek and then knelt on the sofa, facing him as closely as before.

Richard knew she was toying with him, but he couldn't resist her. All the old feelings had returned, and he gave in to his temptress. He kissed Sara on the lips and she responded with a firmer, more passionate kiss. She pushed her body against his, and he embraced her. She allowed him a few more moments, and then she broke free, kneeling back on the sofa.

'Well, Richard, are you going to write back to Mr Barton and ask for a position at the hospital? If you say yes, then we can go to my room. We can plan our marriage and our life together. If you decline, then you may leave Plas Gwyn, forever.'

In the heat of that very moment, he was sorely tempted to go to her room.

'We can't go back, Sara, we haven't changed. It wouldn't work.'

'I am prepared to forgive you for rejecting me, but you must give me what I want.'

'We have been through all this agony before.'

'What we have together is very special, and what we could have in London is within grasp. Please don't throw it all away.'

'I am sorry.'

'Then leave. I can plead no more. I was willing to forgive you, not just for breaking your promise to marry me, but also for your illicit love affair with Elin Roberts. I have had your servant girl investigated, and the information will be very useful to my lawyer when I take you to court. You were seeing her when we were still engaged. You are going to be sued for every penny you've got, and your reputation will be in tatters. Now go back to your little maid.'

'You are wrong. Elin was the sister of a patient, and that is how we met. I didn't have any relationship with her until after we parted. I did not dishonour you.'

'Save your excuses for the court; I am not interested. Now will you please leave, or shall I ring for a servant to show you the door?'

Richard fought down the anger boiling inside him and left Plas Gwyn.

***

The next evening, Richard called at Elin's lodgings. John let him in but told him that she had gone home to Rhuddlan. Richard asked for her address.

'I'm sorry, but she doesn't want to see you,' said John. 'Elin told me that she might not return to Llangollen. You need to forget her.'

'I can't do that,' said Richard.

'She's my sister, and I've seen how upset she's been over the last few days. I have to stand by Elin and do as she asks. Please leave her alone.'

Richard knew that was impossible and that he had to find her.

***

It was early on Saturday morning when Richard rode over to Rhuddlan. He went to an inn and made enquiries about Elin's whereabouts. The landlord was hesitant about parting with information to a stranger, but Richard explained that he was a doctor and had been treating Elin's brother following an accident. He had information for Elin about her brother. This seemed to allay the landlord's concerns, and he gave him directions to the Roberts' home.

Richard found the house and knocked on the door. A young girl, about four years old, opened the door just wide enough to poke her head through the gap, and looked up at Richard.

'Hello,' he said. 'I need to speak to Elin Roberts. Is she at home?'

The little girl turned around and called out. 'Mam, it's a man who wants to talk to you.'

Richard thought that he must have misheard; Elin could not possibly be the girl's mother. But a few seconds later, the door fully opened and Elin stood there, almost as shocked as Richard.

'I don't want to see you,' she said. 'I've made it quite clear that we have no future together.'

'Is she the reason why?' asked Richard.

Elin called out to her father and told him that she had to go outside. She strode into the road and Richard followed her. When they were out of earshot of the house and the neighbours, Elin stopped and looked at him.

'I didn't want you to know about Lily,' said Elin. 'You always respected me and treated me as an equal. I didn't want to lose your respect.'

'You were prepared to lose me though,' said Richard.

'But I would have lost you anyway if I'd told you about Lily.'

'I assume that the father is not around anymore.'

'He has never seen her.'

'Did you love him? I remember you saying that you loved someone once. Do you still love him?'

'I loved him with all my heart, and he told me that he loved me too. I believed him, but it was his family who broke us up. I was in service in their big house, and I saw him when he came home from school for the holidays. He was sixteen and I had turned fifteen.'

'He didn't force you to do anything that you didn't want to do?'

'Oh no, he was always very considerate and kind-hearted. We were just friends at first but then, during one holiday, things changed between us and we fell in love. When I told him that I was pregnant, he said that we would get married. He promised that he would look after the baby and me. We agreed that if it was a girl then we would call her Lily.'

'What happened?'

'His family found out that I was pregnant with his child. He was sent back to school immediately and I was dismissed from the house. I never saw him again. There wasn't even a letter. That was almost five years ago, and I have never heard from him since. But I still have Lily.'

'I am sorry, Elin.'

Richard's initial annoyance with Elin's deceit regarding her past had quickly become genuine concern for someone he deeply loved.

'I hoped that when he had completed his schooling and was independent from his family that he might come back for us.'

Elin became tearful and Richard put his arms around her and held her close.

'Even now, you are still kind to me.' And she hugged him as well.

'How were your parents when they found out?'

'Dad told me I wasn't welcome in his house and I would bring disgrace to the family and the chapel. Mam said that she would look after the baby and that I could go out to work. I told them that he would be back for both of us soon, but Dad laughed at me and told me to leave. Mam persuaded Dad to have me back. Dad was right though; I did bring disgrace to the family, and the deacons made sure that I was not welcome in the chapel anymore.'

Richard walked back with Elin to her parents' house. He didn't go in and they did not kiss goodbye.

On the ride back to Berwyn, he considered whether he still had any hope of a relationship with Elin. She had made it quite clear that it had ended, but he loved her, despite everything. If there was any way he could get her back, he would find it.

Chapter 26

While Richard was in Rhuddlan discovering Elin's past, Evan began to find out why he was losing business at the mill. His initial enquiries had been met with a wall of silence. The breakthrough came when another customer, Harry, who Evan had known for a long time, wrote to Evan saying that he would be having his corn milled elsewhere. Evan rode over to see him.

'Who's got your business now then?' asked Evan. 'You're the third customer I've lost in the past month.'

'That's awkward, I've been told not to reveal the mill or the details of the deal,' said Harry.

'Come on, Harry, we go back a long way, I need to know. I'll go out of business unless I can find out what is going on. I won't mention your name.'

'I'll tell you what I can, and I'll trust you to keep my name out of it. A man called Alun Williams visited me. He said that he was an agent for various corn mills in Cheshire and North Wales and was employed to generate new customers for the mills. He was able to offer generous discounts on normal milling costs.'

'Will you be paying one-fifth less than my price for milling?'

'I got a better price than that,' replied Harry.

'That doesn't make sense – the mill cannot be making any profit.'

'I have a twelve-month contract with John Parry's mill.'

Evan rode home, planning what to do next. He'd have to try to find out more about Williams and who was employing him.

He asked Owen to go to John Parry's mill. Owen had to pretend to be a corn grower and say that Alun Williams had offered him a better deal than he was getting with the Llangollen corn mill.

John Parry readily agreed to give him a contract. Owen asked him how he could afford to provide such a low price. The miller looked annoyed and told Owen to take the offer and ask no questions.

'I don't want you going out of business and then having to find a new mill at short notice,' said Owen.

'Don't worry about this mill,' replied Parry with a grin. 'It's the Llangollen corn mill that needs to worry. By all accounts, they'll be finished by Christmas.'

'It was a good day when Alun Williams told me about this deal,' said Owen. 'I know that he's an agent, but who does he work for?'

'If you want this deal then take it, but no more questions,' said Parry.

Owen knew that he wasn't going to get any more information from Parry, and left the mill to report back to Evan.

'You've done a good job,' said Evan. 'My suspicions were correct. Someone is paying the millers to undercut our prices and wants our mill to collapse. I can only think of one man who would pay a lot of money to make sure that happens.'

***

In the days following the Ann Jones court hearing, the local newspapers reported the case in some detail. As

Richard had feared, the news reports focussed on the mistake over the morphine dosage. In one paper, the report repeated Mr Probert's accusation that Richard was responsible for Mary Jenkins' death, and that he had been negligent in his prescription of the morphine.

A week after the court hearing, the Board of Guardians of the Corwen Union held a special meeting to discuss the adverse publicity affecting the workhouse. Richard was instructed to attend the meeting to answer some questions about the situation.

Richard arrived at the workhouse at six-thirty in the evening. The porter asked him to take a seat in the waiting hall and said that he would be called in due course. About five minutes later, he was surprised to see Ann Jones come down the stairs from the boardroom. She was wearing her plain workhouse uniform rather than her nursing clothes. He hadn't seen her for a few days and asked how she had been after the court case.

'The master has put me to work in the pigsty. He says that I'm only fit to care for pigs.'

'I'm sorry to hear that. Tell me, Ann, how did Mr Probert, the solicitor, come to defend you at the court hearing?'

'I don't know. It's still a mystery to me. He came to see me at Rhuthun gaol and said that someone wanted to help me. But I have no family or friends who could afford to pay his costs. It's very strange.'

'When he saw you in gaol, did he ask you about the dosage of Mary Jenkins' medicine?'

'Yes, he said that we must tell the court that you told me to give Mary two spoons of morphine. He said that it was important for my case.'

Richard was no longer interested in arguing with Ann about the dosage. His interest lay in John Probert and whoever had instructed him to act on Ann's behalf. It was becoming clear that John Probert had not been appointed to help Ann's defence but to cause harm to him. Probert's final outburst about him in court had been deliberate and planned.

Enoch Evans came down the stairs and told Richard that the board was ready to meet him.

Samuel Vaughan thanked Richard for attending at short notice and asked him to take a seat.

'Dr Lloyd, you will be very aware of the recent newspaper reports concerning the death of Mrs Jenkins and the mistakes made in the administration of her medication. Whilst this may not have directly led to her death, this situation has damaged the reputation of the Corwen Union. It is the board's responsibility now to ascertain the facts and take any action necessary to restore confidence in this institution.'

'I will, of course, answer any questions you may have and give you the facts as I know them,' Richard told the board.

'We all know the circumstances of the case. This evening, Mr Evans has given us a detailed account, and Mrs Ann Jones has told us of her involvement. Mrs Jones is certain that you told her that the dose was two spoonfuls of morphine solution to be taken twice a day. What is your view of Mrs Jones' statement?'

'I do not wish to say that Mrs Jones is lying, but she is most definitely mistaken. I would not make such a basic error.'

'How long have you been a qualified doctor?' asked the chairman.

'I qualified in London in 1861.'

'And what experience have you gained since then?'

'I am surprised that you are questioning my experience, Mr Chairman. Surely all of this was dealt with when I was appointed to this position almost two years ago?'

'Many members of this board were not involved in your appointment, so the question is relevant and we would appreciate an answer.'

'Very well,' said Richard. 'At the London Hospital, I specialised in surgery, and on qualification, I was offered a permanent post as a surgeon. However, the opportunity to purchase a practice in the Dee Valley was too good to turn down, so I returned to Berwyn and have been building up my practice over the last two years.'

'Is your practice successful?'

'It provides a living, but many of my patients are poor and they pay according to their means.'

'Is that why you needed this job as medical officer at the workhouse infirmary?'

'No, I applied for this job because I believe that the people in this place deserve care and good medical attention just as much as anyone else. Workhouses are notorious for paying such low salaries that only the worst doctors are employed. The sick people here also deserve skilled and qualified doctors.'

'You mean doctors like you?' Vaughan said with a hint of sarcasm.

Richard, getting increasingly annoyed and frustrated, replied crossly to his inquisitor, 'I don't do this job for the money. Do you realise that I also have to provide all the medication for the infirmary out of my salary?'

'You will appreciate, Dr Lloyd, that the board has very little resources to pay wages or fund medicines.'

'Of course I do. My point is that I do this job not for the money but because I want to help these people.'

Samuel Vaughan asked the other guardians whether they had any questions to ask Dr Lloyd. A Justice of the Peace and a local landowner sought further information about the medication.

Richard was asked to return to the waiting hall while the board considered the situation.

He had his supporters on the board. They knew that he was a good doctor and that the union would struggle to find a better medical officer. The chairman let everyone have their say, and listened to the discussion and their views. He then spoke.

'I have listened carefully, and I can see merit on both sides of the argument. There is however one factor that I didn't want to bring up unless absolutely necessary. I believe that I must now do so. I have had to reprimand Dr Lloyd for his handling of the recent scarlet fever outbreak. He failed to notify me of a contagious disease in the infirmary, and I had to question his professional care and attention to patients. You will be aware that two inmates died of the fever. I am therefore certain that, regrettably, Dr Lloyd has to be dismissed from his post. Dr Lloyd has now failed in his job on two recent occasions. Whatever the rights and wrongs of the Ann Jones case, he has damaged the reputation of the Corwen Union.'

Several members were in immediate agreement with the chairman, whilst others felt that Richard's dismissal was too drastic a step. Some were swayed by the mood of the meeting and the chairman's insistence that the board must be firm and do its duty for the union. The show of hands confirmed that the majority wanted him to be dismissed. Samuel Vaughan summoned Richard back to the meeting.

'Dr Lloyd, we have reached a decision. The board has lost confidence in you as the union's medical officer, and therefore, with regret, your employment will be ended. You will—'

Richard stood up and interrupted Vaughan's statement. 'This is disgraceful. You are making a scapegoat of me, as you want to hold someone to account and I am your only option. Well, you are not going to dismiss me as I resign my position with immediate effect.'

Before the chairman could continue his statement, Richard walked briskly out of the boardroom, down the stairs and out into the cool evening air.

'The bloody fools,' he said to himself.

The board then agreed on a brief statement for the local press saying that Dr Richard Lloyd's employment had been terminated. The inference was clear. The public would know that the board had acted, and that Richard was culpable.

Samuel Vaughan had one more task to do before he went home. After the other members had left the boardroom, he took a sheet of paper and wrote:

My dear William,

The deed is done. Richard Lloyd has been dismissed from his post as Medical Officer. The press will be notified.

I shall expect a bottle of fine brandy next time we meet.

Yours ever,

Samuel Vaughan.

Chapter 27

Richard was downcast as he read a letter from Sara's solicitor. Sara had wasted no time with her latest instructions regarding Richard's breach of promise. Evan joined Richard for breakfast.

'Bad news then?' he asked.

Richard looked up at his brother. 'Sara's offered to settle out of court for one hundred and fifty pounds. She also wants me to admit my guilt and make a full apology for my behaviour towards her. Her solicitor wants the details of this settlement to be placed as a notice in the local newspapers. My reputation, or what's left of it, will be ruined.'

'How much might you have to pay if you went to court and lost?'

'I don't know. I was hoping to persuade Sara to drop the matter but that seems very unlikely. I don't have that sort of money; I'll have to borrow it.'

'I shall have to take out a loan to keep the mill running,' said Evan. 'Two more customers have been lost and I'm no closer to proving that William is behind it. The whole business stinks of Griffiths-Ellis but he has kept his tracks well hidden. I'm barely covering my running costs, and the first repayment on the repair work is due soon.'

'Any luck with your challenge on the rent increase?'

'North Wales Land Holdings has said that it has every right to increase the rent and that the new rent is reasonable. I'll just have to find the money.'

'At least the farm is still doing well,' said Richard.

Evan said nothing and looked away. Richard did not see the deep frown on his face.

***

Richard met Moses Cadwalader, the family solicitor, the following day. He showed him the letter that he had received.

'I need your advice,' said Richard. 'One hundred and fifty pounds seems high, but I have no idea what I might have to pay if I went to court and lost the case. I'm also very concerned about making a public apology and admitting my guilt. My reputation has already suffered badly over the workhouse nonsense.'

'This is a specialist area,' Cadwalader told him. 'If you go to court then you will need an expert lawyer to represent you, and that will be costly. Whether you win the case or not, you will not avoid adverse publicity in the press. The newspapers love these cases and your personal life with Sara will be there for everyone to read. If you lose, then you could face damages in excess of one hundred and fifty pounds.'

'This is absurd,' said Richard. 'I have done nothing worse than prevent a marriage that would have been a disaster for both of us.'

'I'm sorry, but this is going to cost you one way or another. The only way to avoid it is to persuade Sara to drop the case.'

'I have already tried that and failed.'

'My advice then is to try and secure the out-of-court settlement. Even if that doesn't work, the fact that you have tried will help your case in court. An offer of one hundred pounds should be acceptable, together with an apology for ending the engagement and causing Sara distress. We can also say that you agree to make public your apology. If there are no sensational revelations, the newspapers will probably place it in the back pages.'

Reluctantly, Richard agreed to his lawyer's advice.

Sara responded quickly to Richard's comments about the settlement, and Moses Cadwalader visited Richard at Ty Celyn to address her new demands.

'I'm not going to admit to having an affair with Elin when I was engaged because it's simply not true,' said Richard.

'I understand your irritation,' said Cadwalader, 'but we must settle this quickly. They have said that if we don't have an agreement within seven days then they will apply for a court date. You cannot allow this to go to court. We need to agree on a statement that satisfies Sara's need for your admission of guilt and also limits the damage to your reputation. A court case, and the newspapers will destroy your reputation as a doctor. I see that the local papers have already reported on your dismissal from the workhouse.'

'I know that,' retorted Richard with annoyance. 'That is why I am so concerned about this so-called admission of guilt.'

'At least Sara has agreed to settle for one hundred pounds; that's good news.'

But Richard was in no mood for this attempt to raise his spirits. As far as he was concerned there was nothing good about any of this. He sat quietly as Cadwalader drafted an admission that might be acceptable to Sara. The lawyer read out his proposal.

'My client, Richard Lloyd, admits that he had a relationship with Miss Elin Roberts and is sorry that this has caused distress to his former fiancée Miss Sara Griffiths-Ellis, to whom he sincerely apologises.'

Richard was less than impressed.

'We'll have to see what Sara says about it,' said Cadwalader. 'She may insist that the word "affair" remains and that your liaison with Elin Roberts did start while you were still engaged.'

'And I shall have to see what Elin says about it before you send the letter. She has a right to know that she may be publicly humiliated. In fact, if she objects then we need to think again.'

'In my opinion, the proposed statement and admission is the very best that we shall get away with. If that is not sent, then you are facing a court case and that will be far more humiliating and damaging. Please let me know as soon as possible when the letter can be sent.'

'If you don't hear from me by four p.m. tomorrow then send it,' said Richard.

***

That evening, Richard went to Elin's lodgings. He told her about Sara's intention to sue him for breach of promise and that as part of an out-of-court settlement, she wanted him to admit that he had been unfaithful to her. Elin would be named.

Elin listened intently and only spoke when he had finished.

'You must do whatever you think is best. I trust you to do the right thing for both of us.'

'Anyone else would be concerned about the humiliation of being named in the newspapers,' said Richard.

'Having Lily has taught me that as long as I am happy with how I live my life then what others think of me doesn't matter. I'm more concerned about your position as a doctor.'

'My solicitor is trying to get Sara to accept a less damaging admission of guilt, and if he succeeds then it might not be too bad.'

'I hope that this gets sorted out for you.'

'Thank you.' Richard paused for a moment. 'I don't suppose that you would like to go for a walk sometime? Just as friends.'

'Only as friends, and providing it isn't up to Dinas Bran again. It took me a week to recover from the climb up that mountain.'

They both smiled.

***

The morning's post did nothing to lift Richard's mood. He had received a letter from Moses Cadwalader regarding the breach of promise settlement. Sara was insisting that the word 'affair' had to be included in the admission of guilt, and Cadwalader advised Richard to accept the change. Another letter was even more alarming. Dr Bevan had written to Richard, out of professional courtesy, to tell him that three of Richard's patients had asked to join Bevan's practice.

Richard passed the letter to Evan, who had joined him for breakfast.

'We haven't had much luck lately in keeping our customers either,' said Evan. 'I've lost two more this week at the mill.'

'And we know who's to blame for all of this. I am sure that Griffiths-Ellis is behind everything: ruining my reputation and forcing you to sell the mill.'

'How serious is this for your practice?' asked Evan.

'It depends on how many patients leave. The three mentioned in the letter are amongst my better-off clients who pay the full fees. I can't afford to lose many of those.'

Evan shook his head. 'It's so unfair; you've put your heart and soul into that practice.'

'The practice is my life and I shall fight to save it.'

Evan didn't tell Richard that the bank had refused to extend his loan to keep the mill running. The manager had warned him about his level of debt and the impact on the rest of the Ty Celyn business. He was already concerned about the effect on the farm, and the bank's warning was the final straw. Evan instructed Moses Cadwalader to put the mill up for sale.

That evening, Evan told his father and Richard about the crisis at the mill and that he had been forced to find a buyer.

Richard thumped the table with his fist. 'I thought that we were going to fight Griffiths-Ellis all the way. You've given up! He'll get his way and buy the mill now.'

'I have asked Cadwalader to sell the mill, not offer it to William. He could find another purchaser,' said Evan.

'I can't see anyone other than him being interested in it.'

'I had no choice. The mill has to be sold while it still has a value, and William is clearly determined to force us to sell. Another few weeks and the mill will be worthless and Ty Celyn itself would be under threat.'

***

A week passed with no interest in the sale of the mill. However, that morning, Evan received a letter from Cadwalader saying that he had received an offer from North Wales Land Holdings, the freeholder, and asked Evan to see him at his earliest convenience. The offer price was lower than Evan had wanted, but it was a starting point for possible negotiation.

Later that morning, Moses Cadwalader explained to Evan that North Wales Land Holdings wanted to marry the freehold and leasehold interests so as to increase the overall value of the property. They discussed an acceptable price for the mill. The lawyer said that he would put this to North Wales Land Holdings, and hoped he would have some good news for Evan before his wedding.

CHAPTER 28

It was raining hard as Richard set off on horseback to make his home visits. The first call was at Tyn y Rhos to see Ann Thomas.

'I'll take your wet coat, doctor,' said Jac.

'Thank you. How is Ann?'

'She has good days and bad days. Sometimes she is up and about and you would think there was nothing wrong with her. Other days she doesn't want to get out of bed.'

Richard went up the steep and narrow stairs of the farmhouse to Ann's bedside. He examined Ann and told her that she was doing well and to keep up the good work.

'What do you think?' asked Jac when Richard returned downstairs.

'She is no worse than last time, and that's good news. You know that she'll not get better, Jac.'

There were tears in Jac's eyes. 'Sometimes it's all too much – and now I have had this as well.'

He picked up a piece of paper and passed it to Richard. It was a formal notice. Richard felt sick as he read it.

I, Benjamin James Gordon of 2 Cannon Gate, London, the Valuer acting in the matter of the Enclosure of the Waste Lands of the Hills, Sheepwalks or Commons situate in Berwyn, hereby give you Notice that the land now in your possession is about to be allotted and enclosed. You are at liberty within two calendar months from the service of this notice to take down and remove all buildings, fences and other erections now standing on the land. I further give you Notice that unless peaceable possession of the said premises be given to me on or before the expiration of two calendar months from the service of this Notice, then I shall apply to Her Majesty's Justices of the Peace to issue their Warrant directing the Constable of the District to enter and take possession of the said premises and to eject any person therefrom.

Dated this first day of September 1864

B.J. GORDON

Valuer

When Richard finished reading the notice, he looked up at Jac but didn't know what to say. It was Jac who spoke first.

'I'm not the only farmer to receive a notice. I know of several neighbours, and others further afield, who've had similar letters. We've had officials up here, busy measuring with their chains, poles and pegs. They have already started surveying and dividing the mountain.'

'It's wrong in so many ways,' said Richard. 'You and Ann built this house with your own hands over many years. Your sons helped you reclaim the mountain land through sweat and hard labour to make this little farm, and now they give you just two months to remove all of your home and buildings?'

'Who can rebuild all this on another plot of land in two months? And that assumes that other plots are available, which they're not. No, they are stealing our homes and our farms. They are stealing our mountain.'

'Have they decided who the land will be allotted to, yet?'

'Well, I have a favour to ask of you. It is rumoured that the Griffiths-Ellis estate will get most of the mountain as they have significant land holdings already in the area. They know the authorities that will be allotting the land and have the money to enclose it. Our only hope is to ask Griffiths-Ellis to rent our farm back to us. It's a lot to ask of you, but I know that you have connections with the family, and I hoped that you might be able to speak with someone.'

Richard couldn't keep the shock and dismay from showing on his face.

'I'm not on the best of terms with the family just now,' he said. 'I'm not sure that my intervention would help.'

Jac's hopes were dashed. 'You were our only chance. We don't know anyone else who could speak with them on our behalf.'

'If you want me to speak to Griffiths-Ellis then I shall, but please do not expect too much. I shall do my best for you.'

'We know that we have little chance of succeeding, but a little hope is better than no hope. Thank you, doctor.'

Richard rode away from Tyn y Rhos completely despondent.

***

By mid-afternoon, Richard had finished his home visits in Llangollen, and before heading home, he decided to call in at Plas Gwyn and enquire about Jac's tenancy request. As Richard was ushered in, he found William standing in front of the fireplace and Sara sitting on a sofa. There were no smiles.

'What can we do for you?' asked William.

'I have come on behalf of a patient who is very ill.'

Richard outlined the plight of Ann and Jac Thomas.

'So, on behalf of my patients, I have come to ask whether you would grant them a tenancy of the farm and part of what used to be the common land. You would be gaining a rent.'

'How do they know that our estate has been allotted it?'

'The rumours are that you will get the land.'

'Why should I grant them a tenancy? These small farms are not profitable and the rental income is poor. Small farms have no role in the future of the Plas Gwyn estate. Why are you meddling in the matter anyway?'

'As I said, I am concerned for the health of my patients. I do worry for the family and the real threat of poverty and being homeless. The little farm may not be a good business proposition but it provides a good home and is self-sufficient. This is the family's way of life.'

'Just yesterday, I instructed my estate manager to draw up a new tenancy agreement,' said William.

Richard was puzzled, but with a little renewed hope, he allowed a smile.

William noticed his expression and laughed. 'Don't get your hopes up, Lloyd. The new tenancy is for an enlarged farm of over one hundred acres that will incorporate Tyn y Rhos. I already have an existing farmer who will take on the tenancy and pay a decent rent. It's good business.'

'And what about Jac Thomas and his sick wife?'

'Look, it's the Enclosure Acts taking away their farm and not me. They are not my responsibility, but if they are homeless and ill then there is always the workhouse. Unfortunately, though, I understand that the infirmary is without a doctor at the present time.'

William laughed again, and Sara smiled and walked to his side. Richard watched as she took his hand.

For a few moments, Richard was silent. The cruel quips about the workhouse and the infirmary angered him. Sara and William's intimacy towards one another confused him. He then spoke loudly and forcefully.

'It's downright theft and you know it. The land and the livelihoods of poor, voiceless people are being stolen from them. That isn't good business; it's based on greed and corrupt laws.'

'What do you know about business? I've heard that you've had some trouble with the corn mill. Losing customers to other mills is what I call bad business.'

Richard stepped forward. William dropped Sara's hand and moved towards him. The two men glared at one another.

'That's enough,' said Sara, coming between them. 'Richard, please leave now.'

Richard left and rode down the long drive at a gallop.

***

Richard had to inform Jac and Ann Thomas about yesterday's failure to get them a tenancy. While he was riding up the lane that led to Tyn y Rhos, he saw a large cart coming towards him. As it got nearer, Richard could see that it was heavily laden with furniture and equipment. There was a young man driving the wagon and an older woman sitting alongside. A boy and a girl walked next to the cart. Richard pulled his horse over to allow the wagon to pass. The driver stopped to thank him.

'You have a full cart there,' said Richard.

'It's the contents of Pen y Bryn. We were evicted this morning. We had an hour to load up what we could from the house and buildings. They said that they had given us two months' notice to leave the farm and that was up today. As soon as the house was emptied of everything we could take, they knocked every window out and part of the roof as well. It took the men ten minutes to do that. Ten minutes to ruin a house that Dad had built and kept for us all those years. At least Dad didn't see them do it; he died last year. They want to make sure that we don't return. A winter's wind, rain and snow will soon turn our old home into a ruin.'

'I am very sorry,' said Richard. 'What will you do?'

'My aunt has said that we can stay with her until we find somewhere else. I'm going back for the sheep later in the week and selling them at market. I'll have to get labouring work on a farm, but it's not like having your own place, is it?'

'Well, good luck to you, and I hope you find work soon. I'm Dr Lloyd, by the way, and on my way to Tyn y Rhos to see Ann Thomas.'

'Ann has been very ill, but I thought she looked a bit better this morning,' said the woman.

Richard didn't comment but smiled and went on his way. Ann was not going to get better.

At Tyn y Rhos, Richard explained to Jac what William had told him. Jac thanked him for trying.

'We had better plan for the worst now. We don't want an early morning eviction like Pen y Bryn. We'll leave before the last day.'

Richard rode away from Tyn y Rhos feeling helpless and hopeless for Ann and Jac. He had seen their future that morning.

CHAPTER 29

Elizabeth and Evan's wedding day soon arrived – Saturday 1st October. There was great excitement at Berwyn Hall as young bridesmaids couldn't wait to get dressed, the horses and carriages were being prepared and the final touches were made to the great hall where the wedding breakfast would be held. Elizabeth felt a little apprehensive and was also sorry that her brother Grant's army leave had been withdrawn and he was unable to attend. Lady Davenport was still organising everything and everyone.

A couple of hours later, Richard and Evan were at Berwyn Church talking to the ushers and a couple of early guests. Moses Cadwalader also arrived early and had some news for Evan.

'North Wales Land Holdings have accepted our price. I had a letter from them, late yesterday afternoon. I have sent the contract to their lawyers and I'm pleased to say that the deal is done. The mill is not your problem anymore.'

Evan grabbed his hand and shook it vigorously.

'What a relief,' he said. 'That's the best possible news. You've made my day.'

'Don't tell Elizabeth that,' replied Cadwalader with a grin. 'I think that she'll be hoping she'll be the one to make your day.'

'So you're happy with the price then?' asked Richard.

'It's a bit less than we paid, but it's enough to pay off the loans and it will please the bank. We've lost money but we live to fight another day.'

The little church was filling up fast, and Evan and Richard sat in the front pew to wait for Elizabeth and Sir Clayton.

A few minutes later the congregation fell quiet as the bride and her father arrived.

'No going back now,' whispered Richard.

'I don't want to. I've always known that Elizabeth was the girl for me. It's just a pity about the mother-in-law.'

Berwyn Hall looked splendid for the wedding breakfast. The speeches went down well, especially Richard's as best man. Richard reminded his older brother of some of the pranks he had played as a boy, including scrumping apples from the orchard at Berwyn Hall. With a wry smile, Sir Clayton said that he wouldn't have given his consent for the marriage if he'd known Elizabeth was marrying a thief. The guests laughed. Lady Davenport did not.

Neither Evan nor Richard had spoken to William and Sara so far that day. Elizabeth went over to see them after the wedding breakfast. While Elizabeth and Sara talked about the wedding, William made a beeline for Richard and Evan.

'Gentlemen, may I have a word? I have some news that will interest you,' said William. 'I am now the owner of the Llangollen mill. Or I will be in a few days' time when the transfer takes place.'

'But my solicitor told me that North Wales Land Holdings was buying the mill,' said Evan.

'Yes, and now the land and all the buildings will be transferred to me. The old mill will be back in the Griffiths-Ellis family again.'

'But why would North Wales Land Holdings buy the mill and then sell it to you?' asked Evan.

William smiled. 'Friends in high places, Lloyd; let's just say that.'

'So you really were behind the stealing of my customers and the rent rise then,' said Evan. 'I guessed as much.'

'I don't know what you're talking about.' William grinned.

Evan lunged at William, but Richard took hold of his arm and held him back. 'Not today, Evan; he's not worth spoiling your day. But one day you'll have your revenge.'

'Thank you for carrying out the repairs to the mill,' said William.

Evan desperately wanted to remove the satisfied smirk from William's face, but heeded his brother's advice and walked away.

Richard stayed. 'We will get you back for this,' he told William. 'You'll not win in the long term.'

'I have already won. You just don't see it yet.' William moved closer to Richard and said quietly, 'Samuel Vaughan is a director of North Wales Land Holdings. As you are well aware, he is also the chairman of the Corwen Union workhouse.'

William laughed as Richard took in what he had just said. Ignoring his own advice to his brother, Richard stepped forward with the intention of landing his fist firmly on William's jaw.

Sara intervened just in time to prevent an embarrassing scene.

'Now, boys, no fighting today, please. I hope you weren't fighting over me. You must behave.'

Richard unclenched his fist and stood back.

'Have you seen today's newspaper, Richard?' Sara asked. 'I thought the statement about your affair with the chambermaid and the end of our engagement was very prominently placed. They often place these notices at the back of the paper, but my lawyer specifically requested that it should be at the top of the second page. I am sure that everyone will see it. I just hope that it will not cause you too much harm.' She smiled at him.

'I haven't seen it yet,' he said curtly. He knew that it would cause him great harm. His practice was already on the brink of ruin, and this could very well be the final straw.

Sara took William's arm and led him away to talk to Sir Clayton. Richard watched them and wondered what it all meant. They had held hands at Plas Gwyn, and now there was Sara's strange comment about them fighting over her. Was there really something going on between them?

***

After the wedding and back at Ty Celyn, Richard sat in his surgery and poured another brandy. It was all becoming obvious that William had a vendetta against him and had involved Sara and Vaughan in his carefully laid plans. The question that remained was how would it all end, and what would be left of his practice?

As Richard was considering his predicament, Sian entered the room and said that Jed James was at the door and wanted to speak to him. This was all he needed.

Jed told Richard that Will had fallen into the old quarry and was badly injured.

As Richard and Jed rode up the hill towards the James farm, Jed explained what had happened. A sheep had got through the fence and had been in danger of falling from a narrow ledge into the quarry below. Will had tried to get the sheep back, but it had struggled and Will lost his footing and fell to the quarry floor.

Half an hour later, they reached the old quarry. Richard assessed Will's injuries and looked up at the ledge from where he had fallen.

'You're lucky that you're still alive after falling from that height,' said Richard. 'You've broken your arm but thankfully the head wounds aren't serious.'

'Is he going to be alright then?' asked Jed.

'He'll be fine but not able to do much for a few weeks.'

'Let's get him back to the house.'

Richard cleaned and bandaged the head wounds and set Will's arm. He had suffered from concussion but seemed to be over the worst.

'Will you have a brandy, doctor?' asked Jed. 'As it's your brother's wedding day.'

'Well, just a small one then,' said Richard.

Jed poured a very large brandy for him. Richard took a good sip and laughed.

'Duw, that's just what I needed.' And he laughed again.

'You've had a few already today, then,' said Mrs James. 'Was it a lovely wedding?'

'It was lovely until William Griffiths-Ellis turned up,' said Richard. 'That man wants to ruin me. He has already cost us hundreds of pounds. He won't rest until he has driven me out of this valley, but I'm not going without a fight.'

Richard realised that he had already said too much and drank too much. He apologised for his ramblings, thanked his hosts and said he should go.

Jed saw him to his horse and made sure that he was facing the right way. Somehow, the horse got back to Ty Celyn.

CHAPTER 30

Serving breakfast at The Hand Inn meant an early start, and it was still dark when Elin left her lodgings for work. A coal cart stood in the road, and the carter humped a full sack over his shoulder to take into a back yard. Elin was walking behind the cart when the carthorse jolted, startling her. She stepped into the middle of the road to get out of the way. She didn't see the fast gig approaching until it struck her. Elin was thrown sideways and fell under the vehicle.

The gig driver stopped and found Elin lying face down in the road. The coal carrier had heard the accident and hurried back. Together they moved her to the side of the road. Elin was motionless, blood running from a gash on her head. The driver grabbed a small blanket from his gig and wrapped it tightly around her head. A boy who had seen the accident stared at the scene in shock, and then realised that the driver was talking to him.

'Boy, do you know the doctor's house in Abbey Road? Run over there now. Quickly, there's no time to lose.' The boy nodded and ran off to get Dr Bevan.

A few more people had gathered at the side of the road.

'Does anyone know who she is?' asked the gig driver.

'I recognise her from The Hand Inn,' said one of the men, 'I think she works there but I don't know her name.'

'We've sent for a doctor,' said the driver to Elin. 'You're going to be alright.'

There was no reaction from her. He nevertheless continued to talk to Elin until Dr Bevan arrived.

The doctor felt for a pulse and quickly checked her over.

'She's alive but has had a significant blow to the head,' he told the gig driver.

Dr Bevan took Elin's limp body back to his house while the driver went to The Hand to make enquiries about the girl. The landlord confirmed that the girl's description matched that of Elin Roberts and that she had not turned up for work. He said that she lived with her brother, who worked on the new railway line, and gave him her address.

At his surgery in Abbey Road, Dr Bevan examined the head wound. It was worse than he had expected. It looked as if the gig wheel had hit her head as she fell, and caused a deep cut. However, there was a second wound where her head had hit the ground, and the impact had left her unconscious. Elin lay in a bed in the doctor's surgery while he cleaned the wounds and applied bandages. He sat with her for over an hour, but Elin did not move or open her eyes.

The driver of the gig had gone to the railway office to inform Elin Robert's brother. John was at Berwyn Tunnel, but when the message reached him, he downed tools and headed to Llangollen. When he arrived at the doctor's house, the maid showed him to the surgery where Dr Bevan was still sitting next to Elin's bed. The doctor told John what had happened and the extent of her injuries. He said that it was too early to make any accurate prognosis.

John took the doctor's place at Elin's bedside and took her hand, pleading with her to wake up and get better. He sat with his sister all day and night.

In the morning, Dr Bevan examined her injuries.

'How is she, doctor?' John asked. 'When do you think she'll wake up?'

'Head injuries are unpredictable. Elin could come round at any time and be perfectly well or it could be serious. I'm afraid it is just a question of waiting.'

'I'll stay with Elin again today.'

'If you wish, but there is no need as I shall be here for much of the day, and if I do go out, then a maid will sit with her. You could come back to see how she is after work.'

John thought for a moment and decided to go to work. They needed the money. Elin clearly would not be working for some time, and there would be doctor's bills to pay.

All day in Berwyn Tunnel, John worried about Elin. He remembered that she had planned to meet Richard for a walk on Saturday. He needed to know about Elin's accident.

Richard wasn't home when John called at Ty Celyn, but he told Sian what had happened. Sian was shocked to hear the awful news, and tearful when telling John she would pray for poor Elin.

When Richard returned home, Sian asked him to sit down as she had bad news. Richard listened in horror, then went straight to the stables and asked Owen to saddle and bridle the horse again as quickly as possible. He rode at speed to Dr Bevan's house.

'I am very sorry, Richard, but she has not regained consciousness,' Bevan told him. 'Elin has suffered significant head injuries.'

'Can I see her?'

'Of course. Her brother, John, is sitting with her.'

Richard entered the room and exchanged worried smiles with John. He went over to see Elin. Despite her injuries and bandaged head, she still looked beautiful and strangely peaceful.

'There has been no change since the accident,' said John.

'Do you want to have a rest,' said Richard, 'and I'll sit with Elin?'

John left and Dr Bevan told Richard what he knew about the accident and her injuries.

'She has been unconscious now for thirty-six hours, and she'll be getting weaker.'

'I'll talk to her and see if a different voice brings any reaction,' Richard said.

'I'll leave you for now then. If you need anything, let me know.'

Richard talked gently to Elin about all the times that they had shared. At one point he thought that her eyelid fluttered slightly, but if it had, there was no further movement. Richard sighed deeply.

Dr Bevan returned to the room. 'Any change?'

'No, not yet.'

'I am sorry to add to your worries, but I do need to tell you about two more of your patients who have asked to join my practice,' said Dr Bevan. 'I couldn't help seeing the notice in the newspaper at the weekend about the ending of your engagement. Some of our female patients do not care for younger single doctors. I fear that your disclosure will cause you further damage. What will you do?'

'I shall have to weather the storm and hope that I still have a viable practice left at the end.'

'Would you consider selling the practice?'

'This is my life and home. I don't want to leave Berwyn.'

'What's the matter?' said a weak voice. 'Why are you leaving?'

Richard turned away from Bevan and looked at Elin. He smiled broadly, his eyes lighting up.

'Elin, *cariad*, you are back with us.'

'Why must you leave?' Elin asked again.

'I'm not going anywhere.' Richard sat at her side, kissed her cheek and held her hand.

Elin smiled at him.

Bevan spoke over his shoulder. 'I'm Dr Bevan, and I'm afraid you've had an accident, but we're looking after you.'

'Two doctors are looking after me. I am blessed,' she said slowly and then fell asleep again.

'Let her sleep,' Bevan told Richard. 'Hopefully, this is the breakthrough that we have been praying for.'

About an hour later, Elin again regained consciousness. Richard was alone with her.

'I love you, Elin, and when you are well, I want us to be together,' he told her.

'It would all end in tears again.'

'Not this time, as we both know the truth. We have no secrets. We should be married, and if you would let me, I'd like to be a father to your dear little Lily.'

'I should love you to be Lily's father.' Elin paused, fighting the strong urge for sleep. 'I'm sorry, but I can't marry you. Start again, Richard.'

Elin could not resist the call for sleep any longer.

When John returned to the doctor's house, Dr Bevan greeted him with the news that Elin had woken up and that she'd been talking. John's mood was immediately lifted and he went through to see Richard, who was sitting next to Elin. He sat on the other side of the bed.

A few minutes later, Elin may have heard John speaking to Richard, as she opened her eyes and saw her brother. She reached her arm out to him, and he held her hand and kissed it.

'Thank you for sitting with me, John.'

'Where else would I be but with my dear sister? Are you hungry?'

'No, I just want to sleep.' She looked across to Richard and smiled.

Elin fell asleep. She did not wake again.

Minutes later, Elin left the two men that she loved most in the world. And those two men, sitting either side of her, loved her more than any other woman.

CHAPTER 31

Richard had a fitful sleep after Elin's death. He had drunk too much brandy and eventually fallen asleep in a chair in his surgery. He dreamt that it was William who had driven the gig that caused Elin's accident, and that William had put her body in a coffin he then delivered personally to Richard at Ty Celyn. But, when Richard opened the coffin, it was Sara lying there, and she sat up in the box, laughing at him. And then William started to laugh.

Richard woke up with a start and looked at his watch; it was five o'clock.

He rode into Llangollen an hour later, stabled the horse, and started the long walk up to Castell Dinas Bran. He needed to be close to Elin. When he reached the castle ruins, he sat down in the same spot where they had kissed and declared their love for one another. It was still early and quiet, except for the occasional cawing crow flying overhead.

Richard heard a girl's gentle voice behind him. He turned around expecting to see Elin. There was nobody there. It must have been the sound of the wind blowing through the stone ruins, playing tricks on him. He descended from the eerie place, pausing after a few minutes to look back. A shiver ran down his back as if someone was looking down on him from the castle.

As Richard approached the town, he was glad to see people again. He was also pleased that he knew what he had to do for Elin and Lily. He couldn't be a father to Lily now, but he could still help her.

He went into the bank and explained that he wanted a sum of money to be sent to Mr and Mrs Roberts in Rhuddlan for their granddaughter Lily. This was to happen every six months until she was sixteen years old.

'I don't wish to be awkward, Dr Lloyd, but can you afford to do that?' asked the manager, looking at Richard's account.

'My conscience tells me that I must afford it,' replied Richard, 'but obviously you are saying that the figures don't look good.'

'Your reserve has been cleared out by the recent payment to Miss Griffiths-Ellis. A new loan has been taken out to fund the rest of that payment. You've made no payments into your account for three weeks. The monthly repayment on your practice loan is due next Friday and there are insufficient funds to meet it. I see that you no longer receive any income from the Corwen Union. I'm afraid it does not look good at all.'

'I've been very busy lately and I apologise that I have not paid in any income. I'll put that right in the next couple of days,' said Richard.

'That's good, but you should also review your income and expenditure very carefully over the coming months. You have been living on the edge financially for some time and it wouldn't take much to tip you into a serious crisis. I hope you don't mind me saying that I have noticed some unfortunate newspaper articles in recent days. If you lose clients as a result, then your income and the value of your practice could be badly affected. Please treat all this as well-intentioned advice.'

Richard said that he would address the matter of financial help for Lily Roberts when he had sorted out his affairs, and he assured the manager that it was only a temporary problem. He tried to maintain an air of confidence, but the manager remained unconvinced.

Sorrow descended once more as he realised that his financial problems meant he was unable to help little Lily and feel just that bit closer to Elin. The weight of his grief felt greater than when he had awakened earlier that morning to the darkest of days.

Arriving back at Ty Celyn he checked the cash box in his surgery. As he had feared, there was not enough to make next week's loan repayments. He would face a charge for defaulting on his loans. The bank could even withdraw his loan arrangement, thereby threatening his practice. He considered his options, which were either impractical or unpalatable, or both. Evan was on honeymoon with Elizabeth and did not return until next Saturday. In any case he did not want to borrow from his brother, who had his own financial worries after the losses incurred with the corn mill.

Reluctantly he turned to his father. He knew that he would help him, but he didn't want to admit that his circumstances had come to this. Edward agreed immediately to lend Richard the requested sum. It was done kindly and there was no mention of interest or date for repayment. Nevertheless, Richard was apologetic for the situation.

That same day, Richard received a letter from his old friend and colleague, James Morton. He read with interest that James had left the London Hospital, where they had both trained, and was now working at the Liverpool Royal Infirmary. James had been in Liverpool for about a month and wondered whether they could meet and talk over old times and new. He said that he was free next Saturday and Sunday.

Richard immediately penned him a reply inviting him to stay at Ty Celyn. He would meet him off the train at Llangollen.

***

Elin's funeral took place at the chapel in Rhuddlan, where she had been baptised barely twenty years earlier. Her parents and the rest of her family, including John, sat in the front pew. Little Lily sat next to her Nain. Richard had intended to be near the back of the chapel but John insisted that he sit in the pew behind the family, saying that Elin would want him near her. Those words, the sight of Lily and then Elin's coffin almost broke Richard, but he focussed even harder on the job in hand. This was not about him; it was for Elin and all those who had loved her.

After the service, the minister and the mourners followed the coffin bearers to the graveyard and the mound of recently dug earth. They watched the coffin as it was lowered into the ground. Many couldn't hold back the tears, but Richard again fought his sadness and grief.

Richard went back to the Roberts' family home after the funeral, and after a respectful period, he took his leave and walked towards the stables where he had left his horse. He passed the graveyard, which was now empty of mourners. Something made him stop and turn around, and he walked up the path between the gravestones.

Richard stood in front of Elin's grave. The dark earth had already been refilled. Richard dropped to his knees and they sank into the soft soil. He wept uncontrollably; his chest heaved and his body ached.

He didn't know how long he wept for Elin. Eventually, he stood up and told her that he loved her.

Richard rode back to Berwyn at a slow trot. He had nothing to rush back for, and he was alone with his thoughts. Perhaps because he had just spoken to Elin for the last time at her graveside, he recalled their last words before she died. He had asked her to marry him and she had again refused. She had told him to start again.

Elin is probably right, thought Richard. *It may be that I have no other options anyway. But where do I start?*

CHAPTER 32

Richard peered through the steam and smoke for James Morton as his old friend finally emerged from the far end of the train. James was tall and well-built with a thick beard and similar hair. Both always looked as if they needed a good trim. He always dressed smartly in tweed suits. Richard and James had last seen one another just before Richard left London, although they had kept in touch through the occasional letter. They embraced and Richard took James' case from him as they walked towards the gig.

'It is good to see you, James. I was pleased to get your letter.'

'It's really good to see you too. How is the bonny Sara, and have you set a date yet?' asked James in his soft Scottish accent.

'Ah, well that's a long story, and I will tell you what's happened, but the fact is we are no longer engaged.'

James raised his eyebrows at this news.

***

After the evening meal, Richard took James to the parlour and poured them both a brandy.

'Good health, Richard,' said James, holding up his glass.

'And to you too.'

'So, what has happened between you and Sara?' asked James.

'We realised that we wanted very different things. Well, I did anyway. Sara refused to accept that our marriage would have never worked.'

Richard explained their differing expectations of married life. James expressed his surprise at their problems, as he'd thought they always appeared happy and well-matched.

Richard smiled. 'That was because we were in London then.'

'How is the practice doing?' asked James.

Richard grimaced and told James about the recent problems. 'It was never a wealthy practice, and to be honest it's struggling to break even. It's a bit difficult at the moment. Anyway, tell me about Liverpool.'

'I wanted a change after all those years in London. I wasn't ready to return to Scotland and I had heard some good things about the Liverpool Royal Infirmary. It is a progressive hospital and I'm pleased that I made the move. My mother, who still lives in Paisley, hasn't been well, and it's a wee bit quicker to get home to her now.'

'I'm glad that it's working out well for you.'

'Do you still see Sara?' asked James.

'She lives on the other side of Llangollen and our paths cross occasionally. She was at my brother's wedding two weeks ago. I have to tell you though that our separation has turned nasty. Sara threatened to sue me for a breach of promise and I was compelled to settle the case out of court. I was forced to make an admission of guilt that has damaged my reputation and my practice.'

Richard told James all about Elin and then her tragic accident.

'She died, but I was at her side. The funeral was yesterday.'

'Richard, I'm so sorry. My God, that is awful. You've had a bad time these last few months. It sounds to me that you need a fresh start, too. Sell up here and start again somewhere new.'

'You're probably right, but even if I sell up in Berwyn, the money won't be enough to buy another practice.'

'Maybe not straight away, but over time you could save enough to invest in another practice. Take a salaried job for now. Come and work with me in Liverpool. The Infirmary has a vacancy for a surgeon, and with your London Hospital experience, there wouldn't be a better candidate. Think about it. Is there any brandy left in that bottle?'

The conversation continued into the small hours of Sunday morning, and Richard's mood did lift and even some laughter ensued, with reminiscences of medical school and mutual friends. Bed beckoned when the brandy bottle was empty.

***

James had to be back at work on Monday morning, and he caught the last train back to Liverpool on Sunday. At Llangollen Station, Richard thanked James for his visit and his advice.

'I've been thinking about something you said last night about William Griffiths and not wanting him to win,' said James. 'When you get the Liverpool job, you will leave here of your own volition with head held high and a successful career ahead of you – in other words, a winner. Stay here and there is a strong chance that Griffiths will see you lose everything, and witness your despair. Don't let that happen. If you act now, I believe that you can extricate yourself from this awful financial and emotional crisis. Delay and it may not be possible. Here is the name and address you need, to apply for the job.' He checked his watch. 'The train is about to leave, and I'd better go. Good luck, Richard. I hope to see you in Liverpool soon. It will be a new start.'

Richard took the piece of paper and thanked him. He watched the back of the train disappear down the track. He looked again at the piece of paper and wondered.

***

Since returning from honeymoon, Evan and Elizabeth had moved into Ty Mawr, a spacious house with good stabling and large gardens. It had previously been occupied by the late agent for the Berwyn Hall estate, but Sir Clayton had decided to keep it for his daughter and future son-in-law. He had enjoyed planning its modernisation and improvement over the last nine months.

Richard had not seen his brother since the wedding and had important matters to discuss with him. At Ty Mawr he looked around Evan's new home and asked how they were settling in.

'Very well, and Elizabeth is very happy,' said Evan. 'She is over at the hall with her mother, just now, sorting out things for the house.'

'Good, I have some matters to talk through with you. I'd like your opinion on them. Last Saturday, James Morton came to see me. He has recently moved to Liverpool as a surgeon at the Royal Infirmary. After I told him of my recent problems, he urged me to apply for a job there. I sent off my letter of application this afternoon.'

'I'm surprised,' said Evan. 'Not because I don't agree with your decision but because of your change of mind. The last time we spoke you were determined not to leave Berwyn and to fight it out with William.'

'I know, and there is still part of me that wants to do just that. I have only applied for the job. I have not yet decided to take it. Indeed, I may not be offered it.'

'You'll be offered it. Look, I think this opportunity must be heaven-sent. Sell your practice while it is still worth something and get away from the Griffiths-Ellis family before they send you mad. It will be a new beginning.'

'You are the third person to say that, and I think you're right.' Richard idly picked up an ornament that Elizabeth had brought back from the honeymoon, looked at it, then set it back on the mantelpiece. 'Talking about William and Sara, I don't want them to know about this yet, and it might be best not to mention anything to Elizabeth in case she sees Sara. If I get the job, then she can be told.'

Evan agreed and asked whether Richard had spoken to their father about his application.

'I haven't told him yet. I'll tell him if they ask to see me. But he'll be fine about it. He knows all about my problems because I had to ask him for some money. The bank was pressing.'

'He'll miss you, but he'll be pleased, too. I think he always had a small regret that you hadn't continued with surgery after such a promising start. Good luck, and go and get your job in Liverpool.'

***

The Royal Infirmary confirmed its interest in Richard's potential employment, and by Friday he was in Liverpool meeting the hospital's head of surgery, Basil Fortescue. Richard was impressed with the hospital's facilities and Mr Fortescue's plans and ambitions for the Royal Infirmary. Mr Fortescue asked Richard about his reasons for quitting surgery two years ago and moving into country practice. He appeared unimpressed with Richard's response.

However, Richard redeemed the situation with his positive motives for wanting to return to surgery and especially to such a progressive hospital. He talked about his experience at the London Hospital and how his former mentor, Mr Barton, had recently said he would still be welcomed back to the hospital. Fortescue's eyes lit up at the mention of Barton's name. He knew Barton well as they had both worked together at St Thomas' Hospital.

The interview concluded with Fortescue telling Richard that he would be informed of his decision early next week and thanking him for attending.

It was about half past three when Richard left the hospital and walked back to Lime Street Station. He reflected on the meeting with Fortescue but could not tell whether it had been successful. He felt strangely grateful to Sara for writing to Mr Barton and getting that unexpected but useful testimonial. As he neared the station, Richard knew that he really wanted the job.

***

The next day, Richard rode into Llangollen to see Dr Bevan.

'I am considering a new challenge and direction,' Richard told him, 'and I have decided to sell the practice.'

'You're not leaving medicine, are you?' asked Dr Bevan.

'No, but I intend to leave country practice. I may have an opportunity to return to hospital work. I have not yet advertised the practice for sale, but I thought that I would speak to you first, to see if you are still interested in expanding your business.'

Richard gave Bevan a summary of the practice in terms of the number of patients and patient income and promised him full access to his accounts if he wished to proceed. Richard also told him the price that he put on the practice. Bevan said that he could be interested.

'I shall be straight with you,' said Richard. 'Some of my patients are poor and I have always tried to provide a service for everyone, even if they cannot afford to pay the fee. I would wish to sell to someone who would continue this approach. I appreciate that such an arrangement cannot be enforced, but I would put value on such an undertaking, even if only as a gentleman's agreement.'

'Well, that is an easy part of the negotiations,' said Dr Bevan. 'I can assure you that I operate on the same principle for my poorer patients.'

Richard was relieved. Perhaps he needed to rethink his belief that he was so indispensable to his patients.

***

On Tuesday morning, there were two letters addressed to Richard on the breakfast table. When Richard came into the room, he saw the letters immediately and apprehensively opened the first one. It was from the Liverpool Royal Infirmary, and he read the first few words:

'I am pleased to inform you...'

His smile grew wider as he looked up at his father. Richard's feelings were more akin to relief than joy, but they were good feelings anyway.

'I knew you would get the job,' said Edward. 'When do they want you to start?'

'Monday seventh November.'

'Just a couple of weeks then. Congratulations, you've done well, boy, as always.'

Richard thanked his father and opened the second letter. It was from Dr Bevan. Bevan said that he had now considered the matter carefully and had spoken to his bank regarding finance. He invited Richard to join him to discuss terms for the purchase of the practice.

Before setting out on the morning's visits to his patients, Richard wrote a letter to the hospital accepting the position and a note to Bevan to say that he would call the following evening to discuss the sale. He also wrote to James Morton telling him that he had been successful and thanking him for his support.

***

Richard returned home from his meeting with Dr Bevan. The deed was done. The terms for the sale of the practice had been agreed, and both men felt that the price was fair. Nevertheless, Richard was in a gloomy mood, and his father tried to lift him out of it.

'Come on, Richard, you should be celebrating. Your financial woes are almost behind you and you've a great opportunity ahead.'

'I know, and of course I am pleased to have a fresh start. But leaving Berwyn will be hard.'

'You are going to Liverpool, not the other side of the world. It's only a short railway journey, and next year you'll be able to get out at Berwyn Station and have a ten-minute walk home to Ty Celyn.'

'Try and keep me away,' said Richard.

CHAPTER 33

Before breakfast, Richard went to the yard and asked Owen to get the horse and cart ready. He drove up to Berllan and got down to work, tidying each room. He removed all personal and treasured items and loaded them onto the cart. After a good look around the cottage, Richard locked the door.

A short time later he arrived at Tyn y Rhos to see Ann and Jac.

'Have you got anywhere to live yet?' he asked them.

'Ann's brother has offered us a room in his cottage, and we'll move there before the eviction day,' said Jac. 'It's very kind of him to let us stay, but we'll be looking for somewhere else.'

Richard put a key on the table. Puzzled, Jac and Ann looked at the key, and then at Richard.

'What's that?' asked Jac.

'It could be the key to your next home,' said Richard. He explained about the new job in Liverpool. He told them about Ty tan y Berllan and how his grandparents had left it to him.

'So, I'll have no need for the cottage for a while. I have a favour to ask of you. Will you look after it for me; keep it warm and well maintained?'

Ann Thomas looked at Richard with tearfully happy eyes.

'Are you sure? That would be perfect for us, perfect. And you say that it has a big garden?'

'My Taid grew all sorts in the garden, and fruit in the orchard, of course. There is a henhouse and other small buildings. It also has nine acres that are used by my brother. If you wanted to keep some sheep then you could take the fields back. I'll mention it to him before I go to Liverpool.'

Ann Thomas hugged Richard, who felt that the emotion was about to overwhelm them all. He made his way to the door and wished them well. He was aware that he was unlikely to see Ann again.

Richard returned to the cart and headed back to Ty Celyn.

***

Over the next week, Richard made a final visit to all his patients who were ill or undergoing treatment. He sent letters to all the other patients saying that he was leaving and that Dr Bevan would be their new doctor. He received many messages thanking him for his help, and saying that they were sorry to see him go. Many also congratulated him on his apparent success.

Most of his patients had no idea of the torment and anguish he had experienced in recent times. They were unaware that Liverpool was his only option in order to avoid personal disaster. He recalled James Morton's words about moving on with head held high, a winner to the outside world. James was right, and now he had to believe it too.

***

Evan took Richard in the gig to Llangollen Station to catch the Sunday afternoon train. Merryman wished him well in his new venture.

'Mary and all the family are sorry to see you leave,' he said.

'At least you do know Dr Bevan, and he's an excellent doctor,' said Richard.

'Yes, of course, but we are not just losing our doctor, we are losing a very good friend.'

Richard thanked him.

'So you'll be staying with James Morton,' said Evan. 'That's better than having to find lodgings on your own.'

'James wrote saying that there was a vacant room in his lodging house and that the landlady would welcome another doctor moving in. Apparently, it's a decent place and we have a shared sitting room as well as our own bedrooms.'

The train was ready to leave, and Richard found a carriage that was occupied by a mature woman and a young couple. The young man and woman were chatting and quietly flirting with one another. The younger woman had blonde hair in a similar fashion to Sara's.

Richard's mind went back to his last visit to Plas Gwyn and how William and Sara had held hands, appearing intimate. He had thought it strange that William's feelings for Sara had developed so quickly after he had ended the engagement. They had known one another for most of their lives, and lived under the same roof for most of that time.

It was then that he understood. William's feelings for Sara had not arisen in the last few weeks. He had loved her for years and must have hated to see Sara and him together.

Richard could now understand why William despised him. It was a powerful mix of jealousy and frustration. William had wanted him out of the picture so that he might have a chance to gain Sara's affection.

William's fights with him were a battle for love, a battle for Sara.

***

While Richard was travelling to Liverpool, Sara had a visit from Elizabeth. The two friends had not met since the wedding and honeymoon, and Sara was keen to hear all about their holiday.

Evan had told Elizabeth about Richard's career move after he had secured the job at the Liverpool Royal Infirmary. Richard had indeed landed an excellent surgeon's post at a progressive hospital, but Evan had dressed it up even more when he informed Elizabeth. He knew his wife would relay the embellished story to Sara, and in turn Sara would tell William.

'Richard's gone to Liverpool?' exclaimed Sara, after Elizabeth started to tell her the news.

'Well, he's going today and he's probably on the train now.'

'Why Liverpool, and what about his practice?' Sara had so many urgent questions.

'He was offered a top surgeon's job at the Liverpool Royal Infirmary. I don't think he could refuse it. It was the chance of a lifetime.'

'But what's happened to his practice?' Sara asked again.

'He sold it to Dr Bevan in Abbey Road. He got a very good price for it, according to Evan.'

Sara's initial surprise was waning as the news sunk in.

'So Richard is quite happy about all this, then? I thought that he didn't want to leave Berwyn.'

'I think that it was such an excellent opportunity for him that all other considerations were less important.

Evan said that he had not seen him so excited about something since he bought his practice. He has had some bad luck in recent times too, with the bad publicity from the workhouse, and of course your separation. And then there was that awful accident when Elin died. I think he was ready for something new.'

Sara's scowl deepened as Elizabeth carried on with her brother-in-law's news. Sara's emotional compass was pointing towards anger.

'Bad luck?' said Sara. 'Our separation was not bad luck. Richard chose to end our engagement. I offered him a fresh start in London and he threw it back at me. He preferred an affair with a cheap little maid. That wasn't bad luck. Why choose Liverpool when we could have had London?'

The anger soon turned to tears, and Elizabeth sat next to Sara and tried to comfort her.

'I'm sorry, Sara, I didn't think that you'd be so upset about Richard's news. I wouldn't have gone on so, if I'd known. I thought that you were finally over your relationship with Richard when you threatened to take him to court for ending the engagement.'

'I knew, really, that there was no way back for us, but I suppose I still hoped for something to happen that would change things. But now he has gone.' And, she thought, without her.

After Elizabeth had left, Sara went to find William to tell him the news. He didn't detect Sara's sombre tone as she told him about Richard's departure. William was delighted. He didn't try to hide his pleasure at having driven Richard out, and that annoyed Sara. His only disappointment was that Richard appeared pleased with his new opportunity. He had looked forward to the day when Richard might be forced out of the area as a broken man. But all that really mattered was that Richard was gone. He would no longer be a competitor for Sara's love.

***

When Richard arrived at Lime Street Station, he took a cab to his lodgings. On arrival he looked up at the three-storey townhouse on Falkner Street and was impressed by its elegance. The owner, Mrs Robertson, invited him into her rooms on the ground floor. She told Richard that her husband had died two years ago, and she had then decided to use the upstairs rooms as a respectable lodging house for professional gentlemen. The young widow showed Richard upstairs into a fine drawing room and explained that this was the gentlemen's sitting room. She also showed him his bedroom, which was large and airy. Richard was pleased with his new lodgings; breakfast and an evening meal were also available if he wanted them.

Richard unpacked his trunk and then went to the sitting room to wait for James. About half an hour later, James returned from hospital and the two doctors went out to celebrate Richard's success and the start of his new career at the Liverpool Royal Infirmary.

CHAPTER 34

It was Richard's fourth day at the Royal Infirmary and he had been in theatre assisting Mr Fortescue. The operation had gone well and Fortescue was pleased with Richard's work. He had carried out the procedure, with the senior man observing and making the occasional comment.

The patient was now back on the male surgical ward and Richard was about to examine him. At the patient's bedside stood a young nurse straightening the sheets at the end of the bed. She wore the distinctive dark grey uniform and white lace cap of a probationer.

'How is he, nurse?' asked Richard, looking closely at the patient and not at her.

'Very sore but in good spirits,' said the nurse cheerfully. 'We're already feeling a bit better, aren't we?'

'Do I detect a North Wales accent?' asked Richard, and he looked at the nurse for the first time.

'Yes, I am from Corwen – Dr Lloyd, it's you!'

'Well, well, Angharad Edwards, how are you? It must be six months since I saw you with your parents at the Owain Glyndwr Hotel. I thought that you were going to St Thomas' Hospital in London for training?'

Richard examined the wound.

'I did write to St Thomas' but they told me that a Nightingale Nursing School had opened in Liverpool last year and I might like to apply to go there instead, as it was nearer to home. I've been here since July and the time has gone so quickly.'

The patient winced as Richard applied the bandage that Angharad had prepared. He told him that the wound would hurt for a day or so but should heal well.

'You like the work then, Nurse Edwards?' said Richard.

Angharad laughed. 'Yes, I do. I like being called Nurse Edwards too, and I've made some good friends at the nurses' home.'

The ward sister noticed Angharad's laughter and came over to tell her that when she was finished, she was needed for another job.

'I'm on male surgical for another two weeks, so I expect I'll see you again, soon,' Angharad told Richard before she went to see what Sister wanted.

The ward sister told Angharad not to be so familiar with the doctors. Angharad tried to explain that Dr Lloyd had been the family doctor back home, and he had helped her with the decision to enter nursing. Sister was unconvinced and reminded her that the doctor and nurse relationship must remain completely professional at all times. Angharad said she understood and went off to do the bedpans as instructed, still smiling.

Angharad was nineteen years old, pretty, with dark hair and brown eyes. She made friends easily and got on well with most of the other probationers and trainees. She was closest, however, to Jane who was from Wrexham, and they had adjoining rooms in the nurses' home. They had started work at the same time and were about a third of the way through the twelve-month period of nurse training. During this year, they would spend two months on each of the surgical and medical wards. All probationers also had to attend a series of lectures given by a senior surgeon in the hospital. Angharad's intelligence and interest in nursing usually meant that she was a very good student, but she had once been caught yawning during a particularly boring lecture.

Angharad and Richard saw one another frequently on the ward over the next few days but there was little opportunity for anything more than passing acknowledgement. She was also mindful of Sister's warning about familiarity with doctors, and therefore her contact with Richard was restricted to medical matters.

Towards the end of Richard's second week, he stopped to talk to Angharad. He said it was a shame they had not had the chance to talk properly.

'Jane and I go to the Bedford Street Welsh Chapel on Sunday mornings and after the service we have tea and cakes in the hall,' Angharad said. 'Would you like to join us, and then we can have a good chat?'

'That's a very good idea,' said Richard. 'I'll look forward to it.'

Angharad explained that the chapel was a few streets away from the hospital and the service started at ten-thirty. They would meet him at twenty past ten outside the chapel.

***

On Sunday morning, Richard arrived at the chapel, which turned out to be only a few minutes' walk from his lodgings. He waited in the faint November sun for Angharad and Jane. At home, he was church rather than chapel, but when he had attended Methodist services for weddings or christenings, he had always been impressed by the emotion and enthusiasm of the congregation. The two young women arrived, and they all went into the chapel together.

Richard was not disappointed by the service; the moving Welsh hymns could have been heard halfway down the street. He was not the only member of the congregation that morning who experienced *hiraeth*, a nostalgic longing, for home and the land of their fathers.

After the service they went through to the adjoining hall, where a few ladies were busy with some very large kettles and plates of bara brith and cakes. Jane selected a table, while Angharad and Richard brought over the tea and cakes.

'How are you getting on in Liverpool, Dr Lloyd? I think you've been here two weeks now,' said Angharad.

'No "Dr Lloyd" when we're off duty, please; it's Richard.'

'Well, you don't have to call me Nurse Edwards then. It's Angharad,'

'I'm getting on very well. I'm enjoying being back in hospital and have been impressed with the Royal Infirmary and all the people.'

'Even the nurses?' joked Angharad.

'Especially the nurses. Only St Thomas' Hospital in London and the Liverpool Royal Infirmary have Nightingale Nurse Training Schools. You are amongst the best nurses in the world.'

Angharad smiled at Jane, as they had heard that more than once from the superintendents.

'Is the training school as you expected?' Richard asked them.

'I didn't know what to expect,' said Jane, 'but I'm really pleased that I came here. You learn something new every day and the work is never boring.'

'Well, apart from the beds,' said Angharad. 'Stripping the beds and then making them up again can be boring after a while. But you're right; it has been very good so far. We get all our board and lodgings provided, and ten pounds a year.'

'It sounds as if you are pleased with your decision to become nurses then,' said Richard.

'I told you in Corwen that I'd rather be a doctor, but as they don't allow women to train to be doctors, this will have to do,' said Angharad. 'One day there will be women doctors, you'll see.'

'I'm sure that there will,' said Richard, 'and I fully support them. I've written to the medical press on the issue. It might be a few more years before there is agreement on allowing women into the profession, but it will happen.'

Angharad was impressed with Richard's views.

'Will you come to chapel again next Sunday?' she asked.

'I have enjoyed the service and the company,' said Richard, 'and if I can, then I'll be here.'

As they were leaving the hall, Angharad spotted a notice on the board and stopped to read it. The heading announced 'A New Wales in Patagonia'. There was to be a meeting at the chapel about the proposed settlement on Thursday evening.

'Look,' said Angharad. 'That'll be interesting. My brother is going to Patagonia and I need to find out more about it. Will you please come to the meeting with me, Jane?'

'I'm working late on Thursday,' said Jane.

'Oh dear, I don't like going out on my own, especially in the dark.'

'I'd happily accompany you,' Richard volunteered.

'You wouldn't want to give up an evening for me.'

'No, really, I'd be interested to hear what they have to say,' he said. 'I'll meet you outside the nurses' home at seven o'clock.'

CHAPTER 35

Richard met Angharad a few yards down the street from the entrance to the nurses' home. She had made him aware that the nurses were discouraged from going out with men, and it would be inappropriate for him to wait outside the entrance. Neither of them considered their evening together in any way romantic, but it was nevertheless best if they were discreet.

'Thank you for coming with me,' said Angharad as they walked along the gaslit streets. There was a cold mist coming in from the Mersey. Angharad shivered. 'I'll be glad to get to the chapel.'

'I'm interested as to why your brother wants to go to Patagonia,' said Richard.

'So am I – that's one of the reasons why I was so determined to attend this meeting. I know that they're offering a lot of land to every settler, and that is important to him. Getting a farm is very difficult around Corwen and the rents are high. Llewelyn was hoping that he might have the tenancy of our father's farm in a few years, but the agent has said that the land would be taken over by a neighbouring farmer. That was a big blow for him.'

'So if he could get a farm in Wales, he would stay?'

'I think so, but he is quite excited about the prospects of going to Patagonia. You know, the idea of being part of a new Wales. He and his wife, Mary, hope for a family, and the thought of being able to bring up their children on their own large farm appealed to him a lot.'

When they arrived, Richard was surprised to see around fifty people already there, and a few more came in after them. At seven-thirty prompt, Hugh Jenkins stood up and introduced himself.

'I am here tonight on behalf of Michael Daniel Jones of Bala and the Emigration Society. For the last few years, they have proposed a new settlement that would save the Welsh language from the industrial revolution that is threatening to destroy our culture. The settlement provides wonderful opportunities for families to start a prosperous life on the other side of the Atlantic.

'This dream is becoming a reality. It has been agreed with the government of Argentina that we can create a settlement in the Chubut Valley of Patagonia: a fertile river valley with good rainfall. Every family will be given land to create farms that will be theirs, not enclosed or stolen by greedy landowners, and with no fear of eviction. As well as having their own land, they will have the opportunity to build a new Wales, with chapels, schools and a future for the Welsh language.

'We already have over one hundred men, women and children who want to sail to a new life, next year. There are several people here in Liverpool planning to go. But there is room for more.'

A man in the hall stood up and declared that he was going. A round of applause confirmed the audience's admiration for him. Mr Jenkins continued to tell the audience what was on offer for able-bodied Welsh speakers who wanted to build themselves a new life in Patagonia. At the end of his talk, he invited those who were interested to come and see him. A queue of over twenty people formed at the front of the chapel.

'Shall we leave now?' Richard asked Angharad.

'I want one of the booklets that Mr Jenkins held up'.

Richard returned shortly with a copy of 'Y Wladychfa Gymreig' (The Welsh Settlement). The booklet said that the proposed land had splendid expanses of green forest, herds of animals and rich pastures, and the rainfall was as regular as in Wales.

'You aren't thinking about emigrating, are you?' asked Richard, as he walked with Angharad back to the nurses' home.

'My brother has asked me to go with them to Patagonia.'

'And will you go?' said Richard, quite surprised. 'What about nursing?'

'I don't know, but surely there will be a need for someone with my nursing experience.'

'But there won't be any hospitals,' said Richard.

'All the more reason for me to go then,' said Angharad, smiling at Richard's reaction.

***

The following Sunday, Jane had gone home to Wrexham to see her family, so Richard attended chapel with Angharad alone. After the service, they went into the hall together. Richard felt quite at home in this little part of Wales in Liverpool.

'Do you realise that Christmas is only three weeks away?' he asked her. 'Are you going home at Christmas?'

'I have asked Sister for leave.'

'Angharad, I don't know what you'll think about this, but I have been invited to a ball on Christmas Eve and wondered whether you would like to accompany me. My brother Evan wrote to me this week to say that

Elizabeth, his wife, is arranging the dance at Berwyn Hall.'

Angharad was taken aback. 'You must have lots of people that you could take. Why ask me?'

'Well, I don't, and anyway I'd like to thank you for being such a good friend to me during my first few weeks in Liverpool. I also thought that we could have some fun, away from the disapproving eyes of the ward sisters.'

'I'm sure that it would be fun, and thank you for asking me, but I might have to work on Christmas Eve.'

Richard, although crestfallen, smiled and said, 'Let's hope Sister gives you the time off.'

Angharad told Jane about the Berwyn Ball when she returned later that Sunday.

'I was so surprised. It was the last thing that I expected. I really don't know what to do.'

'Well, do you want to go?' asked Jane, 'It's as simple as that.'

'It's not simple,' said Angharad, 'because if I go, then it changes our friendship, and if I don't go, that might damage our friendship.'

'You're reading too much into it. He has asked you to a Christmas dance, not to marry him. It will only change your relationship with him if you both want it to. Is that what you're scared of?'

'I'm not scared of anything.'

'Go then, and see what happens. It will be good fun. Look, if you turn him down, then I'll offer to accompany him to the dance.'

'Oh no you won't,' said Angharad firmly.

'You know what you want to do. Let's hope you get the leave approved.'

***

The following evening, Richard and James had finished their evening meal and were relaxing in the sitting room.

'Are you going back to Scotland for Christmas?' asked Richard.

'No, I'm working up to the thirtieth and then catching the Glasgow train in time for Hogmanay. That's the real celebration back home at this time of year,' said James. 'What are you doing for the holidays?'

'I'll be home for Christmas Eve and Christmas Day. Evan and Elizabeth are holding a dance on Christmas Eve and I have asked Angharad Edwards to accompany me.'

'What? That's breaking hospital rules, isn't it? Doctors and nurses aren't allowed to fraternise. You could get Angharad into trouble with the nursing school, you old rascal.'

'I've asked her to a dance, that's all. She has been a good friend to me since I came to Liverpool. There's nothing more to it than that.'

'If you say so.' James smiled.

***

Angharad accepted Richard's invitation to the Christmas Eve Ball at Berwyn Hall. She remained unsure as to whether it was the right thing to do, but Angharad always erred on the side of excitement rather than caution. That excitement grew over the next fortnight, as she and Richard made plans for their forthcoming Christmas. She had obtained the same leave as him so they could travel home together, and also return at the same time on Boxing Day.

Angharad wanted to know all about Evan and Elizabeth and Sir Clayton and Lady Davenport and the grandeur of Berwyn Hall. She had never before been to a ball at such a place, but Richard reassured her that she would manage very well in the company of the Davenports and their guests. He knew that Angharad could hold her own against the best, including Lady Margaret.

But it was not Lady Davenport that Richard and Angharad had to worry about. A couple of days before they were due to come home for Christmas, Richard received a letter from Evan. Out of courtesy, Elizabeth had invited Sara to the ball but had expected her to decline as Richard was attending. However, Sara had accepted and to make matters worse, William would be accompanying her. Evan told Richard that he should have prior warning, and be prepared for this unwelcome development.

Richard read the letter with increasing concern. He would have to explain to Angharad about the past year with Sara and William.

He went to bed that night wondering whether he would ever be free from the bitter and belligerent world of William and Sara Griffiths-Ellis.

CHAPTER 36

On the morning of 24th December, Richard and Angharad arrived early at Lime Street Station and went to the refreshment room.

'I have something I need to tell you,' said Richard.

Angharad sipped her tea and looked at him in anticipation.

'I had a letter from Evan two days ago. Elizabeth has invited an old friend, Sara, to the ball. Sara and I were engaged.'

Richard went on to tell Angharad about how the engagement had ended and the hostility between the families.

'This is all very interesting, and I do appreciate your openness, but what does it have to do with me?' asked Angharad.

'Sara and William will be at the ball. If they say bad things about me, then you need to understand what has happened. My biggest concern is that they may say something hurtful to you.'

'Don't worry about me. I can look after myself. Sara will have picked on the wrong person if she says anything to me.'

Richard then told Angharad about Elin and how she had died. Angharad could see in his face that Richard was emotional and struggling to find his words.

'I am so sorry, Richard.' Angharad reached across to touch his hand. 'That must have been a very sad time for you.'

'It was the final blow. I had been prepared to fight for the practice, but I had nothing left to carry on. William would have bankrupted me and almost did. Before she died, Elin told me to start my life again. Soon after, James and Evan said much the same thing, and that was why I applied to the Royal Infirmary.'

'I'm glad that you did, and that you got the job.' Angharad reached over to him again and, this time, held his hand.

***

At eight o'clock on Christmas Eve, Richard and Angharad arrived by carriage at Berwyn Hall. Evan welcomed them warmly and introduced Elizabeth. She took Angharad's arm and showed her into the great hall, which also served as the ballroom. The room looked splendidly festive with a large Christmas tree in the corner covered in decorations and glass beads that reflected the light from the candles. There was mistletoe hanging from the chandeliers, and holly and ivy on the walls. Around the sides of the room were tables decorated with holly and crackers, and there was a quartet playing music. A few early guests sat talking.

'What a beautiful room,' said Angharad to her hostess. 'I have never seen such wonderful Christmas decorations.'

'Thank you, Angharad, I'm glad that you like it, and I'm really pleased that you came with Richard tonight. I hope that you both have a good time. Now, where have those brothers gone? Honestly, leave them together for a minute and they'll be up to no good.'

Richard and Evan entered the room and joined Elizabeth and Angharad in conversation.

'Some more guests have arrived,' said Elizabeth after a while. 'I must go and welcome them.'

Evan watched her go. 'It's them,' he said, voice low, 'Sara and William are here.'

'Wouldn't it be good if they just kept their distance?' said Richard.

'William will no doubt have something he'll want to share with us. I heard that he was buying into the Pentrefelin slate works.'

'That man will own the entire valley before he's finished.'

A group of local children came into the room with lanterns and candles and sang carols. The guests applauded the singers, and Elizabeth gave their conductor a basket of crackers, sweets and pennies for the children to take home. Angharad went over to talk to the children.

Sir Clayton joined Richard and Evan and asked about the new job. Richard told him that it had been a very good move.

A familiar voice then announced his presence.

'Good evening, Sir Clayton and gentlemen,' said William. 'May I compliment you on Berwyn Hall looking so fine tonight?'

'I cannot take any credit for that,' said Sir Clayton. 'Elizabeth and Lady Margaret are responsible for everything this evening.'

'How is the railway progressing?' asked Richard.

'Very well,' said Sir Clayton. 'The work is almost complete and the chairman has arranged a private excursion next month for board members and guests. We'll travel down the line to Corwen and have lunch at the Owain Glyndwr. Are you going, William?'

'Yes, it will be a significant occasion.'

'I was coming back from Carrog on the main road earlier, and Berwyn Station looks magnificent,' said Richard.

'The architect has done a good job,' said Sir Clayton. 'The chairman and I are very pleased with the result. It will be a landmark for travellers on both the road and the railway. People will certainly know that they are in Berwyn.'

The music quartet restarted and the dancing got underway. William said he must return to Sara.

Within a few minutes, Angharad and Richard were dancing.

'Who is that with Richard?' Sara asked William.

'I don't know, but she was with Elizabeth when I passed them just now. Perhaps Lloyd has found a new lady in Liverpool. He doesn't waste any time, does he?'

Sara said nothing but she was cross with William's flippant remarks. At the end of the dance, she went back to the table.

After a few minutes, she saw that Elizabeth was on her own and went to talk to her friend. After a few pleasantries, Sara got to the point.

'Who is Richard's dancing partner?'

'Angharad,' said Elizabeth. 'She's a friend from the hospital – a nurse. Her parents live in Carrog and Richard knows the family as he used to be their doctor. She's a very nice girl.'

'There's nothing serious between them?'

'I doubt it. Richard has only been in Liverpool for two months.'

'Would you please let Richard know that I'd like to speak to him this evening?' asked Sara.

'Yes, of course, but do you think that's a good idea? You know I don't want you to get upset again.' Elizabeth reached out to touch her friend's hand.

'Thank you,' said Sara, ignoring the question, 'I'd better get back to William.'

'It's wonderful here,' said Angharad as she and Richard had their fourth consecutive dance. 'Thank you so much for inviting me.'

'I'm glad that you agreed to come,' said Richard. 'Shall we sit down for a few minutes?'

Elizabeth whispered to Richard that Sara wanted to speak to him. He wasn't pleased, but a little later he decided to see what Sara wanted. William had left her alone for a few minutes.

'Elizabeth says that you want to see me,' said Richard.

'I want to hear how you are. Is Liverpool to your liking?'

'Yes, the job is going very well.'

'I see that you have made friends,' said Sara, glancing over in Angharad's direction.

'Angharad is a good friend.'

'Do you ever think about me, Richard?'

'We were together for a long time. It would be unusual if I didn't.'

William returned to the table.

'We were just saying that it would be strange if we didn't think of one another now and then,' Sara told him. 'After such a long time together.'

'Damn you, Lloyd,' said William. 'I go to have a brandy and a cigar with Sir Clayton in his library and come back to find you two together again. You had your chance with Sara, and you lost her. Losing is something that you are good at. You lost your reputation with your patients. You lost your job at the workhouse. You are a loser.'

'And you were the cause of that, weren't you?' said Richard. 'But look, I have better things to do tonight than argue with you. It's Christmas, the season of goodwill to all men, even you. I wish you both a merry Christmas. I am now going to ask Angharad if she would like another dance.'

Sara told William that she wanted to go home. She had a headache. William arranged for the carriage and they said goodnight to Lady Davenport and Elizabeth.

Richard and Angharad had several more dances together that evening. As the night progressed, they both sensed the beginning of something romantic between them. Each dance became more than just light fun.

Much later, Richard accompanied Angharad back to Carrog in the carriage. She told him again how much she had enjoyed the evening.

Richard held her hand. 'I have enjoyed being with you tonight, Angharad. I would like to spend more time with you.'

'I should like that too,' said Angharad.

They kissed. It was only one brief kiss, but it was their first.

***

Christmas Day at Ty Celyn found Richard in an excellent mood. He walked with his father to church in the fresh morning air. The sky was blue and the sun was doing its best to shine. They sat alongside Evan and Elizabeth in church.

While Evan and Elizabeth dined at Berwyn Hall with her father and mother, Sian and Owen joined Edward and Richard for Christmas dinner at Ty Celyn. They enjoyed the goose, and then the plum pudding. Apart from a few Christmas cards on the mantelpiece, there was little in the way of festive decorations at Ty Celyn, but the feast itself was second to none.

***

The next day, Edward took Richard to Llangollen Station for his return to Liverpool. Merryman Christmas, still acting as stationmaster, came over to them.

'Your special time of the year,' said Richard. 'Merry Christmas to you.'

'A special time for lots of jokes and leg pulling,' replied Merryman with a grin. 'My mother has a lot to answer for. Her maiden name was Merryman.'

'Your boss isn't back at work yet,' said Richard. 'You've had a good run as stationmaster.'

'Yes, over four months, but he returns on the first of January and I then go back to being foreman porter. But this experience made me think that I should apply for a stationmaster's job at one of the new stations down the line. I would like to have the job at Berwyn, really.'

'Your knowledge of managing a station like Llangollen must give you a very good chance,' said Richard.

'That's what Mary says too, but I've told her that it depends on who else applies, and I have only worked here, you see. I think Mary has an eye on that stationmaster's house.'

'I don't blame her,' said Richard. 'It looks splendid.'

'It would mean a bedroom for our Myfanwy and no more sharing with her brothers. But I mustn't get ahead of myself, as usual.'

'Good luck to you for the new year; it seems as if it could be a very good one,' said Richard.

Angharad came down the platform, half walking and half running. Her father brought over the case and Richard introduced him to Edward.

'I hear you had a good time on Christmas Eve,' said Mr Edwards. 'Angharad told us all about it. She said that she'd never danced so much in her life. Thank you for taking her.'

'I can assure you that the pleasure was all mine.'

The train was due to depart in less than five minutes, so they said goodbye to their fathers and boarded the train.

As they left Llangollen, they had the little train carriage to themselves. Angharad explained that Christmas Day hadn't been the best. Her brother Llewelyn and his wife, Mary, had dinner with them and the main talking point had been Patagonia.

'Mam got so upset that Dad had to tell Llewelyn to stop talking about it,' said Angharad. 'This Christmas was probably their last ever in Carrog. I said that I had been to a talk about Patagonia and was thinking about going, too. Mam said that never seeing her children again would be like us having died.'

'What does your father think about it?'

'Dad was cross with me for considering it and said that it was no place for a girl. But he understands why Llewelyn wants to go and the chance for him to have his own farm.'

'And your poor mother?'

'It will break her heart.'

Richard said no more. Understandably, Angharad appeared distressed, and he didn't want to pursue how serious she really was about leaving for Patagonia.

CHAPTER 37

Without Sundays and chapel, their romance would not have blossomed. It provided the main opportunity for Richard and Angharad to meet and socialise, without any questions being asked. The Bedford Street Chapel had become an important part of their lives, as it had for many people in the Welsh-speaking community of that area. The chapel had already been expanded in the 1840s when it had over two hundred members. At a meeting in January to discuss the provision of a completely new, larger chapel, over one thousand people crowded into the Bedford Street building. Richard and Angharad were amongst them and pledged to give some money to support the building of a new church in nearby Princes Road.

Every Sunday, Angharad and Richard met for the service. They would usually go for a walk afterwards to make the most of their time together. There was one subject that came up most often during their Sunday walks.

'Have you thought any more about Patagonia?' asked Richard.

'I think about it all the time and I'm still keen to go, even though Mam and Dad are against it.'

'Don't you think that they may be right? It will be hard work building houses and digging land. Is that what you want from your life?'

Angharad looked cross. 'Not all of my life, no, but I do want an adventure while I am still young. I am strong and healthy. As a nurse, I have to move big men in bed – why can't I move earth and stone and help put up buildings? If I were a man, you and Dad wouldn't question it. I want to play a part in building this new land. I can't do anything like that here because women are prevented from doing things that are considered to be a man's job.'

'I do understand why you want to do this. I believe you can do it, but I'm just not sure that it will live up to your expectations. You are right that women have limited rights and opportunities, and you know that I also want to see that change. With your spirit and determination, I think you could help to change things here. It is possible, you know. Look at what Florence Nightingale and Betsi Cadwaladr have done for hospitals and nursing.'

Angharad thought for a moment.

'You aren't interested in going to Patagonia then?' she asked.

'I'm a doctor and not a farmer or builder. Medicine is my life and I don't want to give it up. I also need to do what I can for the future of our language and culture in Wales.'

'But the settlement is going to need a doctor. You could be the very first one. Look what a team we could be.'

'Yes, but the main job for all the settlers in the early years is going to be building and establishing farms. There is nothing there yet but untouched land.'

'I don't know anything about building either, but I can learn while I'm helping others. Don't you feel any excitement about it all?'

'Not as much as you, but I can see that you have enough excitement for both of us.'

'You're coming then?' Angharad smiled.

'I didn't say that,' said Richard.

***

Heavy snow fell during the last week of January. Richard was dismayed to find on Sunday morning that there had been a further snowfall during the night. Looking out from the sitting room window, he could see that the wind had caused drifting on the road and pavement. Richard had brought his heavy country boots from Berwyn, and in the last few days had worn them to tramp through the snow to get to the infirmary. It wasn't far from Falkner Street to the chapel, but he was concerned whether Angharad, at the nurses' home, would be able to manage half a mile or so of snowy pavements in her little boots. He sadly resigned himself to the fact that he wouldn't see her this Sunday.

Arriving at the chapel, he knocked the snow off his boots and coat and went inside. A cheerful voice piped up from the pew where they usually sat.

'Hello, Richard, isn't it beautiful? I love fresh snow,' said Angharad.

Richard sat down beside her and whispered, 'It isn't as beautiful as you. I didn't think that you would manage to get to chapel this morning. Your poor little feet must be wet and cold.'

'They're quite dry – look,' replied Angharad. She lifted her skirt to her knees to reveal a pair of long, black riding boots. 'The bottom of my skirt and coat are wet from the snow but my riding boots have kept my legs and feet warm and dry. Mam sent them to me this week when the snow came. She said it's very deep in Carrog.'

'I didn't know you could ride,' said Richard.

'There are a lot of things you don't know about me.'

It was a good congregation despite the weather. They went into the hall after the service had finished. Richard asked after Jane and whether the snow had stopped her from coming to chapel.

'She has a cold, but the weather didn't help,' said Angharad.

'A pair of your boots would have been helpful, too,' said Richard. 'How long have you been riding, by the way?'

'As a very young child, I pestered Dad for a pony, and he'd tell me that he would think about it. And then I'd ask him again, and he would say that he was still thinking about it. They didn't have much money, but Dad didn't want to say no. Then I had scarlet fever and was in bed for weeks, but Dad said that when I was well, he would get me a pony. I was even more determined to leave my bed. When I was able to get up and walk again, Dad took my hand and took me to the stables and there was a small brown pony. I cried, and then Mam and Dad cried too.'

'So, that little pony was the start of your love of horses?'

'Yes, I called her Scarlet because if it hadn't been for the fever, I wouldn't have got her. Scarlet and I were the best of friends. I rode her everywhere and she helped me fully recover, and after a few months I got strong again. Do you want to know how I got these boots?'

Richard laughed. Angharad's stories often meandered.

'What did I say? Have I said something funny?'

'I just love you, Angharad. If we weren't in chapel now, I would kiss you. Go on, tell me how you got your boots.'

‘Well, after Scarlet, I had a bigger pony and then a horse which had belonged to the vicar’s wife. She had got too old to ride.’

‘Who – the horse or the vicar’s wife?’

‘Do you want to hear this story or not?’ said Angharad.

‘Of course I do, carry on.’

‘Mrs Harris, the vicar’s wife, had arthritis and had fallen off her horse called Champion.’

Richard laughed, and apologised for again interrupting her story.

‘Anyway, the Reverend Harris said that it was time for Champion to go to a new home, and Dad and I went to see him. Dad had known Reverend Harris since they were at school together and he knew that we would look after Champion. While Dad agreed a price with the vicar, I sat talking to Mrs Harris. She looked at my feet and pulled out these boots from behind her chair. She told me to try them on, and they fitted perfectly. She said that they were obviously meant to be mine. They had not been worn very often and she told me that they were the best quality leather. Mam said that they were worth more than the horse.’

Richard looked around the hall. Everyone, except the ladies washing up the cups and plates in the back scullery, had gone home.

‘We’ll have to go soon,’ said Richard. ‘They’ll be locking up.’

‘Let’s wait until then,’ said Angharad, ‘because I want to carry on talking. When we leave here, it will be another week before we can have a proper chat.’

After a few more minutes, they went outside and paused at the side of the chapel.

‘Nobody can see us here, Richard,’ said Angharad. ‘You can kiss me if you want.’

Their lips were cold from the wintry wind. Their hearts were warm and happy.

***

The snow and cold weather continued into February, and the hills above the Dee Valley saw heavier falls and deeper drifts than Liverpool. The very low temperatures over lying snow were particularly perilous for the poor, who were unable to afford the cost of fuel. The railway board became aware of the plight of many living in villages to the west of Corwen and wanted to do something to help. A gift of coal was to be delivered to the villagers of Llandrillo and Llandderfel. On a cold morning in February, the first-ever goods train ran on the new railway line through Llangollen Station on its way to Corwen. A tender locomotive pulled seven wagons of coal for the villagers.

Amongst the onlookers at Llangollen Station stood Merryman Christmas. He shivered as he watched the historic event. It wasn't just the cold that caused him to shiver but nervousness. He had a meeting later with the manager about the position of stationmaster at Berwyn. This was the opportunity of a lifetime. It meant a station of his own, higher wages and a new home for him and his family.

At eleven o'clock the manager invited Merryman into a small room at the back of the station. He made it clear to Merryman that while he had done a good job in running Llangollen station, setting up and managing a new station at Berwyn would be a different task altogether. Merryman told the manager how he would go about setting up new procedures and training for staff. The manager nodded, which gave Merryman some reassurance that the interview was not going too badly. Thirty minutes later it was all over, and the manager thanked him and said that he had three more candidates to see that afternoon before a decision would be made.

While the meeting had gone quickly, the afternoon passed painfully slowly. Merryman remembered things that he had meant to tell the manager but had forgotten to mention. He began to agonise over his responses to some of the questions. At the end of the interview, he'd thought it had gone quite well. By two o'clock he was unsure, and by three he felt that it had been a disaster.

At almost four, the manager asked him to come into the room. He was not smiling. Merryman feared the worst. He could already imagine Mary's disappointed face.

'Mr Christmas, please will you take a seat. I'm afraid that it's not all good news…'

Merryman interrupted. 'Well, I knew that might be so—'

'What I mean is that you are going to be a very busy man setting up a new station at Berwyn and moving house.'

For the first time, the manager smiled.

'Congratulations,' he said. 'I have no doubts that you'll do a fine job.'

Mary had also been anxious as she waited for her husband's news and his return home. As the door opened, she looked at him for any indication of the outcome. He couldn't contain the smile any longer; it was as wide as Llangollen Bridge. They hugged one another as the reality of the situation became clear. Mary began to cry.

'What's the matter, Mam?' asked Myfanwy, who had come downstairs.

'Oh, nothing, I'm being silly. It's good news that your clever father has brought home,' said Mary. 'Go and get your brothers and he'll tell you all about it.'

A few minutes later, Merryman told his family about his new job.

'We shall have a new house at the station,' he explained.

'How many bedrooms has the house got?' asked Myfanwy with hope in her voice.

'Three bedrooms,' said her father, 'and one will be just for you.'

'With room for your books and your writing, isn't it?' said Mary.

Myfanwy clapped her hands together in joy.

'And you boys will have a much bigger bedroom, too, and plenty of places to play. Your school will be across the road from the house.'

'I'd like to stay at my old school with my friends,' said Gareth.

'Berwyn isn't too far away, so you can still see your old friends sometimes,' said his mother, 'but you'll soon make new friends, too.'

'When are we moving to Berwyn?' asked Geraint.

'Next month, but we'll go and have a look at the new house soon,' said Merryman.

Myfanwy went back upstairs to her books and to think about her new bedroom. Mr and Mrs Christmas were happier than they could ever remember being.

CHAPTER 38

'I expect that I'll have to reserve my passage on the ship soon,' said Angharad to Richard, quite casually, during their Sunday walk. 'Llewelyn and Mary have already put their names down. I don't suppose you have had any further thoughts about going.'

'You talk about going to Patagonia as if it's a day trip to Rhyl. This is a dangerous journey and a complete change of life.'

'I know all that, and you insult me by suggesting that I have not thought it through properly. If you don't want to come with me then that's fine, but don't put down my hopes and plans.'

Angharad walked away from Richard, who quickly caught up with her.

'I'm sorry and I would never intend to insult you. I'm worried about you and I care about you. I love you and I don't want you to go to Patagonia. There, I've said it now.'

'I love you too. This is difficult for me as well, you know. I want you to come with me and share my dream. I don't want anyone else to share my dream, only you.'

'But that's the problem: it's your dream and not mine.'

'So you want me to follow your plans? Your ideas are the only ones that are important and mine don't count?'

'I didn't mean that. Of course, your ideas count. What I mean is that I do not want to emigrate to Patagonia.'

'Please think about it again. I so want to see a new world and help improve life for all those who are struggling now and deserve a chance at something better. This is their opportunity as well as ours.'

***

In the sitting room of their Falkner Street lodgings, Richard and James relaxed after a busy day at the infirmary.

'You're thoughtful again tonight,' said James. 'What's on your mind? Anything to do with your good friend Angharad?'

'I think that we've passed the stage of good friends.'

'It sounds as if you've fallen in love'.

'I didn't intend it to happen, but over the last two months I have grown very close to her,' Richard admitted. 'I do love her.'

'But you don't think she feels the same way towards you?'

'I'm not sure, but she told me that she loves me.'

'So what's the problem?' asked James.

Richard paused, struggling to bring himself to say it.

'Angharad wants to emigrate with her brother and sister-in-law.'

'To America?'

Richard nodded.

'Well, you should go with her. There are some good hospitals in America. At least there were before the civil war. The newspapers say that the war will be over within weeks. They are going to need the best surgeons for their hospitals.'

'South America,' said Richard. 'Patagonia in southern Argentina, and there are no hospitals.'

'Why does Angharad want to go there?'

'She wants adventure and to play a part in achieving a piece of history: the creation of a new Welsh settlement. In fairness, Angharad believes that it will do a lot of good for many people. The Argentine government has promised the settlers generous grants of land. Her own brother is emigrating because he has little hope of getting a farm in Wales.'

'And you don't want to join her in this adventure? She is brave to consider such a life.'

'I really admire her bravery and ambition. But medicine is my one vocation and I want to change things for people here, not in some distant colony.'

'But now you love Angharad, the situation is different?'

'I don't want to lose her, and the ship sails in a couple of months.'

There was no easy solution, and thoughts of it plagued Richard long into the night.

***

The Christmas family moved into the stationmaster's house at Berwyn. Although the line would not be fully operational for some weeks yet, Merryman was busy preparing for that day. The station would have a modest staff and serve a small, dispersed rural community. However, the fine station building reflected one of much greater status. The chairman of the railway company lived nearby, and he had insisted on a building that looked more like a grand lodge to his mansion than a railway station.

The stationmaster's house was of a black-and-white timbered style on three floors. It was attached to the station, which had a general waiting room, another one for first-class travellers and a booking office. The station buildings, sandwiched between the main road and the railway line, stood high above the deep river valley below. On the opposite riverbank was The Chain Bridge Inn, which mirrored the station's architectural style.

Mrs Christmas took great pleasure in sorting out the new house. Whether running up new curtains, arranging the furniture or allocating the bedrooms, she had never been happier. She and Merryman had the bedroom with the large bay window that overlooked the platform and the beautiful valley below. The three boys shared a large bedroom overlooking the road, while Myfanwy had her own attic room on the top floor.

On the other side of the road stood Bethania Chapel with an attached schoolroom that the boys attended. In those first few weeks, after school, Dafydd, Geraint and Gareth stayed outside until dusk. They played trains on the line, making chugging and whistling sounds as they drove their imaginary engines towards Berwyn Tunnel. They would then dare one another as to who would go furthest into the dark tunnel and frighten poor little Gareth with stories of monsters and witches.

***

In recent times, Edward Lloyd had taken to walking from Ty Celyn over to Berwyn Station to watch the completion of the building work. On this occasion, as Edward approached the station, he saw Merryman on the platform. Edward congratulated him on his new job and asked how they were settling in. Merryman invited him to meet Mary.

Drinking his tea, Edward asked Myfanwy about her intentions now that she had moved to Berwyn.

'I have left school and will have to find a job.'

'Are you sorry to leave school?'

'I helped the headmaster with the young children and liked to show them how to read and write words. I want to be a teacher one day.'

'It sounds as if you're already a teacher,' said Edward.

'Books, isn't it?' said Mary. 'You can't get enough of them, can you, *cariad*? The headmaster used to lend her all sorts of books but leaving school has ended that. Still, you have a few of your own.'

'But I have read them all, Mam, and at least five times over,' said Myfanwy. 'Would you like to see my books, Mr Lloyd?'

Mary told Myfanwy not to bother Mr Lloyd, but Edward smiled. 'I would indeed, Myfanwy.'

Myfanwy took his hand and led Edward up the two flights of stairs to her bedroom. Merryman followed them.

'That is quite a library,' said Edward, looking at her shelf of seven very worn books. 'You have Dickens and Bronte; I'm impressed. You haven't really read *Oliver Twist*, have you? Poor Oliver has such a hard time.'

'Oh yes, but he is happy at the end,' said Myfanwy.

'I have some books at home, and I shall choose two or three for you. When you have read the books, we can discuss them.'

'Oh thank you, Mr Lloyd, thank you very much,' said Myfanwy.

'You have made a little girl very happy,' said Merryman, as he was showing Edward out of the house.

'Nonsense, she is more than welcome to the books. Perhaps they will help her achieve her wish to become a teacher one day.'

'Myfanwy was a pupil teacher at Penllyn and has ideas that she is going to help the teacher at Bethania. I fear that she will be disappointed.'

'Ambition is good, Merryman. The girl knows what she wants. She needs to be encouraged,' said Edward.

CHAPTER 39

Angharad took Richard's arm as they entered the park. There was a sharp northerly wind, so she snuggled against him and gained some warmth from his heavy coat. Richard kissed her gently.

As usual, Angharad was bubbling with enthusiasm about everything that was going on in her life: recent events at the nurses' home and incidents on the ward. Richard listened politely. And then, amongst all her chatter, she announced it. Richard could not believe that he had heard correctly.

'You've done what?' he demanded.

'I've booked my passage,' Angharad repeated. 'I had to, in case all the places got taken, but I told them about your situation and they will keep a place for you. They really need a doctor.'

'But you know that I don't want to go. How many times do I have to tell you? I do not want to spend months on a ship and then years in Patagonia.'

'But we'll be together and we'll have one another.'

She tried to kiss him, but in annoyance he avoided her attempt.

'How could you sign up without talking to me first?'

'I don't need your permission,' said Angharad, now equally annoyed. 'I have been clear with you these last two months that I am going to Patagonia. I will not be told what I have to do. My life is as important as yours. I'm going back to the nurses' home.'

'I'll walk with you. We need to talk.'

'I don't want your company and I don't need you to escort me anywhere; not to the nurses' home, nor to Patagonia.'

Angharad walked off briskly. Richard followed her, but as he got close, she quickened her pace. He ran in front of her and made her stop. She dodged around him and ran down the road. He wanted to follow her, but not to the south Atlantic.

Angharad got back to her room. Her annoyance with Richard was wearing off, and she could see his face pleading with her to stop and talk to him. She lay face down on her bed and cried. But then she turned over and wiped her eyes with her hands. She looked up at the ceiling and asserted, 'Damn you, Richard Lloyd, I shall go.'

***

In the days that followed their quarrel, Richard and Angharad were both hurting. They passed like strangers in the hospital wards and corridors. On one occasion, Richard did stop to speak to her but Angharad walked by.

In the evenings, James did his best to lift Richard's mood and listened to him trying to resolve his dilemma.

'You've got to make a decision, man, or you'll drive yourself mad,' said James.

'I have made my decision, and I am not going to South America. It's living with the consequences of that decision that's so hard.'

'But you made that decision months ago, and before you realised how much you love Angharad. The facts are different now.'

'You said that I'd be wasting my career and my life if I gave up surgery.'

'Wasting your career, aye, but not your life. Your life is far more important.'

'You are right though. After Elin died, I believed that I would never find love again. I was wrong, and Angharad has brought me love and a new life. I need her love.'

'More than anything else?'

'Yes, I believe so.'

'Even if you spend the next ten years as a builder and working the land in Brazil?'

'Not ten years, but I'd give it five. And it's Argentina, not Brazil.'

There was a light knock on the door and Mrs Robertson entered the room. She told Richard that Jane was downstairs asking to see him. Richard ran down the stairs to see Jane in the hall, clearly agitated and anxious.

'Jane, what are you doing here? Is it Angharad?' asked Richard.

'She isn't well. She hasn't been sleeping or eating properly and has made herself ill. She has gone home to Carrog and will be with her parents now.'

'I must go and see her. I shall go tomorrow morning.'

***

It was mid-afternoon when Richard arrived at the Edwards' farm and spoke to Angharad's mother.

'I heard last night that Angharad wasn't well and had returned home. I'm very worried about her.'

'The poor girl is exhausted. She has been working too hard and not getting enough sleep or food. And, of course, she is very upset that you have argued over

Patagonia. I wish she would see sense about emigrating. It's no place for a young woman.'

There was movement upstairs, and shortly afterwards, Angharad appeared in the kitchen in her nightclothes.

'I thought I heard your voice,' she said with a weak smile, 'but I decided I must have been dreaming. I have had such bad dreams lately. I'm glad that you've come to see me.'

She sat down at the table and her mother poured them both a cup of tea before leaving the two of them to talk.

Richard began. 'I've been very sad, and worried about you after Jane came to see me.'

'I've missed you,' said Angharad, 'and I have been miserable since we quarrelled.'

'I've missed you too. Anyway, I have something to show you.'

Richard took a piece of paper from his pocket and handed it to Angharad. It was a receipt for £1 and she knew immediately what it was, but still could not believe it. She looked at him but couldn't find any words.

Richard spoke instead.

'I reserved my passage this morning and paid my deposit. I shall be sailing with you next month.' He paused. 'You do still want me to come with you?'

Finally, Angharad found her voice.

'Oh yes. Oh, Richard, I love you.' She threw her arms around him and they kissed.

'And I love you too, very much. That brings me onto another matter. Will you marry me, Angharad Edwards?'

'Yes please, Dr Lloyd.' And she kissed him again.

'I had better see your father, then,' said Richard.

Angharad's father was in the cowshed.

'I would like your permission to marry Angharad, Mr Edwards,' said Richard, 'and we plan to settle in Patagonia.'

'Angharad has always been a strong-willed girl,' said her father. 'She knows her mind and is determined to get what she wants. She needs a husband who is not afraid to challenge her wants, but who will also give her what she needs. Otherwise, I fear it will be an unhappy marriage.'

'I respect her strength of character and I recognise the determination that you describe. I love Angharad, and I believe that we will be happy.'

'If anybody can make her happy, then I think it is you, Richard. But to be fair, I felt that I should warn you.' He gave a wry grin. 'As far as Patagonia is concerned, both her mother and I would prefer that she stayed here. But if she has to go, then I should prefer it to be with you than any other man. Look after her.'

'Thank you. I promise that I will look after her,' said Richard.

The two men shook hands, and Mr Edwards invited Richard to stay and have a meal with the family.

The news about Patagonia had a mixed reception. On hearing about Richard's marriage proposal, Angharad's poor mother wrongly assumed that this meant that the couple were staying. She became very upset when she realised their true intentions. On the other hand, Llewelyn was delighted to hear that his sister and Richard would be sailing with them. Mr Edwards declared that Patagonia wouldn't be talked about again that evening.

Soon after, Richard said that he had better go and see his father at Ty Celyn. He went outside with Angharad, and they kissed.

'I cannot believe what has happened today,' she said. 'I woke up sad and miserable, and tonight I am engaged to the best man in the world.'

'I woke up as a respected surgeon and shall go to bed with a receipt for a life in the wilderness. But also for a life with the woman that I love with all my heart.'

***

Richard and his father talked for a couple of hours. The news about his engagement pleased Edward. However, the announcement about their plans to go to Patagonia was not met with enthusiasm. Richard knew that his father would hate the idea but voice no objections. Both men went to their beds with very mixed emotions.

The next day, they went to the station. Edward still had not spoken to Richard about his concerns for Patagonia.

'Your life is yours to live, Richard, but I am your father and I worry about you. Life will be very hard. Is it really what you want?'

Richard thought for a moment or two.

'Not really,' he admitted, 'but I have struggled with this for weeks. I think that I can make a go of it, and Angharad's belief is strong enough for two. In my head, I have told myself to give it five years and if it's not working, then we'll come home. I love Angharad and I want to be with her, and that means Patagonia.'

'So you would rather stay in Liverpool, if Angharad agreed?'

'I would rather have stayed in Berwyn, but yes, I would much prefer to work at the Liverpool Royal Infirmary than go to Patagonia.'

'Look, boy, if you do go but need to return home, just let me or Evan know and we'll arrange a passage for you and Angharad. There will always be a home for you here at Ty Celyn.'

Richard hugged his father and thanked him.

Edward waved goodbye to his son. He was only going to Liverpool today. Very soon, Edward thought, Richard's journey would take him far further.

CHAPTER 40

Less than a week later, grave news brought Richard back to Ty Celyn.

'How is he?' asked Richard.

'Not well,' said Evan.

'It is his heart then?'

'He had pain in his chest after breakfast yesterday and then he collapsed.'

'What did Dr Bevan have to say?'

'He confirmed that it was down to his heart disease. He asked me if Dad had any worries or felt any pressure that might have troubled him.'

'Well, I haven't helped, have I?' said Richard. 'I told him about Patagonia last Friday before going back to Liverpool. I knew that he was worried about it. Has he mentioned Patagonia?'

'Sian said that he talked to her about it.'

'I have brought this on. It's my fault.'

'You know, better than I do, that he had a weakness already from his earlier illness. Dr Bevan said that was the underlying cause.'

'Yes, but my news last weekend caused the pressure that triggered it. Can I see him?'

'He's sleeping. Sian's sitting with him.'

Later, Richard took Sian's place at his father's bedside. The night was long with only periods of light sleep and a lot of time to think. In the darkness, the dilemma of emigration had returned, but it now seemed larger than ever, a matter of life and death.

Just before dawn, Richard made a decision. He could not go to Patagonia and leave his father like this. Angharad could still travel with her brother next month and he would follow on later. He hoped that she would understand.

Richard stayed with his father for two days, during which time Edward became aware of his presence and Richard was able to talk to him. Edward was too weak to talk but he squeezed his son's hand ever so lightly to show he understood. Richard had to return to Liverpool but said that he would be back as soon as work allowed.

***

At the Royal Infirmary, Richard left a note asking Angharad to visit him at his lodgings that evening. She called in at seven o'clock and asked about his father. Richard told her he had improved slightly.

'I am so relieved,' she said. 'I know that it's early days but at least there is hope. And how are you? You must stop blaming yourself for this.'

'I cannot leave Dad at this time, and I know that this will be a big disappointment, but I shall have to sail on a later ship. You must still go as planned. I am so sorry.'

Angharad had anticipated that this would be the likely outcome of Edward's illness. She turned to look out of the window and thought for a few moments before facing Richard. 'I agree that you cannot leave your father. Will there be other ships going to Patagonia?'

'I don't know, but if necessary I'll travel to Buenos Aires and get to Patagonia somehow, across sea or land. I'll come to you, Angharad, however long it takes. I promise.'

'I'd rather that you and I travelled together, but we can discuss that over the next few days. When are you going back to see your father?'

Richard said that he was to return on Friday evening, and Angharad said that she would go with him.

***

On Friday evening, Lime Street Station was extremely busy, and their train was packed. They had to change trains at Ruabon for the last part of the journey to Llangollen. Ruabon station was quiet after the hubbub of Lime Street and the cramped railway carriage. Richard and Angharad sat on a platform bench waiting for the train.

'I have cancelled our marriage in the Liverpool registry office. I want to be married in my chapel in Corwen,' said Angharad.

'But there's no time; the ship sails in three weeks.'

'I'm not going on the ship.'

'Well, it would be good if we could both travel together, at a later date. Are you sure?' asked Richard.

'Yes, but I'm not talking about going at a later date. We shouldn't go to Patagonia at all. Your father's illness has made me think. I have been selfish to you, your family and to my own parents.'

'But your dream?' said Richard.

'You were prepared to let me have my dream, even though it wasn't what you wanted. You were prepared to make big sacrifices for me. I realised how much I really loved you. The dream is not important now. I want reality, and I want you to be my reality. I shall love you anywhere, Richard, and Liverpool will be fine. It doesn't matter as long as we are together.'

Richard had not expected this turn of events but was quietly relieved at Angharad's change of heart. It had been Angharad's decision, and that was what mattered.

'I love you so much, Angharad.' Richard smiled.

'And I love you too. That's why I have come home with you this weekend. We can see your dad together and give him the good news. My parents will be relieved, too, especially Mam. I thought we could ask the minister on Sunday morning when we can be married.'

Richard put his arms around Angharad and kissed her.

***

Angharad's mother and father were delighted that she was not going to Patagonia. Llewelyn was sorry that she would not be joining him, but he was pleased for his mother that Angharad would be staying. Angharad told him that she would be home again in two weeks' time. It would be the last opportunity for the family to be together. The official opening of the new railway was also planned that weekend, and special celebrations were being held in Corwen.

***

Edward's discovery that they were not emigrating marked a turning point in his recovery, and he began to make good progress. As neighbours realised he was getting better, Edward began to receive visitors. Sir Clayton was the latest to call.

'You've had us all worried, Edward. It's good to see that you're on the mend. Evan tells me that Richard has changed his plans regarding Patagonia. That must be a relief.'

'It is a huge weight off my mind. There's another matter that I have been thinking about over the last few days,' said Edward. 'Have you met Merryman's daughter, Myfanwy? She wants to be a teacher.'

'Merryman told me about her. She loves reading, apparently.'

'I have lent her some difficult books and she has coped very well. She is a clever girl. She has an aptitude for teaching and it would be a waste if she went into service. I have an idea that would be good for her and the local children. Bethania Chapel School has a full school roll and a good reputation but has only one teacher and little funds. It would benefit from having an assistant.'

'I can see where this is heading.'

'Well, you donate funds to the church school in the village, so why not make a small annual contribution to Bethania?'

'But I am church like you; why should I give to the chapel?'

'Many of your estate workers and tenant farmers are chapel members, and their children will go to Bethania School. It would be a great gesture to support Bethania and sponsor a talented young girl at the same time.'

'There will be many church members who will object to me doing this, including the vicar. It will no doubt cause trouble.'

'Why tell the vicar? When it gets out, then I'll share the hostility, but it will be a done deed.'

'You are feeling better, Edward Lloyd. Lying in this bed, you've been thinking and plotting. Let's talk to the people at the chapel. If we all think it's a good idea, I'll consider it. You're a crafty old fox.'

CHAPTER 41

Merryman awoke early and had a lot on his mind. Today was the official opening of the Llangollen to Corwen Railway and a big event for the Dee Valley. Every station on the line, including Berwyn, was marking the occasion in some way.

Richard had arranged to meet Angharad in Corwen, where the main celebrations were taking place.

Evan, Elizabeth and Richard stood on Berwyn Station platform, surrounded by flags and bunting, waiting for the special train to Corwen. Children from Bethania sang in front of the stationmaster's house until the approaching locomotive could be seen. There was a loud cheer as it came into the station.

Arriving at Corwen Station, everyone admired the commemorative decorations including an arch erected near the station. Richard eventually spotted Angharad and her parents in the crowd.

They all walked towards the market square. The town had been decorated with flags and banners for the occasion. In the square, a fine pavilion had been erected near the Owain Glyndwr Hotel. Evan and Elizabeth had been invited to the special lunch to be served in the pavilion. They joined the important people associated with the railway company, together with various local dignitaries. Elizabeth and Evan met her father who was talking to William and Sara.

'Well, we've done it, William,' said Sir Clayton. 'We have completed the line, and now it's time to celebrate.'

'Indeed so, but I consider this just another part of the bigger picture,' said William. 'There's still much more to do. I was talking to the chairman a few minutes ago, and we agreed that we need to push on now with the next stage and build the line up to Bala. We've also got to finish the new station for Corwen.'

'You will not rest on your laurels, will you? That's good, but let's take stock of our achievements. What do you make of it all, Sara?'

'I have never seen Corwen look so busy or so pretty as it is today, and let's hope that's a sign of good times for the future.'

'The railway will improve the town and its people's lives for years to come. I expect that it will give you new opportunities too, William,' said Sir Clayton.

'Without doubt,' said William. 'After Bala, let's hope we can press on to Dolgellau and after that, the coast.'

Sir Clayton laughed, but Evan did not appreciate William's hopes for even more business.

***

Richard and Angharad had a pleasant time ambling around Corwen and just enjoying the occasion. He took her into a shop that sold, amongst other things, items of jewellery. Richard asked the shopkeeper if they could see the rings. He brought out a small tray containing a dozen or so different styles and stones.

'I know that you cannot show a ring yet in Liverpool, but if you like one of these, then you can wear it this weekend,' Richard told Angharad.

'Oh, Richard, this one is lovely, can I have it?'

'That style is very popular at the moment,' said the shopkeeper. 'It has a central garnet with six pearls in a flower pattern. The band is gold, of course.'

'I love the red stone.' Angharad looked imploringly at Richard.

He smiled back. 'We'll have it then.'

When they met up with her parents at the Crown for lunch, Angharad showed them the ring with obvious pride and delight.

After lunch, Richard and Angharad walked back to the station. They were both going to Berwyn to see Richard's father. The train was ready to depart, and Richard was hastily looking for a carriage with two empty seats. He looked into the third carriage, and a voice called out.

'Come and join us. There are two seats in here.'

It was Sara, and opposite her was a glowering William. Angharad stepped into the carriage before Richard could react.

'Thank you very much,' said Angharad. 'It's busy, isn't it?'

She sat next to Sara, meaning Richard had to sit beside William. William shuffled sideways to avoid any contact with Richard.

'I saw you at Christmas at Berwyn Hall. I'm sorry, I cannot remember your name,' said Sara to Angharad, though she knew perfectly well what her name was.

'Wasn't it a lovely evening? Angharad is my name.'

'We left the ball early as I wasn't feeling well, but I gather from Elizabeth that it was a success. I am Sara, by the way, and used to be Richard's fiancée, but I expect that you knew that already.'

Angharad smiled. *This could be an interesting little journey*, she thought.

Richard considered getting off at the next station, Carrog, in order to curtail this agonising situation.

'Have you enjoyed the day?' asked William.

'A day to remember,' said Angharad, thinking especially about her engagement ring. She was relieved to be wearing gloves.

'How was lunch at the pavilion?' Richard asked William, trying to steer the conversation into safer territory.

'Too much backslapping from men who made very little contribution to the railway. Yes, it was good to mark the occasion, but some were only there for the wine and self-congratulations.'

'Well, I enjoyed it immensely,' said Sara. 'The lunch was excellent, and Elizabeth and I could have easily talked for another hour. It finished all too quickly for me.'

With the conversation apparently on safer ground, Richard decided not to get off at Carrog. However, almost as soon as the train left Carrog Station, he realised that the respite had been short-lived.

'Are you still just good friends or have things developed since Christmas?' asked Sara.

Richard and Angharad looked at one another. Richard, taken aback at the direct question, said that they were very good friends. Sara saw the look of hesitant concern in his face.

'I don't think that you are telling me the full story. Come on, Angharad, you can tell me, even if Richard is shy.'

'I don't need to tell you, I'll show you,' said Angharad, and she removed her glove and held her hand out.

Sara's complexion was always pale, but her face was now white. She stared at the ring.

Angharad was pleased with the reaction from Sara, who was finally lost for words. William smiled until he realised that Sara was looking at him. Richard wished dearly that they had got out at Carrog.

'We got engaged this morning,' Angharad announced proudly.

By now, two other passengers in the carriage were smiling and congratulating the couple. Angharad smiled broadly and Richard managed a grin.

Eventually, Sara forced herself to offer meaningless congratulations. She put a very brave face on the situation and reached over to hold William's hand.

The carriage went dark as the train entered Berwyn Tunnel. As daylight returned and the train slowed for the station, Richard said that they would be getting out at Berwyn.

The train came to a stop. Sara still said nothing as Richard stood up and opened the carriage door. Richard and Angharad stepped onto the platform. Looking back through the open window, he met Sara's eyes.

'I hope you will find happiness,' he told her.

'I already have,' said Sara, and she took William's hand again.

The train pulled out of Berwyn Station.

'I'm sorry, Richard, if I handled that badly,' said Angharad. 'It all came so naturally, and she really asked for it.'

'Badly?' said Richard. 'You were magnificent, truly wonderful. They were going to find out anyway, so it was better that we told them.'

Richard kissed her.

***

That evening at Plas Gwyn, Sara hadn't come down for dinner. Aunt Grace went upstairs to her niece's room and heard her crying. She entered to see Sara lying on her bed.

'Whatever is the matter?' asked Grace, sitting beside her.

'He is engaged to her, Aunt. They said that they were just good friends – but they lied to me.'

'Richard is engaged?'

'I have lost Richard to that little nurse. He is not mine anymore,' said Sara, catching her breath after each sob.

'Dear little girl, don't cry,' said Grace, stroking her niece's head.

'My Richard now belongs to her.'

'But Sara, listen – your engagement ended nine months ago.'

'I thought that he'd come back to me. The servant girl died; the nurse was only a friend. Richard was always mine.' She threw herself face down on the bed again.

Grace went to get her a glass of water and a little brandy.

CHAPTER 42

On Sunday, Richard returned alone to Falkner Street. Angharad stayed on in Carrog to spend time with her brother. It was the family's last full day together. The following day, the Edwards would travel to Liverpool and prepare for Llewelyn and Mary's departure for Patagonia.

However, Llewelyn's mother did not go with them to Liverpool. She said goodbye to her son at the gate of the farm where he had lived all his life. She could not bear to see the ship taking her boy away. In her mind, he would forever be just down the lane from the farm, where she had last seen him.

***

The *Halton Castle* had been chartered for the journey to Patagonia and was a new iron ship, much safer than many of the older vessels that sailed to South America. However, by the scheduled departure date, the ship had not returned from its previous voyage. At the last minute, the organisers were forced to decide that an alternative vessel needed to be chartered. This left the hopeful emigrants stranded in Liverpool, and having to find temporary accommodation. The clipper *Mimosa*, an ageing wooden cargo ship, was hired; it needed fitting out for passengers, specifically for this voyage.

The further delay caused many people to withdraw from the voyage, and others had to find money or assistance to stay in the port. Fortunately for Llewelyn and Mary Edwards, there was a spare room at Richard's lodgings, and he obtained favourable terms for them from Mrs Robertson. In order to replace those passengers who had returned home, the organisers decided to re-advertise and offer to help those who could not afford the £12 ticket. The advertisement worked and many more potential emigrants came forward.

Michael Daniel Jones, a minister and a college principal in Bala, was the visionary and leading light for the Patagonian settlement. He and his wife Anne financed much of the voyage, including assisting passengers who could not afford their tickets or temporary accommodation in Liverpool.

***

Angharad's father had gone home to wait for a new sailing date and it was a month later when he returned. On the morning of Sunday 28th May 1865, over one hundred and fifty men, women and children, inspired by Michael Jones and persuaded by the offer of land, were aboard *Mimosa* on the River Mersey and awaiting the start of their voyage to Patagonia. Amongst the passengers, all experiencing varying degrees of sadness, apprehension and excitement, were Llewelyn and Mary Edwards.

Many of the passengers' relatives and friends were at Pier Head to wave them goodbye. Angharad, her father and Richard were in the crowd of hundreds of well-wishers to see them off. The prolonged farewell added to the heartache of the deserted relatives, but they still managed to wave and smile. There were few dry eyes, and most believed that they would never see their loved ones again.

The Welsh flag was flown on *Mimosa* and the passengers sang an anthem specially composed for the occasion. The ship's chains jangled and clanged as the anchor was raised.

Richard turned to Angharad and held her. She was crying.

'Are the tears for Llewelyn or a lost opportunity?' he asked.

'I am crying for Llewelyn and Mary, and my poor parents. I pray for a safe journey for our brave heroes on board *Mimosa*.'

***

On the second day of the seven-thousand-mile voyage, *Mimosa*'s passengers and crew encountered a storm with torrential rain and huge waves in the Irish Sea, off the Anglesey coast. Most passengers, including Llewelyn and Mary, had already been seasick from the rough seas experienced since leaving the Mersey. However, this storm was so strong as to cause a lifeboat to come out and offer to rescue the passengers. *Mimosa*'s captain turned down the offer, and fortunately the storm died down and *Mimosa* began to make progress.

There were many families on board and some very young children. On the 10th of June, Llewelyn and Mary attended the funeral of a girl aged two who had died of croup. The grief-stricken parents watched the small, weighted coffin slide off a plank into the sea. Mary tried to console the poor mother, who wept on her shoulder. Later that day, a boy of the same age also died.

The immense sadness on board was soon met by hope when a baby boy was born on the following day. A young doctor had been appointed by Michael Jones as surgeon to the colony, on a twelve months contract.

The child was delivered in a cabin that the doctor used as his makeshift hospital. He had a medicine chest on board to help treat his patients.

On Sunday 25th June, a tropical storm threatened the ship, and during the height of the storm, a second baby was born on board. Two weeks earlier the parents had lost a son. Sadly, the deaths of infants and young children would continue.

After crossing the equator in early July, the ship entered the Doldrums, an area of very calm and hot weather where the sea was still and there was no wind to fill the clipper's sails. The intense heat, humidity and still air made life below deck even more unpleasant. The poorly ventilated space was overcrowded, and stagnant water added to the stench within the passengers' quarters. The sleeping arrangements consisted of closely fitted bunk beds with rough and ready curtains hung between them to try and provide some privacy. There were only four privies for more than one hundred and fifty passengers, and many suffered from diarrhoea and constipation due to the poor diet. On deck, passenger space was limited and the heat was overpowering. Drinking water became more restricted due to the lack of rain. Even Llewelyn, who had been one of the most fervent of the emigrants, began to wonder whether he had made the right decision. Life on the farm at Carrog seemed idyllic compared to the conditions on *Mimosa*. He reminded himself that the farm would be lost when his father died, and that Patagonia was his only option if he wanted to have his own farm. He had to persevere and remain strong for Mary.

Another storm erupted in mid-July and continued for three days. The passengers were sent below deck and the hatches were closed. Seawater washed over the deck and flowed through the gaps around the hatches, soaking the passengers below. Mountainous waves battered the sailing ship's hull and threatened the lives on board. The creaking of the timbers and the roar of the sea was a fearful sound. Llewelyn held Mary tight, and they were not the only passengers wondering if this was one storm too many for the old ship. At last, the sea became calmer and *Mimosa* could sail south again.

On the morning of Wednesday 26th July, land was spotted, and the passengers were relieved and excited that the long and hard voyage was finally nearing its end. In the evening, the ship entered New Bay, where eventually it would put down anchor. The following day, two men, who were already in New Bay to prepare for the arrival of the settlers, boarded the ship. They had been sent ahead by the organisers to build temporary shelters and organise supplies. They told the passengers that there was lots of work to be done in building houses, erecting fences and clearing the land. The enthusiasm grew and Llewelyn couldn't wait to get started.

Later in the day, the first group of men left *Mimosa* in a rowing boat. Llewelyn was amongst them and keen to reach shore. Another of the eager young men could not wait for the boat to land and jumped into the water to be the first to stand on Patagonian land. He fell to his knees, kissed the beach, and wept.

***

On 28th July, the main group of passengers, including Mary Edwards, came ashore at New Bay, or Porth Madryn as it was later named. There was a cold, sleety wind, and the crude huts offered little protection and shelter. The sixteen huts were unroofed and consisted of wooden planks forced into the ground. Each hut would accommodate about eight people, but any cooking and washing had to take place on the beach. The water in the new well, near the huts, was found to be brackish, and the only other source of water was in ponds of rainwater some three miles away. The excitement of arriving in their new homeland soon turned to disappointment and despondency. Decisions had to be made quickly.

Mimosa remained anchored in New Bay, and it was agreed that women with young children would return to the ship for shelter. The huts would be roofed with timber from the ship's bunks. Additional sleeping accommodation would also be created in the long shed that stored the settlement's provisions of salt meat, flour, potatoes and seeds for planting. The passengers' furniture and belongings from the ship's hold were taken ashore in the rowing boats and placed on the beach. As well as furniture, farming implements and tools, there were other personal items including a harmonium or pedal organ.

The landing site on the beach at New Bay was only a temporary arrangement, and the new settlement was to be built in the Chubut River valley, some forty miles to the south. Small groups went ahead to explore and plan the route through the barren, flat land of low, stunted bushes. Llewelyn joined one group that lost its way in the disorientating landscape. He wondered when he was going to find the splendid expanses of green forest and rich pastures that had been promised in the booklet he had been given in Wales. The group eventually made it back to the beach tired, hungry and very thirsty.

The settlers were at New Bay for several harsh weeks. The cold weather and lack of clean water contributed to the deaths of several more children. It was decided to move to the river location as soon as possible and establish the permanent settlement in the Chubut Valley. Before they left New Bay, they saw the departure of *Mimosa* and the last link with their old lives and homeland.

And so, Angharad's heroes, the men, women and children to whom she waved farewell at Liverpool's Pier Head, set off from the beach and trekked the forty miles to their promised land. Llewelyn's and Mary's new lives were about to begin.

CHAPTER 43

In early June, just one week after *Mimosa* had sailed from Liverpool, Mrs Robertson had a visitor in her parlour at Falkner Street. She heard Richard arrive back from the hospital and went to meet him in the hall. She told him that a young woman wanted to see him. She had not given her name but had said that she was an old friend. He was not expecting anyone but followed Mrs Robertson into the parlour.

Richard saw the back of a young woman and recognised her blonde hair instantly.

'Sara, what brings you here?' he asked.

Sara turned around to face him. She looked serious.

'I have some news for you. Can we talk privately?'

In the sitting room upstairs, Richard asked her about the reason for her visit and her news.

'I still love you. I had to tell you before you marry the nurse.'

'But William loves you, and you love him, don't you?'

'I love you more than William.'

'I thought that we had both moved on; you with William and me with Angharad.' Richard tried to make sense of the situation.

Sara grasped his hands.

'I know you want me,' she whispered.

Richard pulled away. 'That's all in the past.'

'But that is why I am here. It's not in the past and it's not too late to get back what we had. I must go now, but I'll come and see you again tomorrow. When will you be home?'

'I shall be home by six o'clock but—'

Sara put her finger against his lips. 'Don't say anything more. Think about what I have said. You and I have the same destiny. I really must go now. I promised my friend I'd be back by seven. Will you see me to the door?'

On the way out, Richard and Sara met James Morton on the stairs.

'It's good to see you, Sara,' said James.

'And you, James. I can't stop, but there will be future opportunities to talk.'

When Richard returned to the sitting room, James asked about Sara's visit.

'She still wants us to get back together,' Richard told him. 'She's coming back tomorrow evening for my decision.'

'But you are marrying Angharad. Why didn't you tell her?'

'She already knows; the wedding was the reason for her visit.'

'Oh God, I'm sorry. She wrote to me two weeks ago. In my reply, I told her that you were getting married in August. I have caused this.'

'Why didn't you tell me that she had written?'

'She told me not to tell you. I'm glad now that this is in the open because I have another confession to make. Sara wrote to me in London last September saying that your practice was in trouble and that you needed to return to hospital surgery. I had just moved to Liverpool but the letter was forwarded. That was when I wrote to you saying I should like to see you. Again, she was insistent that I mustn't tell you that she had written.'

'Her intention, yet again, was to get me to move to London.'

'I apologise, Richard.'

Richard sighed. 'You were not to know her devious ways.'

***

The next evening, Richard came home before six o'clock but heard the clock chime the hour, the quarter and the half hour, without any sign of Sara. Then he heard a cab draw up in the street. Sara got out and Richard went down to meet her. Sara stepped into the hall, turned to him and kissed him firmly on the lips. He followed her up the stairs to the sitting room.

'Well, Richard, are we to share our future together? You know my feelings. I still want you. There is just one simple question: do you want me?'

'A year ago the answer would have been yes, but now—'

Sara interrupted him, 'There had better not be any buts. I was kind to you last night by giving you twenty-four hours to think about it. I warn you that this is your last chance to get me back.'

'I told you last night that our love was in the past. I'm sorry.'

Sara laughed, but it was a forced, false laugh.

'Don't be sorry for me,' she said. 'I have enjoyed the fun. You didn't think that I was really going to leave William for you? He is twice the man that you are. Remember me in your dreams because you'll never again have a woman like me. I was hoping that you would say that you still wanted me. I was then going to reject you, just like you rejected me last July.'

Richard stepped back to regain some space and gather his composure. He ignored her gibes.

'You were just playing games then? You're better than that.'

'I am very good at playing games. Do you remember the lawyer, John Probert, who defended the workhouse nurse in court? Guess who instructed him. Guess who told him to turn the blame for the overdose on to you. Guess who paid his fee. He was worth every penny. Samuel Vaughan had told William and me, over dinner, about the forthcoming trial of the workhouse nurse and the confusion over the morphine dose.'

'You? I thought it must have been William.'

'No, it was me. After I made sure that the case had caused you public and professional damage, I then told William to use his friendship with Vaughan to have you dismissed from the workhouse.'

'You must have despised me,' said Richard.

'Not really. My true motive was to get you back into my life. Once your pathetic little country practice had been ruined, then you would have no alternative but to accept that surgeon's job in London and we could be married.'

'Dear God, Elin said that yours was a strange, twisted love, but we didn't know the half of it. Go home and spend your life with William. You deserve one another. Go now, before I throw you down the stairs. Get out. Get out!'

Sara moved away briskly. She had never seen Richard so angry. At a safe distance, she turned to look at him before she left the room.

'Enjoy your life with your plain little nurse.'

Richard said no more. He heard her go quickly down the stairs. He heard the front door shut. He watched her from the window as she hailed a cab, and then she was gone.

***

At the nurses' home a week later, Angharad received a letter.

My dear Angharad,

I write to you as one woman to another, and where both of us have known Richard Lloyd as a fiancée. I wish to save you from the pain and heartache that I experienced when Richard left me for someone else. I must warn you that he is not a trustworthy man.

I have recently spent two days in Liverpool visiting a friend and saw Richard at Falkner Street on both of these days. He was of course the perfect gentleman, except that he tried to persuade me to renew our love, and on my second visit, he asked me again to marry him. Whilst sorely tempted by him, I can assure you that, although we kissed passionately, nothing more happened. I love William now and would not jeopardise what we have together.

I hope that you trust my genuine wish to prevent you the hurt that Richard inflicted on me. If you have any doubts as to the honesty of my news then please do talk to James Morton or Mrs Robertson, who will be able to confirm my visits to him last week.

Yours with concern and affection,

Sara Griffiths-Ellis

Angharad did have severe doubts as to the honesty of Sara's letter, but she also had serious concerns as to why Richard hadn't mentioned Sara's visits to him last week. Before she reported on the ward, Angharad went to find Richard. She found him preparing for theatre.

'I need to speak with you now.' She gave him the letter.

He read it with a frown. 'This is poisonous nonsense. I can't believe that she would stoop to such vindictive lies.'

'Oh, I can,' said Angharad. 'And it's not all lies, is it? She did visit you last week, didn't she?

'Well, yes, but it wasn't as she describes.'

'I hope not, but why didn't you tell me about her visits?'

'Because it was of no consequence and would only hurt you.'

'But it does matter because Sara is determined to prevent our marriage; can't you see that?'

'Of course, I know that. It was the sole purpose of her visit.'

'And did you kiss passionately?'

'No, but she kissed me when we met. I know it's all very hurtful, and that's why I didn't tell you. You believe me, don't you?'

'I want to believe you. You should have told me because I think that you have a big problem with Sara. Actually, we've both got a big problem with her. She is dangerous.'

Richard was called into theatre. Angharad said that they would talk again that evening.

She went to the ward and told the sister that she had been up all night with sickness. Sister told her to go back to the nurses' home and get to bed. Angharad went back to her little bedroom and changed out of her nurse's uniform into her Sunday best. Minutes later she was approaching Lime Street Station.

***

Angharad arrived in Llangollen around noon. There were a couple of carriers waiting at the station.

'Can you take me to Plas Gwyn, please?' asked Angharad.

The carrier helped her up.

Within ten minutes, the cart pulled up outside Plas Gwyn. Angharad went to the front door and tapped the brass knocker. A maid came to the door.

'I wish to see Miss Sara, please,' said Angharad.

'I am sorry but Miss Sara is out for the day. Was she expecting you? Could I have your name, please?'

'No, I don't have an appointment. I'm Angharad Edwards. Sara knows me well.'

Grace was in the hall and heard Angharad imply that Sara was a friend.

She went to the door. 'Can I help? I am Sara's aunt. It is a pity that she isn't home. Have you come far to see her?'

'I have come from Liverpool this morning by train,' said Angharad.

'Come in, my dear. Sara would want you to have some refreshment after travelling so far.'

Grace asked for some tea to be brought in. She asked Angharad how she knew Sara.

'I feel that I should be straight with you,' Angharad said. 'I am to be married to Richard Lloyd. He is my connection to Sara.' She shuffled in her chair, unsure as to what would happen next.

Grace liked Angharad's honesty, and she was intrigued to meet the girl who had captured Richard's heart.

'Stay and have some tea at the very least. I always liked Richard and was sorry when he and Sara ended their engagement. She was very hurt when they separated. I know, of course, that you had nothing to do with their separation.'

'I think that she is still hurting. I'm worried about her.'

Angharad told Grace about Sara's visits to Richard last week, and the letter that she had received that morning.

'Oh, poor girl, poor silly girl,' said Grace. 'And I thought that she was getting better now. She suffered with melancholy when Richard ended their engagement. For weeks I sat with her saying that things would improve. Very slowly, she seemed to be getting over Richard.'

'I expect her relationship with William helped too.'

Grace looked confused. 'You mean as cousins?'

'Well, it's more than that, isn't it?' said Angharad. 'According to Sara, they love one another. In her letter, Sara says that she loves William.'

Grace asked if she had Sara's letter and Angharad passed it to her. Grace read it and looked seriously at Angharad.

'William always had a fascination with Sara. I suppose he's infatuated with her. But I do know that Sara does not love William. She was only interested in Richard and it would seem that has not changed. I have probably said more than I should, but Richard and you do need to understand about William and Sara. You must not tell anyone about this.'

Angharad said that they would, of course, respect her confidence.

'William has had a fond regard for Sara since they were children and it has never gone away,' Grace explained. 'Sara never felt the same for him, but she used his weakness for her to get what she wanted. As children it was a fairly harmless game, but when they grew up… well, the games continued.'

'So if Sara does not love William, she either wants to get Richard back or just break us up as a punishment,' said Angharad, trying to understand the situation.

'Sara can be vindictive, but I think that she is making one last attempt to get Richard back. The visits and the letter are part of that. Now drink your tea, dear, before it gets cold.'

'You have been so kind to me. I needed to know what was going on, so that Richard and I can start married life without secrets and doubts.'

'You have been brave to come here this afternoon. It is useful for me too, as I can talk to Sara about her problems and hopefully help her.'

'Will you speak to William about any of this?'

'There is no point. It will upset him and make him angry. The best thing that I can do is take Sara to my sister's house in London for a few months. I need to get her away from both Richard and William. So, if I were you, I should avoid London for your honeymoon.'

They both laughed and Grace offered Angharad a carriage back to the station.

'No, thank you, I shall walk. It's a lovely day now,' said Angharad. She gave Grace a kiss on the cheek and set off down the long drive.

***

Back in Liverpool that evening, Angharad called to see Richard.

'I've been to Plas Gwyn,' she said.

'What! I'd have come with you. You should have told me.'

'You didn't tell me that Sara had visited you, did you? Anyway, the letter was sent to me. It was for me to sort out with her.'

'You've seen Sara?' asked Richard.

'Sara and William were not at home. At first I thought that it had been a wasted journey, but Grace invited me in. She was lovely and couldn't have been more helpful, but she told me everything in strictest confidence. This is just for you and me to know.'

Angharad told Richard about Grace's revelations concerning William and Sara.

'I had realised that William loved Sara,' said Richard, 'although I hadn't thought that it went all the way back to a childhood obsession. But I had no idea that Sara's apparent love for William was a complete fabrication, a lie, presumably to try and hurt me and make me jealous?'

'Yes, and to make you go back to her. However, it was William who was hurting. His love for Sara was not returned and she scorned him. He knew that she had always loved you, and that she still did.'

'No wonder he hates me,' said Richard.

'Now you know the truth. William and Sara are very sad people.'

'You have been wonderful today.'

'And so has Grace, but you must remember my promise to her. This is our secret.'

CHAPTER 44

Edward set foot on the platform at Berwyn station with a tremendous sense of achievement. Six weeks earlier he had been confined to bed, and today he'd walked from Ty Celyn with Sir Clayton. He had conquered the old chain bridge over the river, and then the steep path up the riverbank to the station. He felt as if he'd climbed Snowdon itself.

En route, Sir Clayton had told him about his conversation with the minister and the teacher at Bethania, who both had warmly welcomed the idea of a teaching assistant. The teacher had told him about the increase in pupil numbers in recent years and had said that it was difficult to give both the younger and older children, the attention they needed.

Merryman welcomed his visitors and asked after Edward's health. Sir Clayton explained their proposal for Myfanwy.

'You have done all this for our little girl?' said Merryman. 'Nobody has ever been so kind to our family. I don't know what to say.'

Myfanwy was called down from her bedroom.

'I've almost finished the last book you lent me and shall return it by the end of the week,' she told Edward.

'There's no rush, and we have called about a different matter,' he said. 'Sir Clayton has a job for you to consider.'

'Thank you, sir, I do need to get a job this summer.' She looked at Sir Clayton, expecting an offer of a maid's job at Berwyn Hall.

'You don't know what it is yet,' said Sir Clayton.

'I'd be grateful for any job, sir.'

'Well, Myfanwy, you are clearly a very special young girl. Everyone is impressed with your learning, your success at school and your ambitions for the future. Mr Lloyd and I think that you deserve some encouragement. The teacher at Bethania, Miss Davies, needs an assistant, and she wants to meet you and see whether you could work together. She is an excellent teacher, and you'll learn a lot from her.'

Myfanwy ran to Sir Clayton and hugged him.

'Thank you, thank you! This is everything that I've hoped for.'

'You deserve it. I think Mr Lloyd should have a hug too. This was all his idea.'

Myfanwy duly obliged and then gave her Mam and Dad a big hug as well. There were tears in Merryman's eyes.

When Edward arrived back at Ty Celyn, Evan and Owen were in the yard. Evan came over and asked his father how the day had been.

'Very well. You should know that your father-in-law is a very generous man.'

'He can afford to be; he's a very wealthy man.'

'That's not the point, Evan. There are many wealthy men, many much wealthier than Clayton, who would not have done what he did today. Clayton is generous in spirit and in heart.'

***

Angharad had completed her year's training as a probationer. Four other nurses, including Jane, had started their training around the same time, and they were all due to receive their certificates as qualified Nightingale nurses. They had assembled in the boardroom of the Royal Infirmary.

'Nurse Angharad Edwards,' called out the superintendent, and Angharad walked forward and gratefully accepted her certificate.

Later, at Falkner Street, Angharad showed Richard her award.

'I can't wait for Mam and Dad to see it,' she said. 'They'll be so proud.'

'We can make our engagement public now,' said Richard.

'Yes, but first I need to talk to the superintendent about my job. I shan't be allowed to work in the hospital when we're married. If they'll let me, I'd like to nurse in the district and visit patients in their homes.'

'I think that's a very good idea,' said Richard. 'You will make an excellent district nurse.'

'And then we need to think about where we're going to live when we are married,' Angharad continued. 'I noticed that there is a nice house for sale here on Falkner Street. It's similar to this one. Could we afford to buy it?'

'In time, yes, but we can't afford it now. It will have to be a small rented house to start with.'

'We only need a small house for now anyway,' said Angharad.

Richard could see that she was disappointed. He had seen the house go up for sale, too, and in an ideal world it would have been perfect. However, his personal finances had not yet recovered from the problems he had faced in Berwyn last year.

***

Angharad went to see the superintendent about her future at the Royal Infirmary. She dreaded having to tell her that she was engaged to Richard.

'I assume that you were walking out with Dr Lloyd while you were still a probationer, Nurse Edwards?' said the superintendent. 'You do realise that was against the rules.'

'Yes miss, and I am sorry. Dr Lloyd and I are both from the same part of North Wales and we knew one another before he came to the Royal Infirmary. We saw one another at chapel first and then just as acquaintances. It is only recently that we became more than that.'

'Even so, rules are rules, and nurses are expected to abide by them. I, therefore, find it strange that you are now asking the hospital to bend the rules again so that you may continue working as a nurse.'

'I fully understand that I can't stay working in the hospital as Richard – sorry, Dr Lloyd, will be on the wards, but I thought that working outside as a district nurse might be acceptable,' said Angharad.

'You are quite correct that working on the wards is out of the question. Furthermore, I am minded to apply the rules quite rigidly.'

The superintendent paused for a few moments to consider Angharad's misdemeanour. The moments seemed like hours to Angharad. Surely this couldn't be the end of her nursing career before it had barely started. Finally, the superintendent spoke.

'The assistant superintendents speak very highly of your work as a probationer, and the sisters also have provided good reports on your nursing. It would be a great loss if you couldn't carry on nursing. I am therefore prepared to recommend that you may become a district nurse.'

'Thank you very much,' said Angharad.

***

Later in the same week, Richard told the head of surgery, Basil Fortescue, that he was engaged to Angharad. While Angharad had faced an inquisition for having the audacity to fall in love with a doctor, Richard's experience with his boss was a little different.

'You old dog, Lloyd. You kept that one secret, didn't you?'

'Only for Angharad's sake, sir, in order for her to keep her job,' said Richard.

'Yes, of course, and we'll have to celebrate one evening. I suppose that I should be ticking you off for chasing a nurse. Pretty girl with a pretty name; well done, Richard, and I hope that you'll both be very happy.'

CHAPTER 45

Two days before their wedding, Richard and Angharad travelled home from Liverpool together. Richard kissed her as he left the train at Berwyn. Angharad's father would meet her at Carrog Station in twenty minutes' time.

'I'll see you on Saturday then,' said Richard, talking to her through the open carriage window.

'I hope so. Seion Chapel, remember, at midday.'

Richard laughed, and waved to Angharad as the train pulled out of the station.

***

That evening, Richard had invited William to join him at The Hand for a meal. The invitation had irritated William because he didn't want to go but felt obliged to accept. William had a meeting later that evening at the Pentrefelin slate works.

Richard had ordered a bottle of wine and sat waiting for his guest. William arrived and a waitress showed him to the table. Richard stood up and offered his hand, but William ignored the gesture and sat down.

'What is this all about then?' he asked.

Richard poured him a glass of wine.

'I'm marrying Angharad on Saturday. It's the start of a new era and I should like to end the old one with a truce. We know that we shall never be friends, but we don't have to be declared enemies until the day we die. Now I'm in Liverpool, our paths should not cross that often, but when they do, let's be civil to one another. Let's end our painful war.'

'But you have missed the point, as usual. The war has already ended and I won. I have beaten you. My estate continues to grow and thrive. I have significant shareholdings in the railway, the iron works and now the slate works. I control as much business as any man in the Dee Valley and I'm not finished yet. But crucially, I have driven you out of this valley. I do not need a truce because you have been defeated.'

'I left the valley for an excellent position in a top hospital. Perhaps truce is the wrong word, but you must know what I'm suggesting. Let's raise a glass to the future and an end to our animosity.' Richard raised his wine glass.

William stood up and glared at Richard, his cheeks flushing. He flicked the back of his hand against his full wine glass and knocked it over and across the table towards Richard. William turned and stormed out of The Hand.

The waitress came over, wiped the table and changed the cloth.

'I do apologise but I shall not be dining after all,' Richard told her. 'My guest didn't seem to like the wine.'

They both laughed.

Richard drank his glass of wine. He had tried his best to end the feud with William and could do no more.

***

Richard had arranged to call on Dr Bevan that evening and went to his house in Abbey Road. He apologised for being early, but Bevan welcomed him and thanked him for coming. One of Richard's former patients had developed unusual symptoms, and Bevan wanted his opinion on the case and any relevant history. Bevan had written to him a few days ago, and Richard had offered to call and discuss the case in person. He was also keen to know how his former patients were faring.

'I saw Jac and Ann Thomas yesterday at Ty tan y Berllan,' Bevan told him, 'and they asked me to give you these jars of jam made from your fruit bushes. Mrs Thomas is doing well, all things considered.'

***

About a mile away at Pentrefelin, William was discussing business with the manager of the slate works. As night fell, two men forced a window open at the other end of the building. Neither William nor the manager heard them.

The thinner of the two men climbed through the opening followed by the other, who first passed a bag to his brother. Jed looked at Will and gestured the way without speaking. The next room was a store, and at the far end was a strongroom where the cash was held. Tomorrow was payday for the entire quarry and the slate mill.

Jed looked at the strongroom door and saw gaps between the frame and the wall. There were also air vents at the top of the wall. He rammed blasting powder into the larger gaps.

Jed froze as he heard William talking to the manager in the adjoining room. Will heard it, too.

'I thought the place was supposed to be empty,' he whispered.

'It usually is by now,' said Jed. 'This job has to be done tonight. I'm going to put powder in the air holes as well, just to make sure. There'll be no second chance.'

Jed lit five fuses and they took cover. It seemed an eternity but then, one after another, the explosions went off. Jed counted them and, after the last had blown, went back to see the result. The door to the strongroom had been blown off, but so had the top half of the wall, causing part of the ceiling to collapse. The wall had fallen into the adjoining office where William had been working.

The brothers gathered up the money, stuffed it into the bag and got out of the building as quickly as possible. There was no response from the adjoining office, but they didn't stick around to discover the extent of the damage.

A slate worker who lived nearby heard the explosions and ran to the slate works with his two sons. He found the works manager dazed and bloodied but conscious. William, who had been sitting next to the wall, was partially buried under the rubble and the collapsed ceiling. There was no movement from him. The worker told his eldest boy to get Dr Bevan. Together with his other son, he started to remove the debris off William, well aware that further material could drop at any time.

Dr Bevan and Richard hastily got Bevan's carriage ready and drove over to Pentrefelin. A few more neighbours had arrived at the works and were removing rubble.

Richard went to examine the works manager, who had some bad cuts. Dr Bevan, meanwhile, attended to William. Some of the rubble had been removed, although a ceiling joist kept him pinned to the floor. Bevan was examining the injuries.

'Richard, come over here, this fellow has a few problems.'

'It's William,' said Richard. 'William Griffiths-Ellis of Plas Gwyn. I was with him only two hours ago.'

On hearing his name, William regained consciousness for a few seconds and stared at Richard. He showed no recognition and drifted off again.

'He's losing blood and has several fractures, but it's that cut in his leg that I am most worried about,' said Bevan. 'We have to stem the blood loss, but that joist is in the way.'

One of the men who had helped remove the rubble warned that the joist was the only thing stopping the rest of the wall from falling onto William. Richard asked him to go into the strongroom and take down the wall, brick by brick. Two others went to help.

Richard positioned himself so that he would shield William from any further falling bricks and could also get to his leg to clean and stitch the wounds. He was working only inches from the wall where the men were removing the bricks.

After twenty minutes or so, Richard had completed work on the leg and it was safe to remove the joist and finally free William. Dr Bevan had spotted a flat wagon in the yard that was used to move the slate.

'Can someone bring a horse to pull that wagon to my house? The patient needs to be kept flat on his back. Richard, can you ride with him on the wagon and keep him steady while I take the carriage back?'

Richard sat with William on the back of the slate wagon as one of the men drove the horse carefully to Dr Bevan's surgery. William remained unconscious throughout the one-mile journey and Richard pondered the strangeness of their situation.

'Well, William,' he said. 'Who'd have thought the evening would have ended like this? Me holding you, while you're flat out on a slate wagon.'

William was taken to the back room at Bevan's surgery. It was the same room where Elin had died last October.

The two doctors worked together on their unconscious patient.

'If you hadn't sorted out his leg at Pentrefelin and stopped the bleeding, he wouldn't be with us,' Bevan told Richard. 'Even so, I fear that it is God's will as to whether he sees another day. Is he a religious man?'

'He attends Saint Collen's church most Sundays, but I don't think he has paid much attention to Christ's teachings,' said Richard.

'Well, it's all a matter of time now. We've done what we can for him. I'll sit with him, and you go home.'

'I asked one of the boys back at Pentrefelin to take a message to my father that I shall not be home till late and not to wait up. You get to bed – you'll have a busy day attending to William tomorrow.'

Richard sat at the patient's bedside. After a couple of hours, he fell asleep. In his dream he saw Elin in the bed and not William. She opened her eyes and smiled at him. She spoke.

'I told you to start again and I am so glad that you have. Be happy, Richard.'

Richard awoke with a start and felt very cold in the dark room. He turned up the lamp and shivered. He checked his patient, and William's leg had started bleeding again. Richard attended to the wound and renewed the bandages.

'Thank you, Elin,' he said.

CHAPTER 46

The wedding day had finally arrived: Saturday August 5th, 1865.

Richard had gone out for a stroll before breakfast to get some early morning air. He remembered bygone walks as a child with his grandfather, when Taid would tell him to take in the fresh country air, as he was the first person that day to breathe it. He had sometimes thought about Taid's words as he walked to the hospital each morning along the black city streets, under the smoky Liverpool sky.

Richard stood for a few moments at the Horseshoe Falls, watching the river cascading white water into Telford's weir, and wondering what the day ahead might bring. He decided that as long as Angharad turned up at the chapel, then he would be happy.

He was met by Sian on his return to Ty Celyn and quickly realised that the day ahead might not be so straightforward.

'Your father is not well; he's had a bad night.'

Richard rushed up the stairs to his father's bedroom. Edward told him that he was fine, but Richard was clearly concerned. His father was complaining of chest pains, and Richard feared it was the heart condition again.

'I'm not missing your wedding, Richard.'

'Just rest now and we'll see how you are in an hour.'

Evan, the best man, arrived to hear the news about their father.

'Dad can't walk with us to Berwyn Station as planned. He'll have to go to the wedding with the Davenports in their carriage.'

'That's assuming that he's fit to travel,' said Richard.

'If Dad is forced to miss your wedding, his heart will not cope. He'll be fine in the Davenport's carriage. It will be door-to-door service.'

Evan asked Owen to go to Ty Mawr and tell Elizabeth that the carriage should call for his father.

***

It had been Evan's idea to go by train to the wedding. He had tipped off Merryman that the 10:42 on Saturday would be 'the wedding special' with the groom, best man and some guests all catching the train at Berwyn Station. As Richard arrived at the station, he saw that a homemade banner had been draped on the platform wall with the message 'Good luck to Dr and Mrs Lloyd.'

Merryman, Mary and their boys gave Richard a round of applause, and Sian and Owen joined in. Myfanwy presented him with a small posy of wildflowers for Angharad. Merryman shook Richard's hand vigorously and wished him good luck. When the train came to a halt at the station, several familiar faces appeared at the carriage windows. James, Jane and other guests from Liverpool waved and shouted their best wishes to Richard.

***

The wedding party arrived at Corwen Station at ten past eleven. A few minutes later, Richard and Evan met the minister at Seion Chapel, and then the brothers stood talking outside.

'I had a letter from Sara's Aunt Grace, yesterday,' said Richard. 'She wished Angharad and me good luck for our wedding and in the future.'

'I don't expect you had any good luck wishes from Sara or William though.'

'Sara is in London for a few weeks with Grace. Yesterday afternoon, William was still fighting for his life in Dr Bevan's surgery.'

After a couple of minutes, a short, shabbily dressed woman came down the chapel path towards them. Richard recognised the workhouse uniform and realised that it was Ann Jones.

'Dr Lloyd, can I talk to you, please?' Ann was hesitant and looked down at the ground.

Evan went back into the chapel.

'Of course, Ann,' said Richard. 'The service isn't for another half hour yet.'

'I need to tell you that I am sorry. I am sorry that I lied about the medicine. You always told me the correct dose and I made the mistake. I never thought that you would get into trouble and lose your job. I thought that they would hang me. I was frightened, Dr Lloyd, please forgive me.'

'I cannot forgive you, Ann, because there's nothing to forgive. You didn't cause me to lose my job. There were other people who made that happen and were determined to make me suffer. One of them paid for your lawyer so that he could accuse me of malpractice and damage my reputation. You have nothing to be sorry for. Life is strange. If I hadn't lost the job and sold my practice, I wouldn't have gone to Liverpool and fallen in love with Angharad. I wouldn't be here now, about to make her my wife.'

'You are a good man. I wish you and your wife every happiness, today and always,' said Ann.

She reached into her pocket and took out a wooden love spoon. 'My late husband made it for me, many years ago, and told me that he loved me. Please have it, and I hope it brings you and your wife love and good luck.'

Richard thanked her, and Ann turned around and walked back down the path to the road. He wiped a tear from his eye as he watched her turn left for the workhouse.

'Who was that?' asked Evan as his brother came back into the chapel. 'And why the love spoon?'

'That was Ann Jones, the workhouse nurse who gave the wrong dose to a patient. Ann wanted to say sorry, and she gave me the love spoon to bring us luck on our wedding day. Her husband made it as a gift of his love for her. You know, it could well be her last possession. I doubt that any of the other wedding gifts today could be as meaningful or poignant as that old wooden spoon.'

Richard and Evan had taken their places at the front of the chapel. Edward sat behind them, having had a very comfortable journey in the Davenports' affluently upholstered and well-sprung carriage. He was feeling much better.

Angharad and her father had arrived at the chapel. Richard looked round to see Angharad smiling at everyone. She was beautiful. He noticed that she carried Myfanwy's little posy of wildflowers with her bouquet.

Richard and Angharad stood in front of the minister, who said a few kind words to the couple, and then the marriage ceremony took place. At the end, the minister confirmed that they were now married. Richard kissed Angharad, and they gave the broadest of smiles to each other and to the congregation.

***

Arriving at the Owain Glyndwr Hotel, Richard and Angharad couldn't resist looking into the room where a year last May, they had talked about Florence Nightingale and nursing, over lunch on market day.

The guests had made the short walk from the chapel to the hotel, and Angharad and Richard welcomed them to the wedding breakfast. Dr Bevan congratulated the couple and wished them well.

'How is William?' asked Richard.

'He regained consciousness during the night and is making slow progress. I told him that you saved his life and that he would have bled to death if it hadn't been for your swift actions at the slate works. This morning, before I came here, he asked for a pen and paper.'

Bevan gave Richard a folded sheet of paper. Richard opened it and read the shaky writing: *'You have your truce, W.'*

Richard laughed. 'He nearly dies and he still can't say thank you, but I suppose it's a start.'

'His own physician is with him now examining the bone fractures, and he'll arrange for a nurse to be employed at his home for the next few weeks,' said Dr Bevan. 'It's going to be a long recovery period.'

'Grace and Sara have chosen the right time to go to London,' said Richard. 'He'll be like a bear with a sore head.'

After the meal came the speeches. Richard's was reflective.

'I have a lot of people to thank for this happy day and the start of a wonderful life with Angharad. But there was perhaps one person above all, who was instrumental in getting me here today.'

'The train driver?' quipped Evan, to a polite sound of laughter.

'Well, he was very important too,' said Richard. 'No, if it was not for my very good friend and colleague, James, this day would not have happened. Most of you know that in the recent past, I've suffered some unhappy times. In the midst of those bad times, James not only told me to start again, but he showed me the path to do just that. I didn't want to lose Berwyn, my family, my friends and patients, and I had dug my heels in. But thanks to James, I did return to surgery and joined him at the Liverpool Royal Infirmary. And guess who I found working at the hospital?'

'Florence Nightingale?' shouted Evan, this time to real laughter.

'Well, close enough. She has recently qualified as a Nightingale nurse. My *cariad*, my love, Angharad.'

'Come on,' said Angharad, 'or I shall be crying in a minute. Let's open the presents that all of you have been so kind to give us.'

Richard watched while Angharad opened the first parcel, containing bed linen. The guests were either engrossed in the present opening or otherwise talking amongst themselves. Richard noticed a small, brown paper parcel that was untidily wrapped and tied with string. He picked it up, stepped away from any onlookers and removed the string. Looking inside, he saw several wads of bank notes. Richard took out a separate piece of paper and read what was written:

Doctor Lloyd

We shall never forget what you did for our mother. You must now accept our present for you and your wife.

Jed and Will James

Richard was astonished, but after he put the small package in the inside pocket of his jacket, he could not help but smile to himself.

A few minutes later when Angharad had finished opening the presents, she came over to Richard and asked him what was in the brown parcel.

'I'll tell you later when we're on our own, but you know that house for sale in Falkner Street? We'll go and see it on Monday. If you like it, then we'll buy it. Our first home.'

'I love you, Richard.'

'And I love you, too, *cariad.*'

THE END

Glossary

An English translation of some words in the story:

Bara brith: currant bread (literally translated: speckled bread)
Caban un nos: a simple dwelling that was erected in one night (literally translated: one night cabin)
Cariad: love, lover or sweetheart
Castell: castle
Diolch yn fawr: thank you very much
Duw: God (pronounced 'dew')
Hiraeth: a deep longing or nostalgia for something
Nain: grandmother (pronounced 'nine')
Taid: grandfather (pronounced 'tide')

An English translation of place names in the story:

Ty: house (pronounced 'tea')
Ty Celyn: Holly House (pronounced Kel-in)
Plas Gwyn: White Mansion
Ty tan y Berllan: Orchard House (literally translated: house under the orchard)
Ty'n y Rhos: Moor House (literally translated: house in the moor)
Ty Mawr: Big House

ACKNOWLEDGEMENTS

Various sources were used in the historical research for *Berwyn*, but the following books have been particularly helpful in developing and informing the story:

Cwm Eithin, published in 1931, describes the valley where the author, Hugh Evans, grew up during the 1860s. Some of my ancestors also lived there at that time. He vividly recreated the place, which lies about 15 miles from Berwyn, as well as the people of that period. *The Gorse Glen* is the English translation by E. Morgan Humphreys.

An Illustrated History of Llangollen by Gordon Sherratt, and Paul Lawton's superb series of railway books on the history of the Llangollen to Corwen line, provided background information for many of the stories.

Mimosa: The life and times of the ship that sailed to Patagonia by Susan Wilkinson includes a detailed and evocative description of the voyage undertaken in 1865 by over 150 pioneers to the new settlement in South America.

I should like to thank everyone at Rowanvale Books, Cardiff, who provided excellent publishing services. Many thanks for your help.

WHAT DID YOU THINK OF *BERWYN*?

A big thank you for purchasing this book. It means a lot that you chose this book specifically from such a wide range on offer. I do hope you enjoyed it.

Book reviews are incredibly important for an author. All feedback helps them improve their writing for future projects and for developing this edition. If you are able to spare a few minutes to post a review on Amazon, that would be much appreciated.

Printed in Great Britain
by Amazon